Vi............................question what if?
Or Why? Because the thoughts that ran through her
head kept her from sleeping at night.

"What is this shit...?" The large bulky figure smacked his
hand on the wall like a bull banging his hooves in the narrow
pen. I couldn't bear it, but again, all I could do was stand still
as panic and worry consumed me. "You should be grateful."
He said stone-faced and tight-lipped.

The Shops

R. Pion

Roxatized Studio
Ottawa, Ontario

Roxanne Pion/RoxatizedStudio
Nepean, Ontario K2G 0B7
www.roxatizedstudio@yahoo.com

Publisher's Note: This is a work of fiction. Names, characters, places, and incidents are a product of the author's imagination. Locales and public names are sometimes used for atmospheric purposes. Any resemblance to actual people, living or dead, or to businesses, companies, events, institutions, or locales is completely coincidental.

Ordering Information:
Quantity sales. Special discounts are available on quantity purchases by corporations, associations, and others. For details, contact the "Special Sales Department" at the address above.

The Shops/ Roxanne Pion. – 2nd Edition to Vicky's Witness series.
ISBN 9781703177107

I dedicate this book to my friends in the
West Island & Hudson Qc.

A special acknowledgment to those that believe in my work,
thank you for sharing and inspiring me to keep going.

Finally, thank you to my husband, Daniel Jutras and our sons
for being patient and supportive.

Kings will be tyrants from policy, when subjects are rebels from principle."
—Edmund Burke

"Authority without wisdom is like a heavy axe without an edge, fitter to bruise than polish."
—Anne Bradstreet

"Don't be a victim of negative self-talk, remember you are listening."
—Bob Proctor

"No one is as deaf as the man who will not listen."
— Jewish Proverb

Introduction

"Stop!" My mother shrieked as I ran over the sidewalk and onto the road. She quickly chased after me. I ran as fast as I could. The truck driver didn't see my two-year-old body. Instead, the driver saw my panic-stricken mother and her fearful face as she thought her daughter was going to be mangled and painted all over the street.

Large wheels screech towards me as the driver reacted blindly. The truck slid across the cold pavement. Exposed, I saw terror in my mother's eyes as she threw her hands up in horror.

The high-pitched sound of the breaks stunned me. In that fleeting moment I was almost a statistic.

"Are you listening?" Uncle Don continued, snapping me out of my thoughts.

"Look Rockhead, it's important to measure twice." He ordered and extended the flexible yellow tape. "When a drywall seam is done correctly, you can't see it." He couldn't stress more. "Your goal is to avoid spackle work." Uncle Don pointed.

The basement door opened cautiously. "Your show is on." Sarah reminded me, standing with her younger sister Farley at the foot of the stairs.

"Not now," Uncle Don shouted.

Both of his daughters disappeared around the corner.

"Rockhead... Pay attention!" He said sharply.

I stood there and watched him as he put on another coat of plaster. "You might learn something."

Honestly, I couldn't be more bored. I'm missing my favorite show for this.

"You're nothing without a skill." He pointed to my temple. "Remember that!"

Instead, I imagined what it would be like living with my mother.

CHAPTER ONE
Old School

MONDAY QUARTER TO EIGHT, John Rennie High School. Our school motto was: "When the people lead, the leaders will follow."

I stepped off the school bus and took a good look around. I walked up the path leading to the large building. I examine the size of it. From the corner of my eye, I could see familiar faces. My friends became known as the West End girls; not the first and certainly not the last.

"I thought you were moving?" Donna flicked my shoulder.

"False alarm," I smiled. "Why? Are you trying to get rid of me?" I toyed.

Donna tucked the loose black ebony hair behind her ear. "No, of course not." She nudged. Her slightly slanted eyes rested over me.

"I think I'll stay awhile," I teased.

"I hope so." Donna's skin stood out like porcelain.

1

"I'm still getting to know you," She chuckled.

At that moment another friend leaned in. Her glasses slid down to the ridge of her nose. "How was your summer vacation?" Felisha asked.

I looked up at her beneath my baseball cap. "Good." There weren't enough words to describe my time at camp.

"I went to Toronto for the summer..." Felisha's thick curls bounced from her tightly knit braids while she spoke. "Home of the Maple Leafs."

I cringed and imitated my grandfather's heated facial expression. It was the same reaction when the Montreal Canadiens got a penalty. Papa shouted as if the players could hear him through the radio.

I lived with my grandparents for a short time when I was taken from my home and family. They were a breath of fresh air from the doctors and counselors observing my play time. I remember drinking tea with Momma and watching hockey with Papa. We'd listen to the game being described through the old wood cathedral radio. The announcers spoke about an underdog player that had emerged from a poverty-stricken family during the depression. It was before my time. Momma saved newspaper clippings from the Gazette. The articles written about riots and standing ovation for a player called 'The Rocket'.

I sat with them in the living room and listened. I was coloring in my coloring book when we won the cup in 1993. Papa would rip his hair out over a cocky rookie hockey player named Patrick Roy. He was the only player I knew at the time. I felt like his famous wink was for me.

It was hard to ignore the history of the team. The Canadians moved forums; a symbolic torch was lit up to represent the poem In Flanders Fields.

It's written on the wall, "To you from failing hands we throw the torch; be yours to hold it high."

While grown men cried and said goodbye to one retired building and hello to the future. The torch was carried down the route from the old Montreal Forum to the Molson Centre. The Canadiens played the New York Rangers that year and won.

The people of Montreal say, "let's hope the ghosts of the forum have followed."

There was a time when blue-collar men like my grandfather, with his Irish blood, would have a cold beer after work at Magnan Tavern in Pointe-Saint-Charles.

"Once you visit Toronto, you'll be hooked," Felisha said.

"Really, eh?" I looked at her.

"Watch a Leaf's game... maybe you'll become a fan." Felisha's expression looked superior, as if I were missing something obvious.

"No," I said hastily and didn't elaborate. The Habs aren't just a team. They're the glue that keeps the city together on those cold winter nights. They're the heart of the city.

I didn't know all the players involved but I knew enough that there was a city behind the team.

My gut twisted nervously as I stepped through the large front doors leaving the natural light behind. Shouts of roaring high energized teens returned to their stomping ground. I stood and stared for a moment, the grade elevens strutted around like peacocks, while the grade sevens grouped together like a school of fish, waiting to be told what to do.

John Rennie high school took up the whole corner of the block with a fierce slashing tiger as their logo and mascot. Every person arrived today wearing their best. I instinctively kept to my friends or myself.

So, it begins... My stomach curled. I had no other choice but to run with it as the atmosphere got louder with every step. I told myself not to make a big deal out of it. It was temporary. I held my breath as backpacks and shoulder shoves tested my patience. The crowd ate up my personal space. My fists balled up.

Relax.

I was waiting for any opportunity to gain an edge. Like a teen soap opera, drama wasn't far behind and emotions ran high. I avoided getting worked up and I built up an internal wall. I opened a set of double doors and headed straight down the 'Great Hall'. My breath quickened while I made my way through the pockets of people.

The tables were placed to accommodate the crowd and to help manage the flow. The school pulled out all the stops to make us feel welcomed.

A fruity voice caught my attention by surprise. Unfortunately, I locked eyes with the chirpy girl. She stood behind a table, where she pointed toward her display.

"We have many options." She beamed upbeat. There was no way to avoid her. "Almost all students join one club or another, so why not ours?" Each table offered something different.

I straightened; she was expecting me to answer.

My darting eyes settled for a moment on her cheeky face. "Are you talking to me?" I asked plainly.

"Yes." She offered a dazzling smile. "It's after school..."

I walked away in mid-sentence. I couldn't commit to that.

Some people just don't understand. One by one, teens separated, and the crowd of students with hundreds of footsteps rushed in a mad dash to find their classes.

I walked through the large halls. I couldn't help but notice multiple awards, medals, plaques, and even ribbons presented in blocked glass cases along the wall. Students geared up in team photos wearing their school colors: black and gold.

I prided myself on being "just one of the boys." I'm horrified at the idea of becoming a girly girl. I wasn't much into school activities and sports, but my foster parents signed me up for Taekwondo classes in the evening outside of school.

My case worker thought it may help me channel my anger and work on my behavior. She said it may help me to think and make friends. Maybe teach me some self-discipline and burn some energy.

It's been almost five years and I still haven't spoken to anyone at the gym. I tend to keep to myself; I'm known as a loner. Sensei decided it would be better if I moved up with the adults. I'm guessing because of my height.

"Hey, we have homeroom together." Crystal announced.

"Sweet." I answered, relieved.

I walked to the other end of the classroom and placed my backpack over the back of the chair.

"Welcome, John Rennie High." The principal announced over the crackling intercom. "This year will be a rip-roaring year."

My eyes were fixed on the clock, just under it a large poster read 'Step up so others don't get stepped on and together we can reach for excellence.'

During morning introduction, the head of the elite team strolled in: Carly Tremblay. A prize, known for her work as an extra in a few short commercials. She'll try out for the cheerleading team like some social mountaineer.

I crossed paths with Carly a few weeks ago; outside of school, at the Fairview mall. She made a lasting impression, standing at the spritzer counter. She wore a canary yellow jacket, knee high socks and red lipstick. No Doubt a walking ad for girl power.

I became hypnotized when she exposed her wrists through the potent mist. Instead of watching what I was doing at the time, I had been distracted. I meant to spritz perfume onto a strip used as a fragrance blotter, but when I looked down, I mistakenly sprayed myself in the eye. I hadn't noticed I was holding the bottle backwards. It looked more natural for me to be holding a hockey stick rather than perfume. Though, I never had a chance to skate before. I stuck to street hockey instead.

Carly and her friends walked in class making their fashion statement. If I had to categorize myself into a stereotype, I would describe myself as a tomboy. If you want a detailed description of me; I would say I'm laid-back and a little unconventional.

Before I had been taken and placed into the system, I wore dresses and bows, especially when it was time to go to church in Notre-Dame-de-Grâce, also nicknamed NDG with my siblings. For a short time after I was separated from my family, I moved in with my grandparents and Momma made Sunday mass special. We'd go to St. John Brebeuf Parish and light a candle.

Gone were the days of church and dress up when I moved in with my aunt and uncle. Over the last few years I sank into grudge, the peak of my fashion excitement was by collecting heavy metal shirts and chains.

My choice of color before camp had been dark colors. I decided to make a conscious decision over the summer to widen my palate. I picked up a few much-needed tips from the girls I bunked with. I noticed that my clothes are like my second skin and can affect my mood. I aimed for more fitting clothes rather than extra loose.

Carly was followed by her entourage; they wore the newest fashion hot off the rack. She took the whole label-aware gossip girl vibe literally. Her face said I was a stray cat.

I leaned back as I crossed my arms. I couldn't fake my expression while watching the girls unload their bags.

Carly and her group piled up with outlandish accessories as if they were headed to a beauty pageant. I saw them adding gems and feathery trinkets to their pens, notebooks, and glitz to their agendas.

One girl wore a backpack that resembled a stuffed animal and she wore a solid toy pacifier around her neck. I chuckled to myself, not loud enough for anyone to hear, but Carly shot me a look.

My goal was to avoid attention, but on the bases of doing so; I've become nonexistent.

"What options did you pick?" Crystal asked.

"Applied arts and woodworking." I cleared my throat.

"Same here." Crystal said.

I wasn't allowed inviting Crystal over to the house, even if she lived down the street. My home life was private, and it wasn't opened to the public. We kept family business behind closed doors. It didn't feel natural talking about it... usually I escaped the topic. Whenever a friend asked, I just never answered. Now, they don't ask anymore.

When I was taken and rehomed, I still moved a few more times. I've attended five different schools, eaten in five different cafeterias and whenever I started to make friends, we were on the move again. We've been in the West Island for a while now.

Over time, I've gotten to know a handful of people. Crystal was the first to talk to me. Her small frame and bold character stood out when she introduced me to the other girls on the playground five years earlier.

"Listen up." The teacher entered the classroom and wrote her name on the blackboard in giant longhand. "Please take off your hats." She placed the chalk on the ledge. "I like to see faces."

Really!? It took me a moment. I reluctantly slipped my hat off. I sat back on the chair and watched as the teacher spoke.

Every so often her eyes would roam over us to see who was or wasn't paying attention.

"Do you want to come over tonight?" Crystal whispered.

"Depends if I'm allowed out." I mumbled.

It's hard to ignore Carly and her group, their snickering and whispering comments make me uncomfortable.

Morons! I thought as I heard their superficial remarks.

"Look at that one." Carly pointed at a girl in front of her.

One of my eyebrows shot up and the other arched inward.

I bit my tongue, but I knew the other girl from my special ed. class last year. And I know all too well what it's like being singled out from the other classes.

"I could have coughed up a better outfit." Carly rolled her eyes and landed on me; who just happened to be watching her. "What are you looking at?"

I stared at her clueless face for a moment before dismissing her. This chick was treading on thin ice.

"Who cut your hair, your mom?"

"What?" I straightened and growled at the way she said the last word. The side of my upper lip curled.

I tried to ignore the triggering word. I was already regretting my promise to play it cool. I spent a lot of time by myself for this very reason. It was easier than being with people who didn't understand.

Crystal sat beside me in suspense, taking up a position next to me, undoubtedly, to show support. The pensive look never left her face.

"I can't tell if you're a boy or a girl!" The girls cackled.

"You don't look like the type." I casually said.

"What type is that?" Carly asked.

"The type with shit for brains." I smirked.

"You're one to talk, aren't you from the Bobo class?" The last words out of her mouth stung a little too deep.

I quickly swung over my desk and smacked her across her pearly white chops. I left her golden locks spread awkwardly across her face.

"Oh, shit!" A guy next to me roared.

"What does your smart mouth have to say now, eh?" I said, ready to hit her again. I leaned in close, my voice dropped to almost a whisper. "Watch how you talk to people."

Crystal wasn't surprised when it happened - not at all. She saw me hit someone before. Just not in class.

On the surface, all the eyes in the classroom were shocked, stunned, in awe of the spectacle going on in front of them.

The first day of school and already a scene.

I didn't realize it was going to be this quick before someone tried to push my buttons. I wasn't aiming for bad attention, but whatever got them off my back. Ignoring them wasn't an option.

"You bitch." Carly spit out with her eyes watering. She clenched her jaw and touched her tender cheek.

"Bitch, huh?" I smiled with one brow arched. "So, you recognize I'm a girl now."

"Knock it off." Mrs. Robertson shouted from the front, making her way around the desk.

I cut my eyes at her, already standing; I knew the routine. I could see the teacher making her way towards us.

I looked back at Crystal. "Guess I'll see you later."

"You better watch your back, bitch!" Carly threatened.

"You'll both have to go to the office." Mrs. Robertson said gesturing towards the door.

"Why do I have to go? She's the psycho." Carly shouted, making a spectacle of herself. She stomped out of class. Her hair bounced with every step.

"Douche bag." I said, not far behind her. Maybe next time she'll think twice. I cut my eyes at the back of her head and trailed them down to her butt. I just wanted to boot her in the backside and knock her off her feet.

Do these people think I care? I thought, sitting in the office beside Carly. She sat with her back facing me and folded her arms tightly in front of her chest. I leaned back and fiddled with my thumbs and scanned the room. I saw some last-minute students hustling to class through the crack of the door. I couldn't help but think that Carly was a little uptight. I don't think she ever got hit before – what a princess.

Normally I wouldn't care if they called home. It was usually a big laugh when I fought. If I ended up winning, it became a pat on the back or a tap on the head. But the fact is, the worker said no more fights at school. I should have better control of my anger. I've been going to taekwondo and one of the rules said no fighting at school.

Carly looked at herself in a compact mirror. "I think you scratched my face," she said with a vengeful glare.

"That sounds like a 'you' problem." I said.

The lady behind the desk guided us.

"I'm first." Carly demanded leading the way.

11

Without a care, I stepped on the back of her heel while she walked through the door of the principal's office.

"Watch it," Carly snapped.

"What?" I shrugged sarcastically.

"What seems to be the problem?" The principal stepped behind his desk.

"She's rabid." Carly exclaimed.

The principal looked at me, I seemed to look calmer than Carly. Her manners were chaotic, while mine were collected.

"I want you both to apologize... and Victoria I'll be calling your parents," Mr. Harrison said, tapping his pen on his desk.

How many times must I have to explain this to people? "You mean my Guardians." Clearly, not my first rodeo. "I don't have parents."

"Whoever oversees you at home," he said. "I need to talk to them right away. We can't allow fighting." I heard no anger in his voice, just conviction. "Apologize and move on."

With a stern brow, he added, "Fighting is forbidden here." He pulled his glasses down to emphasize on the forbidden.

I avoided the apology, stubbornly biting my tongue.

"Say sorry for what?" Carly hissed. "This is unbelievable." She added quickly with a slight sneer.

"It's no big deal." I played off with a smirk.

The principal lectured us for a few more minutes. Apparently, I'm supposed to know better... I wonder where he got that notion from and people said I assume too much. How fast adults forgot... this shit was real! As if I had a choice to be here.

"I don't want to see you in my office again," Mr. Harrison ordered. "No more fighting." With that, he walked over to the door and opened it. "If you want to talk, we have a guidance counselor here at the school and we also have a place called the Inner Circle."

"Are we done?" Carly asked irritated.

"Yes, we are." Mr. Harrison said sternly. "You girls have a good day."

We both walked out of the office and into the clear; away from watchful eyes.

"This isn't over." Carly expressed.

"Okay there!" I said easily.

The rest of the day flew by. A few hours later the last bell rang and once again a herd of teens ran through the halls.

Finally, relieved to put the day behind me. I sat on the bus thinking back to what made me lose my cool. Was it their stupidity or my insecurity?

I was silent most of the way home. I had a sick feeling in my stomach. I had a deathly fear of not knowing what I was walking into day to day.

I got into the house and checked the answering machine. A message from the principal was there. I erased it.

I decided to bow out of my chores. I wasn't in the mood. I just had to get around Trisha. She usually told me to piss off anyway. We were usually left on our own during the day.

There isn't a dull moment in this family. Last week, Trisha lost her house key and wanted me to go through the second-floor window to unlock the front door from the inside. In no way, shape, or form was I going to climb up the old rusted gutters of our townhouse.

I imagined myself dangling from the old crummy deck in the backyard, hanging on while Trisha sat back and watched the show. No thank you.

When I stubbornly stood my ground, Trisha didn't hesitate to grab the rake and swing at me. Then she ran after me with it. Threatening me as I quickly ran out of the yard and down the street. I figured I would disappear until my aunt and uncle came back home. I couldn't help but laugh thinking back to the image of Trisha running after me. It either annoyed me or amused me when she tried to tell me what to do. Now I had to get passed her somehow, I couldn't stand to be in the house. I never liked to come in straight after school.

My family isn't a traditional family. In public we seem like a regular family, but on the inside the only thing normal about us is our love for the holidays.

I look forward to Aunt Jane's holiday parties.

"Get your butt inside." Trisha said. "You're supposed to be in the house."

"Uh, who died and made you boss?" I teased, using the dog as a barrier.

"Don't give me any crap," she hissed. "Where are you going? Tell me, now!"

"Out." I boldly replied, daring her to confront me.

"Look, you little shit." She shot back a look. "I better not get in trouble because of you." Trisha added. "I'm not doing your chores you fart-knocker."

"Whatever." I said and didn't pay her any mind.

I left the street as quickly as my feet could move. I made my way around the block. I passed the parking lot and headed to the apartments.

In an instant, I met with Simona and Laura. Laura introduced me to Simona a few weeks back. Simona just moved to our neighborhood from Mexico. She lives in the same buildings as Laura, while Crystal lives in the apartments down the street.

I'm always craving to eat at Simona's house. One whiff, and it instantly triggered a hunger in me, causing my stomach to growl. The tantalizing aroma with its thick spicy stir-fry tempted me every Thursday night.

I had to learn to say thank you and please in Spanish. Her mother's eyes glowed with a hint of yellowish gold. Her thick dark hair and luscious wavy curls could make any girl envious. Simona and her mother found themselves competing at times. I would watch them as they got into deep, hot tempered disagreements, switching from English to Spanish.

Laura had a soft spot for Simona and her family, especially her older brother, Alex. I think I'm the only one that doesn't have a crush on him; though my heart does twitch when he makes eye contact with me. Both Simona and her brother have people swooning over them. Even their friends. Their mother had to get extra locks for Simona's bedroom window; her being on the first floor and all. The boys from the apartment buildings tried to sneak into her room, but when face to face with Simona's mother, they thought twice and ran away.

"Do you want to go swimming with us?" Simona invited me.

I imagined myself wearing close to nothing in front of the apartment windows, while cars pass by with watchful eyes.

"Uh, no thank you." I shivered at the thought of sitting in a collective soup of bacteria. From the look of it, it seems the pool had hit its capacity.

"Just for a bit." Simona said with her sweet accent.

"No, thank you." I protested.

"Come on." Laura said, "It will be fun."

I hesitated for a moment, "No, I can't."

The inground pool was meant for the tenants in the building. "Just come for a dunk."

"I really can't, I have to get back." I replied, not exactly sure how much time I had to play with.

"We'll be here if you change your mind." Laura said as she stepped off the monkey bars. "We're starting to babysit some of the kids in the apartments." Laura said. "Let me know if you're interested."

I replied with no attempt to hide the amusement in my voice. "God, no." I knew the whole fun of having a babysitter was to drive them crazy. A babysitter wasn't a target I wanted to be.

Laura's voice was smooth, "Crystal said you got in a fight today?"

"Yeah." I shrugged. "If it's not one thing, it's another." I said with calm assurance.

"It seems you're always in a problem or you've just left one or your headed towards one." Laura pointed out.

That reminds me, I had to get back to the house. "I got to go." I replied.

Laura didn't miss a beat. "To another problem?"

I just might be stepping into another shit storm. A part of me wanted to stay, but I didn't want to push my luck.

Simona lifted her hand to her ear and stretched out both her thumb and pinky. "Call me." I gave her a wave and headed back to the house.

I quickly walked around the corner and down the street to our ordinary townhouse. On the main floor, a living room and kitchen created a cozy layout. The basement was made-up into the master bedroom, and the unfinished laundry room was off to the side. We have a large backyard, but I wouldn't advise anyone to go in it; due to the collection of dog stool.

No one did lawn care; leaving the grass to grow halfway up to our knees. It's a wild mess out there and the little hobbit shed outback barely fit any practical tools. Uncle Don was busy with his other garden. He left the backyard to us while he took care of what he calls his nursery.

Our attached neighbor is an older lady from Grenada. She wore matching gardening gloves and hat while watering her flowers. She had planted a few different types earlier in the season. When I stood downwind from her, I could smell rose, coconut, sugar and spice. Sometimes I wonder what it's like on the other side of the wall that separated us.

I wondered if she ever thought about us. I could tell she heard some unnerving things; her eyes said a lot. Sometimes I could see the concern and other times a displeasing curiosity. I was unable to say anything. We were discouraged to talk to anyone. Every Sunday afternoon the lady would work in her flower bed happily. When winter was around, we barely saw each other.

I think she knew we weren't allowed to talk to her, so she kept her distance. As did I. Yet every so often she passed me a flower in exchange for a smile. I would play with her dragon flowers, or what some people call snapdragons because of the flowers' fancied resemblance to the face of a dragon that opens and closes its mouth when laterally squeezed.

One of the few times the neighbor spoke to me was when she explained that the average strawberry has 200 seeds. It was common knowledge, just not all that common to me. She informed me that it's the only fruit that bears its seeds on the outside and is a member of the rose family.

Roses has become one of my favorite flowers, graceful yet painful. Traditionally, the rose is a symbol of love and romance, but gardeners know that every rose has its thorn, or should I say prickle.

CHAPTER TWO
Misfits

Numéro de dossier : 083573
Cas de Victoria Lafontaine
Classé par Louise Gagne
Villa-Maria, Montreal, Quebec

The Courts consider custody can be subject to change until the child is of age.

The province decided where I get to call home. I've been in the system for a decade, evaluated and I still haven't found a way out. It's not an institution, but Uncle Don runs the house as his own personal compound. I was never adopted. It seemed we were all just coasting through. Or so I thought...

I approached the house and noticed an unknown car in the driveway.

My uncle owned a garage, an automobile repair shop specializing in bodywork. So, I didn't care, I got used to seeing different vehicles. There were a lot of things I didn't care about. My parents parted ways before I was born. The things cared most about were gone. I was taken from my mom and siblings. I wasn't allowed to see my dad. Sometimes I acted like I didn't care about that either.

I marched into the house and the door shut behind me with a heavy thud. Someone else was here. I could hear a lady talking with Aunt Jane in the living room. There was an empty spot on the couch. I didn't want to sit down. I wanted to go upstairs to my room and be left alone. I stopped and stared at Aunt Jane as her eyes darted towards me.

"Victoria get in here." She demanded. I looked at her.

My stomach sank.

"Your social worker is here." The seat was set for me.

"Caseworker." The lady corrected with a heavy French accent, while stretching her hand out towards me. I just stared. I wasn't into handshakes, but there was no way to avoid it. I raised my hand and she grasped it. With a brief up and down movement, she explained why she wanted to meet. I gave her a solid handshake; conscious not to be weak handed.

"We have some good news; we're closing your file." The caseworker said with a smile.

I slowly sat down under her darting gaze, not knowing what that meant. Nobody told me how it was going to be. I was no longer in the system?

I sat with a blank look, a slack expression. My head tilted to the side. I looked around, I noticed Trisha wasn't here. "What does that mean?"

Aunt Jane shot me a disapproving look. She couldn't put what she was thinking into words, due to our guest. I got the picture just the same.

A few minutes into the meeting the lady started following up on my Taekwondo. "Do you find the classes helping?" She asked me with a large mole on her upper lip. I watched the dark spot as she spoke, and I half expected the mole to fall into her mouth.

"It kicks butt." I answered, pulling my sleeves up. Aunt Jane didn't look happy with my answer. "I haven't had any issues... I find it helps me think." I said as I pictured hitting Carly. Still, that wasn't my fault. I liked to think she fell into my fist. I'd say she provoked me, but my sensei would say otherwise.

"Good." the lady said. "So, it helps with behavior."

"Mm-hmm, yes and we're still working on her vocabulary." Aunt Jane said.

I folded my lower lip into my mouth and bit on it nervously. I didn't remember the last time I could speak freely without being ripped apart. Unless Aunt Jane's idea of working on my vocals were singing along to music.

The social worker then continued, "Is there anything else you want to talk about before I leave?"

I shook my head and shrugged. I didn't expect her to be so straight forward. It wasn't that the question was so outrageous, really. I knew it was a fair question but how did she want me to answer that? The lady was just sniffing around.

Plus, it wasn't a question I could answer if I wanted to. I just looked at her and blinked. I didn't know what to say.

Trisha wanted to report Uncle Don and Aunt Jane to the child labor board. I escaped through television, music and my friends.

"Do you need help with anything else." The lady pressed. "Let me know now before I go." She was prying into something I couldn't possibly get into.

I shrugged, hoping that did the trick. Aunt Jane looked more at ease. She didn't like dealing with social workers, or anything that had to do with the system. 'Fascist pigs' Aunt Jane snarled softly and rolled her eyes. Uncle Don had a lot to say on people poking into family matters and political debates were his game. He weighed out life as if it were a cost. Leaving me to wonder who was paying for me. How was I going to pay my way? I was already indebted and a burden.

"Well I guess, I'll be on my way." Getting up from the table the caseworker smiled and stretched out her hand once again, but this time to say goodbye.

"This is for you." She gave me something while heading to the front door.

I held the envelope up to the light. "What is it?"

"Open it and find out." She said and nodded goodbye. She made her way out the door and to her car. Then disappeared down the street.

I stood there for a moment, wondering what's the point. I looked down at the envelope. Aunt Jane snatched it out of my hand and opened it.

"Hey..." I went to say something but stopped myself.

"You have to learn to watch your mouth." She ordered.

Aunt Jane slid out two tickets. "It's for a wrestling match at the Forum." She said dryly. "I'll hold onto these. You'll lose them."

I rolled my eyes.

"Watch yourself." Aunt Jane snapped. I bit back the urge to argue. "Soon there will be no more social-jerkers coming around here." She huffed. "You're getting older."

I gave her a questioning look. "You mean case worker."

Aunt Jane shot me a death glare.

"Where's Trisha?" I quickly asked changing the subject.

I was answered with a suspicious scowl.

"What?" I said in my head, not daring to question her.

She always said we were going to push her over the edge one day. No one knew what day that was.

Aunt Jane habitually smoked her nerves away, numbing out the day. She'd change from the stepmother in Cinderella to Mother Goose within minutes. She'd bake with her home-made green butter and hum to her music as she rolled dough for freshly baked goods.

After the caseworker left, Aunt Jane made herself an Irish drink. She chose to medicate herself rather than medicate us. On occasion it felt as if she despised children, particularly Trisha, me and Uncle Don's first child, Michael. Though, I don't know anyone that could last watching us without needing a drink. It seemed we turned the mellow into high-strung... or at least that's what we were made to believe.

Michael was from a previous relationship; the two girls are from Aunt Jane. Aunt Jane got pregnant with Sarah when we moved out of Lasalle and Farley was born when we lived in Chomedey, Quebec. They were inseparable from the start.

I had to see the humor in it; I had to find the happiness in our dysfunction. Even through the gritting teeth, I found enjoyment. Maybe it's because we were able to grow some roots, we've been in the West Island for five years. It's the longest place I've lived so far.

"You have to prepare for the future. You're not entitled to anything." The words seemed to mean something else when she said it. Or am I just being sensitive?

"I won't lose them, you know? The tickets." I carried on... "I'm not a kid anymore." I pointed out. "I'm officially a teen."

Aunt Jane's frown deepened, "Get real!" She looked like she needed another time out in the basement. That's what she called it when she disappeared. "You're just a child!" She stopped short. "You want to grow up... then do the dishes." She demanded. "First lesson: don't be in a rush to grow up."

In one hand she told me to grow up and in another told me I'm still a child.

So much for going out! I wanted to ask but I already knew the answer. I tried to imagine what it was like to be the boss of my own home or my own company.

"Chop, Chop." Aunt Jane ordered, "You'll be happy once you're done." She said. I was happy the first time I was allowed and honored the role of dishwasher, but I haven't been happy since.

"Happy, huh." I stepped to the sink in defeat.

"Just do it." Aunt Jane opened the door to the basement and then closed it behind her. I could hear her mumble down the stairs. "Teenagers... they think they know everything."

I can't wait to be an adult, then people will listen to me, I thought to myself, hoping I had better success when I'm older. I picked up the damp dish cloth as if I was allergic to it. Where's Trisha? I thought.

Uncle Don took me off dishes to find a tool for him in the back shed. He replaced me with Michael. "You have to put power into it." Uncle Don ordered from behind. "put your wrist into it," he said firmly.

"God damn it! Just fucking do it. You're like a bad infomercial." Uncle Don shouted; consistently demeaning, he believed he was doing us a service. "Take the dirty pot and fill it with hot water and dish soap and scrub."

Uncle Don enjoyed breaking us down, or as he calls it; training.

"Smile while you work," he ordered.

Michael turned and looked up at him. Uncle Don pinched and widened Michaels cheeks to smile. "Listen," he said. "Don't be a candy ass."

I gave Uncle Don the tool that he told me to get. "That's a good little soldier." He said and patted me on the head. "You two finish up here."

I didn't say anything.

I helped Michael finish the dishes. I didn't just want to get out of here, but I desperately needed to get away. I pictured forever being assigned tasks. Uncle Don says kids are made to work and that we should learn how to earn. Aunt Jane loves to say, children should be seen, not heard.

"Rockhead, don't forget the yard has to be done." Aunt Jane yelled from the basement. "You can't keep slipping out of that one."

I rolled my eyes and took it as an order.

The tears welled up in Michael's eyes and he didn't want anyone to see him cry. He held back the tears and didn't say anything. He scrubbed till his hands were raw and red.

Tears never helped me before. Sometimes I was so angry I couldn't cry; instead I'd find relief in hitting something. One or two times I took my rage out on myself. I aggressively finished the rest of the kitchen without a teardrop. I wasn't going to give anyone the satisfaction. Michael and I finished it together.

I hurried upstairs and dialed the phone before anyone noticed I was on the line. I called Simona, but she didn't answer.

I grabbed the dog leash and headed out the door. Aunt Jane assigned me as the official dog walker. Finally, a chore I didn't mind.

Our dog was already named when we got her. Jesse had been given to us from a family that lived in the back apartments. She was a cross breed between Collie and German Shepherd. Why she was interested in chasing cars was beyond me.

"Why?" I asked automatically, and repeated it, "Why?" I smiled, scratching the back of her furry ears. I planted my feet on the ground as she tried to run off. "No." I commanded her. Pulling on her leash she barked and barked at the guys on the court. "Jesse! Stop it," I said, not knowing if I wanted to go further. I turned her around to bring her back home.

"Hey!" A guy called out as he walked towards me. "You live around here?"

I nodded.

The guy was about my age. His hair faded down the side. "My name is Marcus." He spoke with a natural charm and a red lollipop in his mouth. He reached out his hand, his leather wallet was strapped to his body like a gun holster. He took pride in his style. "Your friends with Simona, right?"

"Yeah," I said holding my dog down from sniffing him. I gritted my teeth and held her back.

Marcus reached his hand out, "your dog must smell my ferret."

"You have a ferret?" I smiled. "That's cool."

"I live across the park," Marcus said. "You can always drop by to see him if you want."

"Sure," I answered.

This suburban block was made up of families. So far, the West Island has been the longest place I've called home. It will be five years this winter. There's no shortage of parks, malls, cinemas, sports, courts, fields and rings.

Some guys down the street called out for Marcus. "I'll see you around." He smiled and twirled his candy in his mouth. He looked thoughtful as he rubbed his chin and walked away with a long stride. At the same time, my arm almost dislocated. Jesse lunged towards a passing car and tugged me forward like some limp toy.

"Wow!" I shouted and pulled back on her leash. "Stop!" I planted my feet and dug my heels into the ground.

I used the key hanging from around my neck and crept into the house, not wanting to be visible. I didn't want to attract attention. I quietly slipped my boots off and walked to the basement door. I wanted to hear what my aunt and uncle were talking about, but I couldn't make out their muffled words. I didn't skip a beat when I grabbed a stemless wine glass and placed the top of it onto the door and the bottom to my ear. To my surprise, I could hear them; still faint, but clear enough to understand.

"I found a place," Uncle Don said in a gruff voice.

"A place?" His words surprised Aunt Jane. "What do you mean? A place?" Her tone changed; I could almost hear her heart leap.

"I'm saying now we can move." Uncle Don's greatest desire was to own his own land. His old school father was an only child of millionaires. He had grown up to be an English professor who played the political scene and won triathlons during his spare time. He believed money was better spent elsewhere; he preached that owning your own home should be a priority but to beware of the pitfalls of being house poor. Uncle Don never agreed with him. Land ownership was the only thing that mattered, as far as he was concerned. "We have a house."

Uncle Don was madly driven with his own vision and desires; still an eager-beaver type of guy like his dad. But when he got an idea in his head, he became borderline obsessive.

With a one-track mind, he pushed the competitive spirit in us and not the creative. He drilled it into our heads to learn a trade. He wanted us to know a skill and understand the importance of farming and the harvest of it. He had acquired a green thumb early in life, fine tuning his craft as years passed.

"So, we're moving." I whispered in dismay, mentally wincing.

"Where is it?" Aunt Jane asked.

"The house on the mountain." He said.

It was the last words I heard before backing away from the door.

I had to call someone. I dialed Crystal's phone number, but nobody answered. The next number I called was Simona. She was excited about a babysitting job.

"I have a job tonight," Simona said proudly. "Do you want to come along?"

"No."

"Come on."

"I'm not up for watching kids," I said.

"You don't have to... I will," Simona pleaded. "Please."

When I took the chance and asked Aunt Jane if I could help babysit. She practically kicked me out the house. I thought for sure I'd have to beg.

Simona and I showed up on time. It was a cozy apartment. They have a large corner deck that looked over Saint-Charles Boulevard and beyond the deck there were dozens of trees.

When we arrived, the parents gave us money for the pizza, and they let us know when they expected to be back. It would be late, nearly four o'clock in the morning. Simona said it wasn't unusual for them. They liked to go to parties that dragged out into the night.

We had our pizza and watched some light T.V. The kids were well behaved. I had seen them around before in the park. They were a lot easier to care for than kids typically that age. They played a lot on the deck and had a small tent made up. The kids spent a lot of time in it and there were nights when their parents would let them camp out on the deck. They had done it a few times when Simona had babysat. Normally in the summer.

We checked on them every so often. The kids were excited about sleeping out on the deck. Their mom had told Simona it would be alright; she had to go check on them every hour. We took shifts, including after they had gone to sleep.

We went back and forth throughout the night. I fell asleep curled up in the corner of the couch. It was around eleven when I heard someone walking around down the hall in the next room. It was weird because the kids were out on the deck and Simona just went to go check on them. I stopped to think if they had a pet. They didn't mention a dog or cat. I heard some footsteps for a couple of moments and then it was quiet again. I figure it was a sound coming from the next apartment.

After ten minutes, I heard someone walking again and I thought I saw a shadow. In an instant I checked the rooms, but I didn't find anything. I turned the T.V. off and went outside, rubbing my eyes. Simona had gone to check the kids and hadn't come back. When I opened the tent, Simona had fallen asleep reading one of them a book. I guess one of them had been awake. I surprised at the size of the tent and I wasn't comfortable waking anyone up, so I was about to find a corner to roll up into when I paused for a moment. There was a light on in one of the kids' rooms. I could see it from the deck, but I had checked that room and turned the light off. I went to go back inside to go turn it off, when I saw the light turn off. This wasn't just my eyes playing tricks on me. I knew I had turned off that light, and I knew I had just seen it on and turned off. I wasn't sure what to do at first. I didn't want to scare Simona and the kids. The phone was inside. I sat on a chair and watched the door and windows. But nobody came. I slowly fell asleep and let my guard down.

I woke to a light tapping at the window. The parents had returned.

"Did you have any trouble?" The mom asked.

"No," I wasn't sure what to say.

Simona slowly crawled out from the tent. The kids were still sleeping.

We made it through the night, I thought, Maybe babysitting and getting paid for it wasn't that bad of a deal.

When we were on our way home, I told Simona what had happened. "And instead of waking you up, I stayed on the deck and kept an eye out." I shrugged.

"But you didn't see anyone?" She asked.

"No," I said. "But something just didn't feel right."

"Nothing happened." She said thoughtfully.

Simona and I split up once we got closer to home. I had to take the dog out before I settled in. It was apart of the deal for going to help babysit in the first place. Aunt Jane and Uncle Don leave the dog care to me or the kids.

I didn't see Trisha till that evening, she had gone to visit mom. When she came back, she was bursting with excitement to show Aunt Jane an art award she received at school.

"Vicky could do better." Aunt Jane said to Trisha; looking over her artwork. I sat up abruptly, unsure of what to do. Trisha looked at me with disgust in her eyes, her face pooled with emotion. She looked at her art and slid off her chair and headed upstairs to her room. Deflated, her shoulders dropped with doubt. "Apparently, my art isn't as good as yours," Trisha grumbled passing me.

"I like it." I said as I got up from my chair and followed closely behind her. Trisha walked as quickly as she could and skipped every other step. She closed the door behind her and shut it in my face. My emotions clawed at me with helplessness. I felt like a fool and I didn't even know what I did.

"Have you seen my jar of wasps?" Michael asked, with a blank expression.

"Gee no, I haven't." I gave him a long, considering look.

Squeezing his hands together, he added, "I'm going to pull a prank on a friend."

"Well... good luck with that," I said and went into my room and closed the door.

Trisha's room was attached to mine. A hanging sheet and a long dresser divided the two rooms, breaking them into two distinct areas, giving us some semblance of privacy. I could slightly see Trisha through the wall to wall sheer sheet. She sat on her bed with a book. Instead of allowing Trisha to read, open and freely, Uncle Don's teasing remarks forced Trisha to read out of sight. I still remember the day when she came to live with us and corrected Uncle Don's spelling. He grabbed his cowboy boot and smacked her in the head with it. "Shut your mouth," He growled and threw her across the room into the living room recliner. With every thump she sank deeper into the chair with a whimper.

Trisha turned a page every few minutes while I sat and looked out the window. I enjoyed observing people walking by the house. I wondered what they were up to and what kind of lives they lived. It reminded me that we weren't the only ones.

In the horizon, the day ended with a streaking color of the sunset reflecting off the buildings. The streetlights switched on as the sky became a darker blue.

Usually, I try not to dodge out of Taekwondo class, but tonight I stayed home. My punishment was cleaning. Hence why I never miss. I wondered if I can pawn work onto Trisha.

By the time I had fallen into relax mode, a thought hit me. Did he say wasps!? I jumped to my feet. I suddenly realized that my cousin was going to unleash a jar of wasps as a practical joke.

I ran out of my room.

He had already left. "Son of a bitch!" I whispered.

Concerned but not enough to inform Aunt Jane or Uncle Don. I ran as fast as I could down the street to the cul-de-sac just around the corner. Michael's friend lived in one of the apartments, just next to Crystal's place. I knocked on the door and was surprised when the two boys opened it. Michael and his buddy, Oliver, were just saying goodbye. I didn't see any jar of wasps and the boys seemed to be fine.

I could see over Oliver's shoulder. I was caught by surprise when I witnessed his mother breastfeeding her other son. It wasn't the fact that she was oddly angled that caught my eye but the fact that she was still breastfeeding a five-year-old boy that caught me off guard. I don't think anyone saw the expression on my face because I picked up my jaw as fast as it fell. I avoided eye contact. What the shit? I almost blurted out, not knowing anything about it. I would be afraid to get my nipple bitten off.

"Your wasps?" I asked Michael as we headed back home.

"I lost them," he said.

"Good, because I don't think that would be a good idea." I smiled. "We can figure out another way to pull a prank."

We walked home, brainstorming mischievous ways to get back at Oliver. Michael wanted to one up him.

Dinner was served just as we walked in. No one mentioned anything about us being out, so I kept my mouth shut. Aunt Jane made corned beef mixed with potatoes and hotdogs for us. "So, I guess Uncle Don isn't coming home tonight." I said after seeing his spot at the table was empty.

"Thank God," Trisha said faintly. "We can eat in peace."

I looked at the food and didn't see much peace in it. I was thankful it wasn't fried eggplant. "Too bad Aunt Jane didn't make her delicious shepherd pie." I said picturing a large bowl of my favorite hearty dish.

"Why did you mention that?" Trisha sighed. Plopping full spoons of food onto our plates, Aunt Jane gave us another option. "Or you could just suck on air." Aunt Jane giggled to herself as she emptied the pot onto our plates. One giant spoon at a time. Plop after plop. "This isn't a restaurant," she snapped.

You could say that again. I couldn't help myself... the words trickled out. "Looks like dog food." I said taking the first spoonful and almost choking on it after Aunt Jane smacked me in the back of the head.

"Be grateful you little shit," she said, pressing her lips to her teeth and biting her tongue. "Little monsters."

Sarah and Farley usually pick off Aunt Janes dish, but today they had their own plates. They were just getting out of their diapers. Sarah seemed girly, while Farley had more fun playing with Michael's trucks in the dirt. I found myself playing fort with them under the tucked sheets of their bunk bed. The girls would create a dome like cave. Some days we would pretend to be a pack of lions roaring for attention. And other days I would draw for them.

"I heard you got wrestling tickets?" Trisha asked.

"Yeah. Cool, eh!?" I grinned, excited to have something to look forward to.

Trisha shook her head. "I guess there isn't one in there for me?" She grumbled as she nudged forward to eat. Clearly not happy with being left out, Trisha toyed with her food.

I didn't answer back at first. "You don't even like wrestling," I said defending the gift.

"And?" she glared. "Why do you get everything?"

"So, you think I shouldn't go?"

"Don't be stupid," Trisha remarked and then that did it.

I yelled back, "I'm not stupid."

"Don't have a cow," she said. "I'm not calling you stupid." Sucking her teeth Trisha stared at her plate. "I can't eat this."

"Just do what I do," I said.

"And what do you do?" Trisha's nose twisted. She lowered her eyebrows and sucked in her chin at the sight of the food in my mouth. "It's not that I don't like it. I'm just not in the mood."

"If I can't swallow the food down, I stuff my mouth and my cheeks and sometimes even under my tongue." I said proudly. "Then I go and spit it out." I thought it was a genius, but Trisha didn't look thrilled.

"Why do you always make me feel like an idiot?" I asked her.

"You do that on your own," She said simply.

Aunt Jane came to check up on us and looked over our plates. "Eat." Her thinned lips told me she wasn't going to leave until our plates were cleared. I smiled somewhat grimly at Aunt Jane.

A hurt look filled Trisha's eyes as she ate with steady indifference.

I started stuffing my cheeks, chipmunk style.

"Trisha, clean up the table after dinner." Aunt Jane ordered before she left the room. I gave Trisha a wink teasingly and scooped up the last of my dinner.

"I'm done." Michael said hastily. He was the first to finish and left the table. I couldn't say a word with my mouth full of food.

When I got up, Trisha stepped out behind me, and quickly reached over both my shoulders. "Ha!" It was too late when I realized what her plan was. Trisha smacked both of my cheeks. Everything that was in my mouth shot out with an explosion of chunky spit, corn beef hash and hotdogs. I froze with shock.

"Ew." Trisha looked at the mess.

"I'm not cleaning that," I said as I wiped the side of my face. I refused to budge. I crossed my arms in protest and stood my ground.

"Yes, you are." Trisha said paying no mind to my silence. "You'll have to explain why it was all in your mouth, if you catch my drift." She muttered, stepping away from the mess. "Clean it."

I pulled myself together. I had a plan. "Whatever," I said pathetically. "Fine, but that's it. I'm not cleaning anything else."

Trisha's eyes narrowed; her nostrils flared. "It's never just it." She said with mock ferocity. "I've had enough of this crap." Trisha didn't elaborate.

I didn't think much of her complaints. She had something to say about everything. Trisha always had a plan and some outlandish idea of escaping.

I got on my knees to clean the mess that splattered all over the side of the counter and floor. What if Trisha was serious? what if she was getting out?

"Are you going to move in with mom?" I asked Trisha.

"Maybe."

"You can't just do that!" I said peevish. "If that was the case, then why can't we both move back in with mom?" Especially after she was released from Tanguay.

"I'll do what I want. And mom can't take both of us." She snapped dismissively. "I'm of age. I don't need Uncle Don or Aunt Jane telling me what to do," she smiled. "I know what to do."

"You really hate living here?" I reached into my pocket and pulled out a few melted jellybeans. I studied her face wondering if she would miss me.

"Yes," she said. "I don't find it cheerful living under a roof with a gas-lighting narcissist." Trisha explained and looked around seeming to notice where she was. "Look... I'm practically an adult and I'm expected to live here as some servant. I've become the live-in babysitter."

"I think that's called chores." I joked. As if on cue, Sarah and Farley left the kitchen.

"You don't realize how bad the situation is," Trisha said with a meaningful arch of her eyebrows. "But I do."

How could I ignore the disdain and bitterness we lived in? I knew there weren't many options for us. But this was ours.

I understood the day police came through the front door when I was four and our family was separated. Once I compared my life to others, I knew my life wasn't peaches and cream.

"Are we still going to see each other?" I asked offering some of my candy from my lint filled pocket. The color of the jellybeans stained my sweaty palm.

"Of course, we'll see each other. We're still sisters," she murmured, refusing my jellybeans. "You can't get rid of me that easily," she grumbled. "I'm never taking orders again." She tossed the cloth aside, "we're not soldiers." She offered no more explanation.

I chewed over the implications of her decision. Where does that leave me? With every dreaded thought, I wondered.

I shivered as if someone stepped over my grave. There was a chill in the air. My eyebrows rose nearly to my hairline. I could feel Aunt Jane's eyes digging into my back as she entered the room. I wiped my mess that much faster.

My heart picked up and my mouth went dry. My mind was nothing but brittle reaction. I disconnected when Uncle Don walked in, like flicking a light switch down, I shut my emotions off. I use my breath as an anchor to steady myself. I had to keep a straight face when his angry voice deepened in agitation. I told myself not to say anything that could be used as leverage. Sometimes it's better to say nothing and let him be the puppeteer.

It took me awhile to fall asleep and when I woke up again in the middle of the night, the room was still dark. I wasn't happy. My door was closed as I liked it.

I slept on my right side now that I was forming. It bothered me to sleep on my stomach.

Something didn't feel right; I noticed my body was stiff and it wasn't like the time my arm locked. This time my eyes were open – I couldn't shut them. My body wasn't registering the command.

Something had tugged on the blanket. It felt like I wasn't the only person in the room. Once again, I felt as if I were being watched. A dread came over me like a dark wave. Fear and terror cupped me, and my gut twisted. An evil presence was in my room. I went to call out for Trisha, but I couldn't speak.

Wide-eyed, I felt the damp bedsheet under me. I was laying in my own sweat. I could see nothing, but I knew I wasn't alone. My breath quickened with a racing pulse. Confused, I fought to move. Paralyzed, a promise of death crept over me.

"Oh, my God!" I shouted inside my head; my mouth didn't want to follow. A bursting frustration swelled inside of me. My heart pounded so rapidly that I passed out.

CHAPTER THREE
Trouble

I woke up in a wicked mood this morning. I haven't been sleeping properly. I'm just not ready for sitting in class today. My stomach twisted in knots as if I was kicked by a horse. Cramps grinded deep inside, like a knife carving me out. Giving me a bad case of 'stay the fuck away from me'.

"Who gives a rat's ass?" A guy shouted to himself as he threw open the doors. It was never a dull moment at school. Apparently, the smoking section was for troubled individuals. An uptight chain smoker stood behind me in a pile of cigarette waste that was sprinkled across the asphalt.

The only time I tried to smoke was when Trisha gave me a cigarette once and I found myself shoulders deep in the toilet.

"What a bitch!" A girl screamed suddenly, clearly in deep conversation with her friend. Their lips moved a mile a minute. It wasn't until I turned around the corner that I realized two guys were spray-painting their signature on the side of the building. I thought creative street art added greatly to the charm of a city; it had its own culture.

"Be fast!" The guy said to his buddy as he looked up at me. He seemed to know what I was thinking. "Do you like it?" he asked.

"Yeah." I shyly answered. I slowly made my way in front of the design. Curiosity got the better of me. I saw the different colors come to life within the crafted letters. It wasn't just a scribble, but an illustration.

"Do you want to try?" His eyes lingered on me, breaking into my brain. "It's not hard," he said.

"Sure." He handed me a spray can. I always wanted to try some graffiti, and without thinking, I did.

I stepped up to the wall as if it were the Wall of Berlin itself. The smile on my face grew wide as the paint coated the brick. A rush came over me as I did something that I've never done before. I released myself from a place which limited my creative freedom. I hummed as I poured my heart out.

"That rocks!" The guy said admiring my work.

At times, I felt useless, especially in class, but when it came to art? It was all me. The brick began to take on the form of Jericho. I felt a victory. I've been so quiet for so long, I just wanted to make some noise. Art gave me a way to express myself.

"Hey! Stop that." The janitor shouted by the garbage bin; making me jump back. My smile evaporated.

"Free expression," the two guys shouted just before running away. Grimly leaving me standing there. Where was I going to run to?

"It's not your building..." The janitor barked; his eyes lit with annoyance. "You come here," he snapped at me.

For a moment, there was nothing. We looked at each other. He inspected the wall while the other students ran off from the smoking section to avoid getting lectured.

"Kids these days," he said, scratching the back of his head as he stared at the art. I took a chance and quickly slipped back into the school before he noticed.

"Where were you?" Laura said. "They almost paired me up with what's her face in the front."

"I got sidetracked." Not to mention, I was caught up with a new thrill. It was like I found another way to express myself. I wanted to take my art to the next level.

"You came just in time." Laura snatched a pen from her pencil case "We're calling him the crocodile hunter." Nodding to the teacher in the front. He quickly wrote his name with messy yellow chalk across the board: Mr. Heart. He wore a beige shirt that gave the impression of someone on safari. This being my first ecology class, I found it fitting. Apparently, we were dissecting worms that day.

We're dissecting already! I thought.

"I wanted to start off with something small today." Mr. Heart announced. "Earthworms are a gardener's best friend." He cleared his throat. "They're like free farm help. Worms increase the amount of air and water that gets into the soil. They break down organic matter, like leaves and grass into things that plants can use. When they eat, they leave behind castings that are a very valuable type of fertilizer."

"I'm not doing this," Carly said, reacting to the news of poking around a worm's insides. "I don't agree with this." Pulling on her plastic pacifier necklace. "It's not right killing something for us to be graded on."

"Then you'll get a zero." Mr. Heart announced. "It's not that difficult and it's not up for debate." He proceeded to inform us on what to expect. "We start with worms, and later in the year, we're moving onto lamb eyes. It'll be fun," he said. "And remember – this could get a little messy."

"Ew!" Carly whimpered.

"What he finds fun, scares me." Laura chuckled uncomfortably and pulled her sleeves up.

"As long as it's not frogs." I said.

"Laura and Victoria!" Mr. Heart called out, directing our attention to him.

"So, this isn't biology!?" A guy whispered.

"No," Carly commented, "It's two different things."

"No shit!" I overheard him say.

"Ecology is a subfield of biology." I was surprised at her answer. "It's pretty obvious." She said. I made a mental note to look up what subfield meant.

The guy blinked slowly. "Oh."

Carly caught me staring. "You need help, creeper?"

Both the guy and Laura simultaneously looked over at me.

I groaned and didn't answer. I sat back and almost fell off the bench. I had forgotten that there was no back.

"Why can't we have a normal class?" Laura complained. "I can't do this." She pressed the scalpel against the wet fleshy worm. "It's pinned down." Laura's words came out in disgust.

"I've got it." I shrugged, nudging her over, confident in my ability to cut it open. "I think." I gave Laura a wink as I sliced open the worm.

A super burger from the cafeteria sounded perfect. I met up with Crystal and the others. Laura passed over lunch due to the worm incident, but nothing could change my mind off John Rennie's menu. From chocolate croissants to their oatmeal cookies down to Jamaican patties; my mouth watered just thinking of all the choices.

"Does anybody have a dollar?" Some guy asked, he blinked slowly like a lizard. His shaggy hair hung over the side of his face.

"Hold on." I pulled out the newly made two-dollar coin.

"Here," I said tossing him a Toonie.

"Thank you." He smiled. "Hey, that art piece in the back... that was you, right?"

I paused. "News travels fast," I said. What else was there to say? I wondered how he got that info.

"I saw it while I was coming in from the shops." His glance didn't waver. "Someone said they saw you." He was about to sit when he changed his mind and prowled slowly away from us. "Uh...thanks again... but I got to go."

I gnawed on my lower lip a moment as my eyes trailed to where he was looking. I noticed two men entering the cafeteria. One being the principal and the other the janitor.

Shit! The custodian spotted me and pointed, curling his finger for me to walk to them.

"What did you do now?" Crystal questioned.

I shrugged. Knowing I didn't have time to explain. I hurried through the lunchroom without a scene. The principal didn't say anything and gestured for me to follow him.

"So, freedom of expression is banned now?" I asked with maddening calm, sliding my backpack over my shoulder.

"Yeah, that's it!" The janitor responded as I walked ahead. "We're trying to suppress your human rights."

I'm delivered like some package to the office. Mr. Harrison barely looked at me before my stomach curled in knots. A little conviction rattled inside me.

"What were you thinking when you did this?" Mr. Harrison asked. All his attention was on me and I just sat there.

At first, I didn't say anything; not wanting things to get this far. My self-control dissipated. I tried to explain myself, "I wanted to try it. I never had the chance to spray paint before." I admitted. Besides at my uncle's shop but painting the car wasn't the same thing as creating graffiti, I thought.

Mr. Harrison's blank expression told me that my answer wasn't good enough.

"I wasn't thinking." I said, knowing that's what he wanted to hear. "I didn't think of the consequences." I answered him like I would Uncle Don. He didn't like thoughtless answers or excuses. He preferred you give it to him straight or keep your mouth shut.

"That's why you think before you act," He said warmly, I smiled at him. "I'll have to call your guardians about this." He lingered for a second over his desk. "On another note, I think you have talent. Maybe we can work something out."

"Like what?" I was a little worried.

"Drama class puts on a production in the auditorium every year. Maybe you can help with the backdrops and set up," He said. "This year they're re-enacting a comedy 'Much Ado About Nothing. It's a play by William Shakespeare.

At last, someone who appears to care. "I'm up for that.."

"Stay out of trouble and I'll see what I can do."

I moved forward eagerly. I forgot I was there for a reason.

"Just a second," he said, looking me over. "The fact is you got caught vandalizing the school."

I grumbled.

"So, you'll have to help clean it."

"Really!?" I said, half to myself.

"It's that or we get the authorities involved." Mr. Harrison threatened.

My eyes widened, "No... no... I'll clean it."

"I still haven't been able to talk to anyone at your residence. Is there any other way to reach your parents?" He corrected, "Guardians."

"No." Good luck with that, I thought to myself. I was surprised. I thought for sure he was going to punish me or at least give me detentions.

"I appreciate that you don't get into any more trouble." He eyeballed me as I left his office once again.

"This is nice. Too bad you have to get rid of it."

"No big deal," I reassured Crystal. "I can always do another piece."

"Not here," she muttered.

"No, not here," I chuckled. "But maybe I'll find a space somewhere else." I got a twinge in my chest having to destroy my art.

"Where are you going to be able to paint on a wall?" Crystal asked.

"I know my father found places to paint; Shops, restaurants and other commissioned work," I sighed. "He taught me some stuff."

"I never heard you speak of your father." Crystal's gaze lifted to meet mine. I held my breath and willed myself to say I didn't know him much.

"There's not much to say. He's known for his talent and he's studied the arts." I shrugged. "But he dropped out and started hustling something else." I smirked. "My family tells me not to waste my talent like he did."

"Whatever you do... don't stop being an artist." Crystal smiled and left me to finish cleaning.

I scrubbed the paint off the brick. The colored liquid ran down my hands and dripped onto my shoes. Everything fed my creative juices. I don't think I can ever run from being an artist. It's in my blood.

There was still last period before the day was done. I went back down the corridor, into my class. Now, this is where I belong. I stepped into the computer class, not knowing what to expect. I put a floppy disk into the wide desk hogged computer and waited for it to download... and waited... and waited.

After the 'Still loading' sign disappeared, I was finally in. With the basic option for painting, I created some constellations for fun while the teacher explained the lesson. Feeling accomplished, I impressively typed as fluently as possible. I scored 37 words per minute. I wasn't sure if that was enough to impress the teacher, but I impressed myself.

Cool course. I thought. I didn't want the class to end; the lights shut off and I was the last one to leave.

As the weeks passed, I was able to focus better in class. I used the breathing exercises I learnt in elementary. The program encouraged me to have quiet time and meditation due to my aggression and anger. The teachers focused on stories; we took the time to read and have group book discussions. I remember starting the program with 'The Three Billy Goats Gruff' and over the weeks ending the last session with 'A Wrinkle in Time.'

"Are you deaf?" Aunt Jane asked turning down the television, MTV was always better with the volume up.

"Aw, man..."

"Just do it now." Her stabbing eyes ordered me.

Tiredness from school was not an option. Aunt Jane never missed a reason to party and especially when it came to her birthday bash.

Uncle Don complained about it every year, like a broken record. It cuts into his work time. Even when he wasn't at the body shop, he had other work to do. He shouted with growls and howls, rummaging through the kitchen drawers looking for the wine opener.

I tied a bag over my boots and walked out back. I wasn't happy being the one having to clean up the yard. It was like shit bombs had been laid out everywhere, leaving no grass untouched. Good thing I'm only told to clean the backyard every few weeks. As the lawn mower bobbed with the bumps and pits in the lawn, I pushed myself to get it done.

I finished the edges with the whipper snipper, it didn't take long before my hands went numb. "Crap!" I walked alongside the fence from the back to the front. I could smell something funky. I looked around and then under my shoes.

"Shit," I shouted, sliding my foot across the grass. "Disgusting." I stomped towards the door.

"You missed a spot," Trisha yelled. "Shit-Shoveller." She slammed the patio door shut; locking me out.

"Oh, come on," I shouted and made my way around the deck. I almost peed my pants when a head popped up behind the fence.

"Hey," Marcus said with a smile that lit his face up.

I paused and blinked at him a couple of times. He seemed to be a nice guy. I had to get rid of him before Uncle Don saw him. It could cause me some serious headaches later.

"What are you doing here?" I asked hoping he didn't hear the urgency in my voice.

"I was just passing through. I wanted to know if you wanted to come over to see my ferret."

"Thank you but I can't. I have Taekwondo," I said shrugging off the anxiety. "Maybe another time."

"You do that stuff?" Marcus asked with both hands in the air. "KARATE CHOP." He attempted a hand samurai strike.

I closed the gate behind me. I gave him an interesting look.

"Yes. After class I'll come by the park and see if you're still around." I said walking up the front steps.

"Just watch out for those guys down the street," he said smoothly and tucked his hands into his pocket. "They're a little rough around the edges."

The gym became a steppingstone for me. I finally got my green belt and upgraded to a higher class.

Tonight, they paired me up with a young man. A red belt who taught the class occasionally. It was my fourth year here and I haven't spoken more than two words since I started.

"Listen her. We don't do those kicks." Sensei Cox spoke with authority to one of the new guys showing off his flying kicks.

"Why not?" The new guy challenged the teacher like he had something to prove.

"Because you're an open target."

"Who says?" The cocky adolescent revved up with his fancy kicks, snapping his feet into the air. He totally disregarding the teacher. What's he trying to prove anyway?

"I want to show you something... attack me." Sensei Cox took his stance and gave a little wave, gesturing the guy to come forward.

The guy leapt forward, towards the teacher with a kick, intending to connect with a blow. As he lifted off the ground with both feet in the air, the teacher threw a high kick that landed directly in the center of the guy's chest. It connected before the guy could land. The guy flew across the room into the mats. A loud thump, with a bang, created a rippling effect as the pads fell off the shelf. The point had been made. You have no control when both your feet were off the ground.

"Try not to leave yourself vulnerable," the sensei carried on. "You should spend less time trying to impress people and more time learning the techniques. Timing is everything."

Every Thursday night we sparred for two hours. It was essentially 'free-form' fighting, with enough rules to make injuries unlikely.

I headed home thinking of tonight's class; it was interesting. I'll never forget that guy's reaction when he realized his moves failed him. I wonder if he'll come back. He seemed pissed that the teacher had made an example out of him. Then again, he was asking for it. Sometimes a good lesson is all someone needs.

CHAPTER FOUR

Guidance

Aggravated and crude, a deep voice growled out with a loud snapping urgency.

"Just walk straight!" Uncle Don shouted with a venomous foul mouth and a sour temper; his voice carried through the house. My instinct was to freeze where I stood but my second thought was to sneak away and avoid him.

"Put your feet like this... point them forward and fucking walk straight." Uncle Don threw his hands beside him like a soldier and walked in a straight line with one foot in front of the other. "How fucking hard can it be?" Bewildered his eyes linger over Trisha with a dark wild stare. His pupils wide and baffled; waving his finger in her face. "Shut up and just fuck-ing do it!"

There was only silence that followed his ripping roar, as he stood there with a clenched fist.

My curiosity got the better of me. I slowly peeked around the corner to see who today's target was. Our eyes met and Trisha put her head down in shame right away.

"Why do you always have that fucking face on you?" Uncle Don knocked his knuckle on Trisha's forehead.

Uncle Don called me Rockhead, but he also called Trisha 'The Face' and Aunt Jane was named 'Burnt Out Jane'. The other kids didn't get a nickname, but Uncle Don used to always call us a bunch of morons.

"Point your feet forward..." With a grunt he took another sip of his beer and paced back and forth like a tiger in a pen. "Useless." Rage gripped him.

Anger stirred within me. I felt useless that I couldn't help. I hoped for Trisha to walk straight but I knew she was doing her best.

Trisha began to walk and headed out of the kitchen.

Uncle Don slammed his hand on the table, making Trish and I jump. He leaned down to face her.

"Where do you think you're going?" Uncle Don pointed to the floor. "I told you to walk straight." He sounded like a broken record; he just couldn't let it go.

Her shoulders crept tightly inward; Trisha moved towards the direction Uncle Don pointed. Facing the floor, she mustered up all her focus and attempted to do what he ordered. Trisha tried to force her pigeon feet straight and will them like he said.

"It's because you're lazy," he snapped.

I could see the emotion behind Trisha's eyes and inwardly she was seething. A resentment festered in her.

Uncle Don hadn't seen me. I was still in the hallway out of his view. I looked at the clock thinking it wasn't is usual time he would get into a state. I quietly turned around to sneak upstairs. Maybe I can avoid a lecture for the night. I slowly took soft steps towards the stairs to avoid being noticed.

"You see?" Uncle Don said with a stern hard frown. "Just walk like that from now on," he said. "Go practice."

Trisha's eyes pooled with pain.

Passing by me, Trisha didn't hesitate to greet me out loud for my uncle to hear.

"Tag! You're it," she mumbled.

What a bitch, I thought as her frown turned into a smirk.

"Rockhead come here," I took in a deep breath and staggered forward, replacing my face with a smile. I didn't speak unless spoken to, and I only spoke when I was asked a question. Keep it simple, stupid, I thought.

"You went to the gym?" Uncle Don continued to drill me with questions. "What did you learn?"

I paused. This was a trick question. I know if I tell him what I learned, he will break it down and take the value out of it. But if I say I learned nothing, I'm wasting time and money and he will call me stupid.

I figured I'd give him what he wanted to hear. "I learned to keep my feet planted." I breathed in deep and fought not to mumble. "And I did pushups and stretches." It was true I learned these things but that's when I first started at the lower level. The level I'm at now had more contact but I wasn't about to tell him that. He'd tell me to throw up my dukes for sure.

"That's good." He grinned. "Show me how you plant your feet." His cheeks and nose were already rich with a red flushness.

I rubbed my gut; which knotted. I'm nauseous. "Okay." I replied without hesitation. I learned once not to volunteer any additional information that might trigger another rant.

"Are you planted?" Uncle Don asked me as he took another swig of beer. "Show me!"

I jumped into a stance potion, known as fighting position and slightly steadied my body.

"Ready." Uncle Don stood in front of me.

I didn't say anything as I waited to be pushed across the room. I not only thought of what I learnt in class, but it was automatic to think of a sumo wrestler because to me, Uncle Don was a giant. I needed to really root into the ground. For a moment, I thought of Bruce Lee and Chuck Norris.

He shoved me back slightly and I kept my ground for the first shove. It wasn't as bad as I thought it would be. Then he did it again, and it was harder; my body jerked. The third time he gave a hard shove and I had to step back. I almost fell to the floor. He still held back; he was just testing.

Uncle Don told me to put my hands up, so I raised my fists. With my feet firmly planted, I gave him my best shot. It didn't faze him, not even a little. "Not bad kid but remember... all you have to do is punch them in the throat, nose and kick their legs out from under them."

"Like this?" I kept a tight rein on my emotions as I went to kick his knees. Jesus, what had I gotten myself into?

"You'll have to keep practicing." Uncle Don showed me where to kick and then he raised his hand and pointed to my temple with a solid finger. "Connect right there after you hit the legs." Uncle Don put pressure on the front of my throat.

"After I hit them in the leg, I hit them in the throat?" I repeated after him. "Like a combo." I amused him.

"Yes." He grinned.

I put on a poker face as his glare was on me. I had to control my breathing. I hope he hadn't sensed my fear. Keeping my chin up and giving my best impression, I decided to ask a question and change the subject. "Can I take the empty bottles to the store tomorrow?"

"Yes, good idea." Uncle Don's eyebrows furrowed. He patted me on the head and sat down to look through his hardware catalog. "What are you using the money for?"

"I would like to get a video," I answered. I didn't want to remind him that it's for tomorrow night. Pamela was coming to sleep over. I hope he's in a better mood tomorrow. I met Pamela at camp a few years ago and then found out we were distant cousins.

"Grab the bottles from the basement," Uncle Don ordered.

"Thank you," I said, calculating the cents I'll get back for returning the empties. Once, his attention fell into the magazine and he didn't say anything else, I took the opportunity to leave the kitchen.

"Rockhead?" Uncle Don said quickly.

I froze. "Yes?"

"Keep up the good work," he said.

It was like I now had allowance to go on with my evening.

I quickly went upstairs; straight to my room. I leapt onto my patched waterbed and reached for my sketchbook. I put some music on; grabbed a pencil and my wrist went with the flow and I just let the creative juices go.

In the days ahead, I buried myself into computer class. I used every minute to sharpen my skills and learn more about it. The principal also got me helping in the theatre department. It gave me a chance to paint.

Today, I took the lunch program off to be with my friends.

"Some of us are going to the shops," Crystal said. "Are you coming?"

"The shops?" wondering what I was agreeing to.

"It's a strip mall with an excellent selection," Crystal added. "Apparently, the restaurant sells slices of pizza."

Instantly, my mouth watered, and I imagined the taste the melted cheese.

"Pizza, huh?" I answered, pleased to be doing something different other than hanging around the school. "Lead the way."

"Maybe we can catch up to the others," Crystal said cheerfully.

We walked down the stairs, passed the locker room where I had spray painted. We made our way through a cloud of cigarette smoke and across the street through dozens of trees. Crystal and I met up with the rest of the girls on the trail and walked down a path alongside St-Jean Boulevard towards the shops.

Not only was there satisfying pizza but there was a candy shop beside the restaurant. I couldn't help myself; I had a bad sweet tooth.

It was a gem hidden away from our school, our own little Candyland. Why didn't anyone show me this sooner? I noticed Carly was there also. She was buying jawbreakers.

Instead of leaving, I walked down the aisle and leisurely scooped candies into a paper bag. Carly and I saw each other. I passed her without any issues; she was distracted, and I felt accepted. It was like I was able to breath. It felt like the candy shop was on neutral ground.

"You have to try this one," Crystal said.

I grabbed a few of the ones she pointed at and some red lipped candies. When it came to candy, most people either savored it or devoured it.

"Do you know why Lifesavers have a hole in the middle of it?" I asked Crystal.

She paused for a moment. "No, I don't."

"So, children don't choke on it," I said. "If it gets stuck, at least you can still breath."

"No way," Crystal said, "Is that true?"

I nodded. "I heard it from a friend." I wasn't sure if that was 100% true, but it fit. It's funny how there was a story behind everything, even a simple piece of candy. Some candies are marketed on their unique ways to eat it. The experience must be just as enjoyable as the flavor.

I slowly finished my candy throughout the day. But that wasn't the best part of it. I walked through an invisible door; a step closer to a social circle. It seemed it was one more thing that set me apart. The Shops were where the cool kids went... but for me it was one step closer to finding a life with friends. I like my alone time, but I don't like being lonely. I looked at my classmates; knowing, in a few months, I'd be gone. Why do we have to move now? It was beyond me.

I got home before Aunt Jane woke up. She slept the day away. Just another night owl in the family. Trisha was in her room talking on the telephone. She cut her eyes at me.

I couldn't have cared less. Uncle Don paid me to check on her and eavesdrop on her conversations. Lately, he'd been occupied with work and other things.

"Don't you have somewhere to go?" Trisha asked.

"Always." But I didn't.

Once again, I was out like a light; right through to morning. It seemed they couldn't wake me and even when I woke, I couldn't shake it.

"Fuck! Who's the idiot that spilled the molasses all over the kitchen floor?" A deep angry voice echoed, a roaring temper, he started his way up the stairs, "you fucking kids need to learn." Agitated, Uncle Don drowned out the faint radio in my room.

Fumbling, I rolled out of bed forcing my eyes wide open. I quickly got up and stood outside my bedroom door, as if it was for an inspection, I straightened like a soldier.

"Wake up!" Uncle Don barked like a drill Sergeant.

Horrified, I looked from Sarah to Farley. I stood ready for an order. Trisha and Michael didn't open their doors yet. I looked at Michael's doorknob, hoping for it to turn.

Uncle Don questioned the girls and then told them to clean up their rooms. He opened Michael's door and told him to get up. "There's work to be done," he shouted.

I didn't blink as I watched him open Trisha's door, but she wasn't there. She was in the bathroom, so he started banging on the door. "The Face get out here."

His eyes drifted to me, before yelling again.

"Come!" He said sharply and made his way heavily downstairs. "Get the fuck up and follow me."

He expected all of us to follow him, so I jumped in line behind him and followed his lead.

"Do you know who did this?" He questioned.

"No." I said, feeling weary.

Trisha trailed in last, her face was white, pale and ill, she looked as shaky as I felt.

Michael couldn't help himself, back against the wall, he stood away, not knowing what to expect. I looked at Uncle Don with a blank stare on my face. I really had no clue, raising my eyebrows.

"Nobody knows who did this?" he shouted.

"No," Trisha said cautiously. We all shrugged in unison.

"Clean it up," he said throwing a cloth at Trisha.

"I'll try," she said wobbly with a scowl.

"I don't want to hear a fucking 'try'," he said with daggers in his eyes. "Just do what your fucking told." He paused, looking at the lot of us. "What's with the long faces?"

I lifted my chin in response.

"I want to see my reflection in it," he growled.

No matter how much this floor would shine, there's no way he'd see his thick-headed mug in it. Looking over at the others, we were all on the same page. Trisha made a face that was to die for, half shocked and in disbelief, her jaw dropped with a hint of disgust, her face was easy to read.

"You could get your toothbrush if it's an issue," he spat out. "When I get back, it better be clean." He left us with a sticky sweet mess and a creepy silence. I wonder who made the mess. I could see ants already forming a line.

"Who did this?" Trisha snapped with no response.

I rolled up my sleeves and grabbed the cloth. "It's not that bad," I answered.

"Did you do it?" Trisha accused, "I need this like I need a hole in the head."

"No." I bent down to give more arm power, wiping the sticky mess with dish soap.

"Brown-noser." Trisha mumbled.

"It's called survival." I smirked.

"It's called stupidity," Trisha added. "You're just a bunch of morons," she said, while throwing her hands up in the air with frustration. She couldn't help herself, she continued, "I can't do this anymore." Rolling her eyes defiantly. "I'm not a soldier or a slave. I need privacy. I want to stop moving and to live in one place long enough to make friends." She bellowed. "I need clothes and my own room."

"Don't hold back." I teased. "You're on a roll." She clearly wasn't in the mood. She punched me in the arm.

"What's with these ridiculous haircuts Aunt Jane gives us." Trisha complained. "My bangs are too short."

"My hair is always cut short," I said without thinking.

"Why do you listen to them?" She stopped and gave me an unhappy look.

"Do I have a choice." Of course, it would be easier to give my opinion and plead a case, but I found it hard to talk. I shrugged, "there's no point in arguing," I said softly. They wouldn't hear me, anyway. They're too quick to give a lecture.

"I have a choice and I choose they could stick it up their ass." Trisha frowned.

I hadn't formed a voice; let alone make decisions. My opinions were dismissed, and my dreams were just that – of dreams. I wanted to impress Uncle Don. I was searching for approval in some way.

It took us about an hour and a half to clean the kitchen. We even cleaned the fridge and stove. When Uncle Don returned, he was in good spirits. "Keep up the good-work," he said pleased, cracking open a beer, and sending us on our way.

Before I left, I bent over to see if I can see my reflection in the floor. I couldn't. But apparently it was clean enough.

When I went upstairs, I went straight into the bathroom to take a bath. A few minutes later, there was a knock.

"Yeah." I answered. I knew it wasn't Uncle Don because I kept my ear out for him. This was someone already upstairs.

"How long are you going to be?" Trisha asked.

"I just turned the water off." I said.

Trisha clunked her teeth. "Are you taking a bath?"

I slowly answered, "yes."

"You bitch." She said, totally at a loss. "I was going to do that."

I couldn't help but relax my body. I sank slowly into the water, dipping my head under while Trisha's voice muffled out. She disappeared with a bitching rant, complaining that she had enough.

The moment I saw the party-line commercial pop on, I grabbed Michael and urged him to the television set. "Carly Tremblay is on our television."

Michael nodded wearily and looked at the screen.

I watched as Carly answered a ringing telephone, while confetti and party poppers went off as she said hello. Her blond hair was in a ponytail off to one side and her bangs teased up. Suddenly, she was on her way and chatting with a new group of friends 24 hours a day, the commercial said as balloons fell around her.

"Who's she?" Michael asked.

"A girl that goes to my school," I leaned back to watch.

"How did she get on T.V.?" Michael asked with raised eyebrows.

"How would I know?" I answered.

I'm sure I wasn't the only one seeing this. That was the problem her head grew bigger by the minute.

I got up and decided to trade Uncle Don's beer bottles in for some cash. I realized I could do four trips to the store. Usually, it was Trisha that was sent on the store run to get a two-four of beer or three bags of milk; sometimes, she had to carry back both.

I was the one who counted the profit of bringing them back. Trisha wasn't into bringing back empties. She didn't want nothing to do with them.

I was looking forward to renting a movie for Pamela's visit. First it will be TGIF and then a movie night. Trisha was going to Mom's place again.

I decided not to wear shoes. I walked barefoot up the concrete sidewalk and then behind the apartments, towards the back parking lot of the strip mall. I entered the dépanneur with the empty bottles. An elderly man slowly approached the cash and I asked him to exchange them. With no issue, the man counted the bottles up and handed me some cash.

"Hey, you go to the Gym up the street?" The old man asked with a Korean accent.

"Yes," I answered. "How did you know?"

"I see you walk on Saturday to the gym, wearing your Gi." he smiled at me and continued, "I am Chung Lee."

I cocked my head and took a step back. "No, you're not!" I said taking a better look at him. I recognized him from his picture on the wall at the gym. I bow to him every time I enter the class.

"Sensei," I naturally bowed, smiling. "What are you doing here?"

"I own the store." He said with a smile, while cleaning out his ice cream section. "Do you want ice cream?" He pointed to the different selections I could choose from.

This is the coolest sensei ever. It was a tossup between chocolate or dark cherry. The bubble gum was low.

I noticed he wasn't going for a cone or a scoop, he slid out the whole bucket and passed it to me.

I looked up from the ice cream to him. "No way."

"Way." He said.

"Thank you." I eagerly hugged the cold bucket.

"Have a good day," he said soft-spoken.

I walked out with cash and a bin of ice cream. It's crazy who you meet in the neighborhood. I find it random but not odd that my Sensei owns both the gym and the dépanneur.

I went over to the video store which was right next door. I headed straight to the new releases. The movie covers sat on display, neatly in order.

There was a poster on the wall that caught my attention. "When you're done with the poster, can I have it?" I asked, fidgeting while asking the guy behind the counter. I pointed to the poster on the wall that matched the video in my hand.

"Hold on," the guy answered and turned around to another customer. The lady butt in front of me to ask a question, as if I was invisible.

Casually the guy behind the counter came back to me. "Yeah, I don't see why not." He looked through the drop-offs and added, "but we can only give it after it's moved from the new releases."

"That's fine." I said cheerfully.

I walked out of the store; accomplished from achieving something on my own. I held on tight to my ice cream and movie. I was even sucked into buying popcorn as I walked out from the buttery scent.

Pamela and I found out we were related through my father's side of the family. I can't help but think back to the last time I saw my dad... feels like a lifetime ago.

I tried to imagine what happened that day when we came back from visiting him, nobody mentioned anything, all I knew was that we weren't allowed to go back. Some people told Trisha to stop telling stories. I guess it all had to do with the night before. Instead of talking about what happened, everyone avoided the topic. The memory of that night slipped from my mind. Buried deep, as if it were too much to bear. I was forbidden to talk about him, like he ceased to exist.

Pamela was picked up at a foster home in Pointe-Fortune, she was recovering from some personal issues at home. The woman that manages the house bought Pamela a sleeveless black velvet dress that hung down around her ankles, it came with a jean jacket. "I love this dress," she said as if she never wore velvet before.

"You look good," I said. It had been almost two months since I've seen Pamela.

When she arrived, we walked to DK restaurant to kill her craving for hotdogs and doughnuts. The last time we saw each other was at camp. It started to get chilly and dark by the time we left.

Excited, Pamela rushed across the lawn. "Superman!" She shouted and skipped forward. Her footing slipped and got the better of her; overstepping, both her feet left the ground as she tumbled over the grass to the cement sidewalk. Staggering and arms flailing, her heel caught in the dress as she attempted to catch herself.

I watched her tumble to the ground.

Still, she raised her hand in the air, the bag dangled in one piece without harm, "I saved the donuts." I couldn't help but laugh as I ran to her aid. Her knees were scraped up.

"Are you okay?" I asked.

"I think so." Pamela looked down at herself. "Crap! My dress is ruined."

"It's just a tear," I replied quickly.

"I'm going to get in trouble for this," Pamela confessed. She blew out a frustrated breath. "I just got this dress."

"Hopefully she won't notice," I murmured.

"At least we still have our doughnuts," Pamela said quickly while picking up the bottom of her dress.

The movie was worth the wait. Both Pamela and I had to get tissue more than once. "We have to do this again." We both agreed as we finished off the last of the chips.

"Have you heard from Derek?" Pamela asked me. The boy I met at camp over the summer.

"No." I shrugged.

Pamela giggled. "What do you mean, no."

"I didn't hear from him," I said. "I see how Uncle Don is with Trisha. Imagine if he found out I was talking to a dude." turning the questions around on her I then asked, "What about Newman?"

"No. We haven't spoken since camp." Pamela's fingers hovered inches over the donuts. She was having a tough time deciding which one to pick.

"Guess what?" I gave Pamela a big grin.

"What?"

"I got tickets to Wrestling," I said, finally having someone to share my excitement with.

"Live?" Pamela said surprised. "How many tickets do you have?"

"Only two... and I think Aunt Jane's bringing me."

"Traitor!" Pamela playfully said. "If it wasn't for me you wouldn't even be watching wrestling."

"You're right. I'd be watching some ..."

"M-M-A!" Pamela and I said simultaneously. She knew I was more into the mixed martial arts.

"How is Uncle Don?" Pamela asked genuinely concerned. "Has he been in a better mood?" Pamela knew what to say without saying too much.

"Sort of." I answered and ground my teeth a little.

"You know he loves you." She smiled again and switched the subject. Pamela wasn't telling me what I didn't already know.

"You know what would be cool?" I sank deeper into the couch.

"Another bowl of chips." Pamela winked.

"If one day I could meet all my brothers and sisters," I said slowly, wondering what sort of person they were becoming.

Pamela slid me an odd little look that I couldn't read. "I never asked you what happened to them?"

"We all split after we were taken from mom. I never really got to know my younger brother." I paused for a moment leaning back. "I haven't been allowed to see or visit my dad, so I never met my siblings on his side," I said simply and filled the bowl with the rest of the chips.

Pamela agreed. "I hope you get to meet them one day."

"Me, too." I always let down my firewall with her. She knew me best. I only let people see what I wanted them to.

By the end of the weekend, I didn't want our time to end. I didn't want Pamela to go.

Once she left, I went upstairs. It didn't take much effort to hide away. I buried myself in my sketchbook. Once again, art filled my lonely hours. I slept well all through the night.

Monday seemed to be the least liked day of the week. It was a little uncomfortable having Carly sitting across from me in such close quarters. Neither of us wanted to be spending our time together.

The counselor introduced himself. I didn't find any point in remembering his name. I wasn't planning on coming back.

Uncle Don said they were just being nosey. What else was there to say? Go against family? Like that was an option.

I fidgeted on the couch for a minute debating, finally telling myself, well, you can face Uncle Don, so you can face this, too.

"Whatever is shared here is under the privacy act." The guidance counselor encouraged. "If anyone gets the urge to speak, don't hesitate." A hush came over the group.

"Is this Inner Circle?" Carly looked worried.

"No." The counselor said lightly.

"So, what exactly is this?" I asked.

"This is for support to let you know we're here to help."

I was still hesitant to trust. I clasped my hands together. "I don't need help."

"Everyone needs help," he admitted "How's the family?"

"Fine." I said defensively. I had been born into a madhouse. Feeling abandoned and alone, like I was made to swallow the world's bullshit. I felt like I was being inspected. How is this guy going to change my scene?

"First of all, I would like you all to say your name and the reason you think you may be here." I angled my head, like it was that simple. I was having trouble taking the whole thing seriously. But I watched as everyone spoke up, one after another.

As time went on, aside from the corny comments, it wasn't that bad. I was ready to erupt with heartfelt complaints. Who put these expectations on me? Boxing me in. I live in two worlds with two faces. The one in public and the one in private. It wasn't about being a rat. It was about being free to be myself. I wanted to take off the mask. To find hope in the shadow.

The counselor looked pleased, "would you like to share?"

Just mentioning about my home life would get me into trouble. In a daze, I questioned the process. The room was quiet. It dawned on me that the group was staring at me waiting for me to speak.

"There's not much to tell," I said quietly. I bent over my knees slouching forward on the couch as we proceeded.

"Why do you think you're here?" The counselor asked.

I figured I'd start with something small. "I tend to get angry." I shrugged, "It gets away from me."

"Okay," he said. "Is there a reason?"

There was a trembling within me. I kept my eyes on him. "I don't think so." My heart rapidly clocked like a rabbit; I knew there was a reason.

He understood what I wasn't saying. "What triggers you?" He said quietly, with a curiosity underneath that made me cautious. I didn't have an answer for him, so he just continued. "You need to recognize your trigger signs."

He was really trying to get to the root of my anger.

I naturally interrupted him. "My martial art classes help."

"Hmm." He didn't look convinced and my attention, however, was on other things.

"You seem secretive."

"Do I?" I repeated without elaborating. I sat there in silence until he got the picture to move on.

"Does anyone else want to share?" He asked softly.

This counseling thing isn't that bad, I thought. As if on cue, Carly stretched upward, and began to talk tentatively.

"I live with an alcoholic." She shrugged, looking at us, not one peep from any of them. She didn't have to draw me a picture. "My dad says I won't amount to much... that I'd have to work that much harder to get ahead. He wants me to marry a rich guy."

"I know how you feel." The words slipped out. I hesitated before continuing. "I know what it's like to live with an alcoholic. My uncle gets angry a lot."

The counselor looked at me with an aha moment.

When I saw their expressions, I wanted to extract. Why had I been so stupid as to confide in them?

"How do you handle it?" Carly asked softly.

I crossed my fingers and rolled my eyes skyward, "I don't," I said into the silence. "I just swallow it."

Carly's eyes were curious, as if we were waiting for the same answer.

Uncle Don drilled into us from the get-go that we were never to speak to people; that we were never to bring up what we do at the house. Ever.

"What's eating you?" Crystal asked while crossing paths. I rubbed my forehead not knowing what to say. I just stared straight ahead. I sat on the bus wondering what the punishment would be if the school decided to call.

CHAPTER FIVE

Live in Babysitter

By the time I got closer to the house, a bitter pang went through me. My knees were rattling from the fear of my aunt and uncle finding out what I had shared with the guidance counselor.

Uncle Don was already home when I arrived, "Sit your ass down," he hollered loudly, walking towards the kitchen table with boxed red wine.

I'm in some serious shit! I thought. I sat down quickly. There was no room for error. It took Trisha a little longer to arrive and the others were still at school. I prepared myself for whatever punishment I had coming.

"Jane and I are going on a trip. You kids have to stay here and behave." The tension in my shoulders melted with his last words. Thank God!

Uncle Don advised that it would be in our best interest to listen to the babysitter.

"Don't do anything stupid," he growled, stepping outside onto the back deck.

"Who's babysitting?" Trisha asked Aunt Jane hesitantly.

"Ebony."

"Ebony!?" Trisha repeated. "Why her?"

Aunt Jane cocked her head like a chicken, "because I said so." She placed her hands on her hips daring Trisha to say something. "We can't have you babysit all week."

"I have to watch them all the time, anyway." Trisha complained.

"You're the oldest." Aunt Jane glared at her. "Get over it."

"When are you leaving?" Trisha asked, trying not to sound overjoyed.

"Tomorrow morning." She continued as she pulled out the meat for dinner.

"You brats be good and no funny business," Uncle Don belched out while stepping in through the patio doors. He just unloaded himself off the back deck.

It was evident that this conversation was over. Uncle Don walked past us to the living room for the nightly news.

I didn't hesitate to call my friends like some hotline, we made plans like a couple of mall rats to cruise Fairview Mall.

I froze once I hung up the receiver back in its cradle and heard unfamiliar voices echoed through the house.

I went downstairs, partially because I was curious and half because I was thirsty. I walked into the kitchen.

"You must be Vicky," a young man said holding a beer. I froze and my stomach sank. I didn't recognize the two men in front of me. They looked to be in their early twenties and ready for a large mountain to snowboard down. One guy had orange hair and the other had green.

"Who wants to know?" I smirked.

"Give them a straight answer," Aunt Jane said annoyed. "And what are you doing out of your room?"

"Getting a drink." I carried on to the fridge and poured myself a glass of O.J. I didn't say anything else as I stood there and downed my juice in a few gulps. I blushed at the thought of them.

I was surprised Uncle Don had people around whose vocabulary had been made up with words such as... gnarly, rad, sick or bro.

"Okay! You have your drink, now get to bed." Aunt Jane said and stepped towards the counter to make herself a drink. Her forehead puckered as she nodded toward the hallway. "Go on." Aunt Jane demanded with a juice and vodka in her hand.

I shrugged and left.

I could see Trisha on the other side of the sheet that hung between our rooms. Her nose was in another book. Many times, she escaped to her room to avoid Uncle Don and Aunt Jane.

I flopped onto the bed, looking at a cookbook. The hearty pictures literally made me drool.

Steadily, I could hear Aunt Jane and the guys laughing outside my window. I open it up to get a better grasp of what they were saying.

"Sorry about that," she sneered. "Vicky doesn't know better. She's just a stupid kid."

I couldn't help myself. I slammed the window shut. It was obvious. Just a stupid kid, huh?

Not a minute too soon, Aunt Jane swung the door open and marched straight towards me and slapped me. "Stupid girl." Her voice venomous as she turned around and slammed the door behind her. "Don't come out."

Shaken but not surprised, my cheek stung.

"You shouldn't have slammed that window." Trisha said faintly. "Stupid move."

I sighed.

I fell asleep to Aunt Jane singing. Her voice carried like a folk singer as she sang along to a song. Looking at the four walls I call my life, I imagined what it would be like to be on my own, swept away. Can time really heal all things?

Again, I can't seem to shake it. I keep waking up in the middle of the night. Shadow people appear without a word, solid and blacked out. Other times, like last night, I dreamed of falling from the sky. It was different from the time I fell asleep and I saw myself from the ceiling. This time, my soul lifted to the sky, looking over the landscape of the city. It seemed once I acknowledged the situation, the spell broke and I fell from the clouds like a rock. Gravity switched; leaving me to drop, like a shot down bird.

I never seem to hit the ground. I always end up waking up. Pulling the panic out with me, leaving me awake with an unexpected rush of adrenaline.

I took the morning to think it over. I couldn't solve it. My thoughts studied what had happened. I guess, in a way I had to meditate on it. It seemed funny to say it that way, but even an analyst was considered someone who meditated. It was a way for me to direct my thoughts and sometimes even ball them up and wash them away.

I wrote my dreams in a hidden notebook I got from school. My handwriting poured out like art, fluid and musical. I fell down the rabbit hole of words. Drawing and writing meshed well, hand in hand, both an instrument to get lost in. I envisioned an understanding... I broke off into thought.

When I was done my morning pause or whatever people called it – reflection, meditation or just a simple personal time out, I made my way downstairs slowly. The voices seemed to be pleasant. My shoulders eased and the pressure in the back of my neck loosened. The usual worry washed away from me.

The guys from last night had left early this morning and Ebony arrived just in time. Aunt Jane and Uncle Don were leaving. They had already loaded their van.

"Remember to get your asses to school and listen to Ebony," Aunt Jane ordered.

Making sure we attend school was one thing, but it was another to expect us to listen to Ebony. We were known for being little shitheads.

"Who's Ebony?" I teased, giving her a wink. She was like an aunt to me. Our families grew up tight-knit on the streets of Little Burgundy and Notre-Dame; a vein to the body of the island of Montreal.

"The kids can be difficult, but..." Aunt Jane laid her eyes on me, "they're going to behave."

I was about to say if she wanted me to behave, she'd have to pay me. But looking at her, Ebony knew all too well how we were. That's why she brought extra bottles of coolers.

"Come on," Uncle Don growled. He seemed strangely eager to leave. "We have to get on the road."

Sarah and Farley refused to unpeel themselves from Aunt Jane's legs. "Get off!" Uncle Don shouted.

Both girls detached reluctantly and dragged their feet to the house. Michael and Trisha didn't come out to see them off. I assume they were having a celebration.

The van disappeared around the corner. Ebony and I squared off on the front lawn.

"Somebody has chores to do." She said automatically.

I laughed at her determined face. "Who?"

"You." Ebony challenged.

My eyebrows shot up with protest. "Me? Are you serious?"

"Like a heart attack." She handed me her bags. "Let's get cracking. I have a show that comes on at seven."

I paused and cocked my head to one side. Adults are obsessed with cleaning. It's not just one adult but a fleet of them. "Are you sure you're not pulling my leg?" I asked Ebony again, she never told me to do anything before. Usually she didn't care what I did.

"What do you think?" She leaned in, her gaze resting on me with obvious curiosity, as if I was some bizarre sight she's ever come across.

"No can do," I answered, shaking my head. I saw how this was going to go, thinking furiously.

"Yes, you will." Ebony said. The words came out a little rancid. Her dark eyes scrutinizing me.

I was no stranger to piercing eyes or presenting a placid expression even when my brain was burning and screaming, so it was not much of an effort to fake a smile.

"I don't see that happening." I answered.

"I don't see you eating pizza with the rest of us," she eye-balled me.

Shit. I stopped and said nothing. I wondered if the pizza was worth the work. My forehead furrowed. "Okay," I sighed dramatically.

"Alright." Her attention switched to the house and my attention switched to the clock.

Once we were inside, I didn't see Ebony for most of the morning. Trisha refused to clean and left twenty minutes after the order was given. My cousins scattered, leaving me to be the schmuck.

I danced and cleaned to pass the time, but once I got to the large aquarium of angelfish... I had enough. Nobody would bat an eyelash if I left. "I'm done," I grumbled heading for the door. To be honest, the house still looked like shit. I slammed the door behind me challenging anyone to say something.

I liked to believe I had a choice. I wondered why some kids were forced to grow up quickly, while others were catered to.

I found myself walking aimlessly, roaming freely. I wondered if I would want to live any other way... I knew this way.

"Vicky! Simona shouted from the lobby of an apartment.

"Hold on." I could see she wasn't alone.

"Hurry," She said waving.

I slightly quickened my pace. I refused to run, not because I couldn't, but because I didn't want to. "What's up?" I asked as I got to her.

"These guys invited me to their place..." I looked over her shoulder at them. "Come with me."

"Seriously?" I whispered, not impressed.

"Please," she said softly. "Look at them."

I rolled my eyes. "Um..." I said, totally at a loss. They were clean cut with a Ruff Ryder style.

Simona strolled back towards them; her hips exaggerated. "Come on," she tugged me forward, "Please."

One guy brushed his eyes over me as if I was going to be his afternoon snack. "Do you know them?" I asked her, noticing she liked the attention.

"Sort of." She said briskly while opening the door to the lobby.

What the crap did that mean? Sort of. "Do you know them or not?"

"Just come," she pleaded as I walked past her.

Well, I don't. "No." I said. "I'll see you later."

Not that I didn't want to hang with her, but my gut said just keep walking. I turned up the street, not far from Simona and her admirers.

A small bell above the door frame rang like a chime as I entered the dépanneur. Mr. Lee stood behind the counter.

"Did you like the ice cream?" he asked.

"Yes," I replied. "Thank you."

He smiled and nodded. He never really said much. It took me awhile to explain to Uncle Don and Aunt Jane how I got the bucket of ice cream in the first place. They didn't believe me when I told them Sensei owned the corner store as well as the gym. Uncle Don roared in laughter and praised me for my sense of humor.

I used up the bit of change I had left. I wasn't out of the store two minutes before I had three pieces of gum in my mouth.

On my way back home, I noticed Simona pulling on the door to the lobby I had left her at. I could see she wasn't enjoying herself. The guys were still trying to persuade her inside. "Come on. Come on. You know us."

I wasn't sure if this was one of her tactics of playing hard to get. I walked close enough for her to call me over. I didn't want those boneheads to think I was eager to see them.

"Vicky!" She said looking at me, her eyes wide with panic.

"I forgot to tell you; your mom is looking for you," I said, giving her a way out. "Come to my place and call her back." I said, hoping the guys would back off. But she didn't hear me, she turned to tell one of them to stop pulling on her arm.

"Hey, enough." I said firmly. "She has to call her mom."

Both guys turned on me and Simona was able get loose. I looked to see if anyone was around to help, but there wasn't. I thought about running over to the house to get Uncle Don, but he wasn't around, either way. Even in the midst of panic, I felt annoyed.

I kept my hands slightly up and stood my ground casually. "It's a great day to be outside," I said firmly. I didn't dare go close to them – best to take time for blood to cool. Simona joined me and we walked away.

One of them cringed. "Come on... where are you going?"

"Uh...none of your business," Simona said.

We made our way to my house. It was the closest option to put distance between us and them.

Simona's expression changed as we walked in.

I'd like to see them try to start shit over here, I thought, looking over her shoulder.

Shock nearly made Simona stammer, "I'm in."

"Just for a few minutes." I warned her questioning gaze.

We made our way upstairs in hopes that no one would notice us. It was nice to finally invite someone in. It felt like I was not only inviting her into the house, but into my life.

"Who's this?" Ebony said. "You know you're not supposed to have anyone over. It's not an open house."

"It's not for long." I said hoping to dilute the tension. She didn't realize how fed up I was of rules. I didn't have to justify myself.

"You have five minutes." Ebony said sharply before heading back to her show.

"You know you're not supposed to have any friends over, right?" Trisha said, clearing her throat.

"Yeah, yeah." I closed the door, but Trisha could still see over if she wanted to.

"A waterbed?" Simona sat down; her weight shifted to one side. "Why aren't we allowed in the house?"

"My uncle and aunt are out of town and they don't want anyone hanging around." I said automatically.

"But you never invited me over before."

"It's a mess..." There was a part of me that wanted to tell her the truth, but I just couldn't. "Plus, those guys were bugging you."

"I told them I changed my mind." She smiled, curling her hair around her fingers, "And that's when they got pushy."

"Bastards," I said. "Just stay away from them." I quickly changed the topic. "I never wanted you to think I lived in a pig pen."

Simona looked around with a shrug. "Who cares? It's not like you're asking me to help you clean."

Knickknacks where all over the house – Aunt Jane couldn't help herself and I wasn't going to clean up unless I was told to. I didn't want to get stuck with another chore. The house looked lived in and then some - worn down.

Simona observed my lack of décor. My bedroom walls were sadly bare compared to Simona's richly decorated room. Her bed and breakfast style made my room looked like it was ready for the dumpster. I didn't even know what a duvet was until I slept over at her house. I discovered that even comforters have covers and that there is more than one kind of sheet.

"No offense, but you need to fix your room up," She mentioned. "It doesn't feel happy."

"No offense taken," I said dryly. "I just don't think I can do anything about it. Shit, I've been cleaning all day."

"Okay there, keep lying." Trisha said from the other side of the sheet that hung between us.

Simona ignored the comment. "So, what do you do when your home?" She looked around.

Besides having to clean, staying out of the way or helping Uncle Don when he called, I just usually sit in my room. When he wasn't home, I watched movies or drove Trisha crazy. "Draw and listen to music," I said, I would have told her I wrote a bit, but I was afraid she'd see my spelling.

"What type of music?"

"I listen to different stuff."

Simona pulled something out of her pocket. "You have to listen to this." She passed me a tape. "It's 'Boyz II Men'."

I placed the cassette in the tape player and pressed play. I relished in the soulful melody.

"Can I see your art?" Simona asked.

"I don't usually show my work."

"But you do draw." Her smile was cool and collective.

"Yes, I draw." I smiled, "I also love crafts."

Trisha laughed unwillingly, "And you play with yourself."

Simona looked at me bewildered. "Don't listen to her, she ate paint chips as a child," I said throwing my pillow at the visual division between us.

"You're one to talk. You were dropped on your head," Trisha replied.

"This is why I can't have people over," I said hastily.

"I want to see your drawings," Simona said, a little more demanding. "Let's lay them all on the bed."

"I don't usually lay it all out." I shrugged.

I slowly slipped my hand under the dresser and slid out three sketchbooks, a few large pieces of paper rolled up from art class. I hid them away from prying eyes. There were a few spots I keep to myself.

"Here." I passed them to Simona.

"Vicky colored in mine." Trisha commented, while we separated my art.

"I thought they needed color." I smirked.

"Bitch." Letting off steam, Trisha snuck a cigarette.

I could have told her I did it to be a jerk, but really, her art caught my eye and I guess I wanted to color it. I always had a coloring book and Momma and Papa had always colored with me.

We spread out my work and the characters and images filled up the room with a story. I hadn't noticed it before, but their seemed to be a theme.

"I love that one." Simona pointed to an image of a female skater doing a trick where the underbelly of the board slides against stairs and a railing. "It's called a board-slide."

"Makes sense," I paused. "How do you know that?"

"My brother."

"Oh, yeah!" I forgot for a second that her brother skated. It made sense that she knew. She liked to hang around and watch him and his friends.

"I want this." She asked, reaching out for the drawing.

"Sure." I added, "just one." I could never hold onto my drawing long enough to finish them.

Smiling, Simona sat down and noticed something in my pillowcase. "What's that?" She asked while reaching for it.

I'm sure my cheeks burned flush red. "It's nothing."

She picked it up before I could grab it. As she opened the pillowcase and pulled out the paper, my heart sank. Without thought, she plucked into my soul.

"What's that?" Simona asked, looking at the picture. Her dark eyebrows shot up so high, I thought they'd leave her forehead.

"It's just a house." I reached for it and slowly took it out her hands.

"Are you moving?" Stunned, I wasn't sure if I should answer. "Is this your new place?" She asked anxiously.

"I wish." I ran my thumb over the image and folded it back up. "This is the house I plan on owning one day."

"Keep dreaming!" Trisha interrupted.

I could have yelled, but I didn't want to talk about it anymore. I placed the picture back into my pillowcase.

"I like looking at houses and auto magazines." I shrugged. "For fun."

The image stayed with me. The vision of a long driveway that led to a place I could call home.

I slowly put my drawings away. The combination of Trisha smoking and Simona's prying hands were too much to handle. I had to get out of here. The air seemed to be choking me. "Let's go."

She hesitated, then agreed when she saw I wasn't waiting for an answer.

"What's in that room?" Simona pointed to the light shining outside the bottom of another door across the hall. "That light's bright..."

Avoiding the door and the question I walked downstairs right away, assuming she would follow me but to my surprise, she didn't. She stepped towards the door and reached for the handle. Simona almost jumped out of her skin when Trisha, Michael and the two girls jumped out of their rooms and shouted at her.

Simona jumped back as I made my way to her. She smiled and, oddly, the expression wasn't startling. "What's up?"

"Um... Ebony's staying in that room, we don't want to disturb her," Trisha explained, her voice slipped a notch. "She needs a brighter light to read."

We hoped Simona bought that. I nearly knocked her down the stairs and went straight out the front door.

The street was clear. The guys were gone.

"Hey!" A familiar voice shouted from up the street. Marcus appeared with his pet ferret.

"Hi," I nodded.

"Hello," Simona said, her accent made the simplest word sound sultry.

"Have you seen those guys around?" I asked.

"The guys up the street?" Marcus looked over. "I haven't seen them." He frowned. "Why?"

"They were bugging Simona."

"Did they hurt you?" Was it me or did Marcuse's voice change every time he spoke to Simona? It seemed he spoke smoother. I would say he drowned himself in cologne for her, but he did that anyway. He liked to smell sharp.

"Just a little." Simona batted her eyes.

"Stay clear from them. You don't want to get mixed up in that." He stretched. "They have a bad rep."

"What kind of bad rep?" Simona asked.

"They're known for some shady stuff," Marcus muttered, changing the subject he volunteered some neighbourhood gossip. "You know that old lady that lives down the street with all the cats?"

"Yeah." I answered, I counted nineteen cats on her front lawn once.

"She smokes pot," he smiled.

"No," Simona dismissed.

"Apparently, it helps with her pain." He admitted.

"How do you know that?" Simona asked.

"She told me," he explained. "My ball fell in her yard and we got to talking."

I snuck out of the conversation and left them behind.

"I have to go," I told Simona and turned to pet Marcus' ferret goodbye. "I'll see you later."

Simona gave me an odd look, she knew I didn't have any-where to go, or do anything. I was hoping she thought I was leaving them to talk. Marcus didn't have a problem with it.

CHAPTER SIX

The Switch

Once back inside, Ebony gave me an earful. "You know, Rockhead, you're not allowed people over," she warned.

"Won't happen again." I was unfazed.

"I have to step out for a minute," Ebony informed me, expected me to listen to Trisha, adding before she left, "I won't be long."

I fell silent. I had no idea what to do with myself.

"You should know better," Trisha teased. "You can't just bring whoever over."

"Yeah, sure." I sarcastically pouring out the sand from my shoes onto the floor.

"Oh yeah. You can do whatever you want. It's me they have a problem with." She rolled her eyes, her voice rumbling deep in her chest.

"Would it make you happier if I got into more trouble?" I teased. "You're the one that doesn't listen."

"Stop stressing me out," she said, glaring at me. "I can't help myself... I'm a Taurus and stubborn. Nobody is going to tell me what to think."

"Then stop stressing me out." I grinned. "I'm a Capricorn and apparently just as hard-headed."

"Whatever. Just don't make any plans for next week. You may be busy." Trisha said dryly.

"I'm sure I won't be." I was only half-listening.

"I wouldn't be so sure about that," She insisted.

"What are you talking about?" I could feel my temper rise. "What's with the riddles?"

Grinning, Trisha got up and left the room without another word and she didn't say much for the next few days. Come to think of it, she wasn't around much.

During the week, the girls brought home a bounty of apples from a school trip. It was the season for apple picking. I pictured a freshly baked apple-pie sitting on a thick wood ledge; cooling down by a windowsill. We were expecting Uncle Don and Aunt Jane to be back any day now.

I opened my eyes and looked out our window with no ledge and a pathetic excuse for a view. The sight of the neighbours' brick wall had etched into my memory. Apple juice dripped down my bottom lip. The bittersweet fruitful taste filled my mouth.

I went upstairs to my room and let my body fall onto the waterbed. It formed under me, creating a floating effect. The heater was still broken, waiting to be fixed and the patches and duct tape had to be replaced every few days. I laid down with my eyes closed and listened to Simona's cassette.

Someone answered the phone.

"Rockhead, it's for you." Being that the phone was off bounds and I was used to sneaking calls. It was weird having Ebony address me for it.

"Really!?" I grumbled. Simona insisted that I go with her on another babysitting job. "I feel better to have you with me. It's my first time babysitting for this family."

"What about Crystal or Laura?"

"They're both busy tonight." Simona said. "They also got two other girls, Donna and Felisha, babysitting as well."

"Yeah, they're friends from school." I smiled. "You see, it's just another reason you should be going to JR."

"No way, Saint Thomas is the best." Simona continued; her focus didn't falter. "Just come with me tonight. I don't want to be alone."

"Fine." I shrugged, not particularly excited that I agreed to it. I was curious about making money, I wonder how the girls were all coming along. "JR is an old school."

"My school's old."

"Not as old as mine." I smiled, promising I'd meet up with her later in the evening.

We headed to the house. We arrived just in time. It wasn't far from where we lived. It was a smaller family. They paid Simona upfront and gave us some extra money to order dinner.

"Thank you for doing this." The woman smiled.

"My wife and I don't get out much," the man carried on. "The baby's sleeping for the night. She shouldn't wake up." He said distantly.

The mother added to the introduction. "Our other daughter, Misty, is nine years old and in her bedroom. Brandon's seventeen. He's been going through some hard times," she sighed. "When he was eleven, he witnessed a gruesome murder... a man killed his wife in front of a convenience store and shot himself... and we're still coping with the loss of our other child. Our daughter went missing two years ago."

"That's horrible," Simona gasped.

"She was a sweet girl." The mother spoke softly with her eyes about to spill out. "A year after her disappearance, police were no closer to solving the mystery. Her body has never turned up."

"It's time to go." The father had crow's feet etched around his eyes. He didn't meet my gaze. All eyes were on Simona as he handed her flyers to order from.

"Our son should have been back from his appointment by now but sometimes he strolls in late," the woman said a little jumpy.

The guy gave Simona a paper. "This is my number if you need help," he said before the couple walked out the door.

We ordered fast food as soon as they left.

It wasn't long before the delivery guy arrived.

"We didn't order this," Simona said, refusing to accept it. "We called for two poutines, not a pizza."

He stood there stupefied. "Are you sure?"

"I know what I ordered." Simona barked.

He gave Simona a ghoulish smile for a moment and turned around. "I got the wrong order." He headed back to his car.

He returned with another order and oddly enough it still wasn't the right one.

We didn't bother calling back, we were so hungry that we accepted and ate the order we got. I was reluctant but after smelling the hot cheese, I had to have some.

Twenty minutes later, the doorbell rang. It was the delivery guy. "You underpaid me for the pizza." He slurred.

"Dude! We didn't order pizza." Simona quickly closed the door and locked it.

I shook my head. "What a nutcase."

We weren't sure if the doorbell woke the baby. I headed to the room to check on her, while Simona flipped through the channels. I didn't hear anything as I walked down the hall. I realized I didn't know which room it was. I slowly opened one door to sneak a peek. Not wanting to wake her, I tiptoed in.

Relieved, I saw a small form under the blankets.

I looked around her room for a moment and was just about to leave when something made me hesitate. Something didn't seem right. I stared into the crib and saw no movement, just a bump under the blanket. I reached my hand in to check. As my hand got close to the bundle, I realized there was no heat. There was something wrong.

A rush of adrenaline cranked my heart up. Biting my lip, I threw aside the small blanket to get a better look. I stared in horror at the eyes of a doll. I looked around the room to see if this was some sort of prank. Where was the baby?

I ran out of the room and howled. "The baby isn't here."

Simona laughed. "Stop! That's not funny."

"I wish I was joking," I said, in shock, thinking that would be a twisted joke. I turned to check the other rooms.

Brandon's door was locked and the sign read 'Stay Out'.

"Didn't they say the baby was asleep?" Simona questioned.

We entered Misty's room. She didn't seem surprised to see us, but she was surprised to hear we were looking for the baby.

"There's a doll in the crib but no baby." I said.

Misty winced. "Where's my brother?" The crease on her forehead gave me the impression she was worried. "He's not supposed to be playing with that doll. It's our old nanny cam and mom says it has a bad influence on him."

The last room to check was the master bedroom. A crisp air came from the bottom of the door. "Shh!" I said.

Simona checked along with me. "Do you think somebody is in the house," she said ready to run to the phone.

I motioned for her to be quiet and grounded myself before I opened the door. I embraced for a blow as I opened the door quickly. To our surprise, there was nobody creeping around, and we were able to breath when we saw a bundle on the bed between two large pillows. The warm milky scent of the baby calmed me. We all relaxed at the sight of a sleeping baby.

"Where's Brandon?" Misty asked.

"Your dad said he may get in late." Simona and I walked Misty back to her room. "Good thing we found the baby."

Simona and I sat in the living room and watched television. I looked through the pile of albums under the coffee table. I found it odd that there weren't any pictures of their son or baby. I did find one picture of the father, standing next to a red corvette. It looked like a great image to draw.

I slipped the picture out of the album and pocketed it. I couldn't help myself and my sticky fingers. The tough looking car got the better of me.

The babysitting job was done before midnight and Brandon never came home. The father offered to drop us off.

I got back home in one piece and I went straight up to my room. I drifted off to sleep while drawing the slick car.

I woke up to shouting. My door flung open with a bang.

"Where's your sister?" Ebony panicked. "Where's Trisha?" She stumbled back against the door frame.

Laughing, I joked. "Why, did she finally runaway?" Even before my mind registered, I knew she wasn't there. I rolled over and covered myself with the blanket.

Ebony yanked me off the bed. "What?" she shouted, turning to Scott with worry. "You see... she's gone."

Scott must have just arrived. They've been together for as long as I could remember.

I didn't say anything.

Sadly, Ebony didn't take the hint, she froze; staring. After a moment, she continued, "We need to find her now. Where do you think she went?"

"You're asking me?" I shrugged, raising my eyebrows.

"She's your sister," Ebony snorted.

"And?" I waved her away.

"We have to call them." She said meaning; Aunt Jane and Uncle Don.

A dozen needles danced their way across my forehead.

"You don't understand," I barked. "Trisha isn't going to tell me crap. I didn't even know she left; she didn't even say goodbye."

"It's hard to believe you don't know," Ebony spit, her reasonable voice clearly surprised. "Where is she?"

I shrugged. "She probably made a break for it."

"What does that mean?" Ebony demanded.

My stomach churned at the idea of Trisha as a runaway. I pictured her sneaking out, taking her things and tiptoeing out the door.

I got up and moved the curtain that divided our bedroom. Her backpack, glasses, books and personal belongings were gone. Even her stuffed Garfield wasn't there.

"It's not looking good." My frown turned puzzled.

From my reaction, Ebony eyes grew even wider and Scott ran out of the house. She was in a tizzy talking nonsense.

After my eyes adjusted to the morning light, I went to see if Trisha's shoes were missing, and they were.

She was gone.

"What's going on?" The girls asked. Sarah already making breakfast for herself, while Farley made orange juice. Michael was remarkably detached from the drama unfolding.

"They're looking for Trisha," I mumbled. It's a long shot, but maybe the girls saw something. "Do you know where she is?"

"No," Sarah said, while Farley shook her head.

"And what about you?" I asked Michael.

"No," he said dryly and turned his head back to the tube.

I sat down wondering what to do. Where did she go?

Ebony and Scott went looking for her. I went up to Trisha's room to grab dibs on whatever she left behind. I knew that even if she was found that she wouldn't be staying here anymore.

I was afraid for her thinking of Uncle Don's reaction.

Uncle Don and Aunt Janes road trip was cut short. "What the fuck kind of Shenanigans are going on here?"

The sound of his voice made me pee a little.

As soon as Uncle Don returned, he drilled me about it.

"Tell me or I'll beat it out of you." Fuming, his face beat red and roaring something fierce. "Spit it out!" He repeatedly knocked my forehead and continued to question me. "Where is she... that bitch?" He squeezed my arm tighter. "We haven't even been gone long."

My stomach sank and I went white with fear.

Aunt Jane blew a fuse, her nostrils flared. "We're missing plants!" Her face turned scarlet red. Still, I didn't know what to say. I stood there with a blank expression on my face.

Who cared about plants? I thought.

"Find her." Uncle Don growled.

He let go of me and shoved me across the room. "This isn't a fucking game," he snapped, throwing the chair and looking for something else to hit. In one sweep, he kicked a hole in the door.

I froze to the sound of the impact.

"This is our life." He pointed at me, his eyes cut through me, stabbing me with hatred.

My reaction was to run, I wanted to hide from his venomous glare. I had to stand firm. I looked at the ground... just don't make eye contact. I forced myself to swallow my worry.

"She should be shot." Uncle Don stopped and leaned down to face me. "You'll go a long way if you just listen and learn. Otherwise, go back to your deadbeat diddler dad or shoplifting mom." He shouted, stabbing his finger in the air toward me. "Your sister doesn't give a shit about you... tell me where she went. I know you know."

"If she gets caught with those plants... we're all in trouble. And you will be shipped off to some group home." Aunt Jane bit her lip as she looked down on me.

It wasn't long before they decided to go look for her. "Stay here and don't fucking move!" Uncle Don ordered.

I wasn't going to test his patience. I sat in a daze with nobody in sight. They went out looking for Trisha. I felt like a wave of doom over me. Am I going to be kicked out as well?

They found Trisha waiting at a public bus stop. She was on her way to meet her boyfriend on the reserve. Now, the best choice was to send her away.

In the end, Trisha got what she wanted and that was to be far from here. Uncle Don and Aunt Jane got their plants back and Ebony decided that this was the last time she was going to babysit us. She went to get a bottle of wine for the night.

Uncle Don ordered me to clean up and watch the kids. I was next in line to be drafted to babysit.

"Trisha's in La-la land." Aunt Jane grumbled.

I didn't say anything.

"I knew there was something wrong with her. That girl has never been normal," Uncle Don growled.

All the adults left me to babysit and everything was going smoothly, until I attempted to do the dishes. I figured I'd score points for a clean kitchen. I ran with arms out towards the sink. I couldn't stop the dishwasher. The water was pissing out everywhere. The sink didn't drain, it just overflowed with the sound of water slapping onto the floor.

I couldn't help but panic.

I ran outside desperately. "You!" I reached out to the first person I saw. "It won't stop..." I cried with a fish-eyed view lens and shouted even louder. "Water's everywhere!"

The guy I grabbed lived at the end of the block. He was walking by with his son. He quickly reacted and turned off the dishwasher and the tap.

I panicked.

My stomach churned at the thought of Uncle Don finding out. He'd hang me for this.

"Thank you," I said, standing in embarrassment.

"Next time... just turn it all off." The guy smiled.

I walked to the door, hoping he'd leave right away. Uncle Don wouldn't be welcoming if he saw this man here.

"Thank you again," I said and closed the door as soon as he stepped out.

I dreaded what was heading my way. I cleaned up the watery mess and then made my way to my room. I was done for the day. I threw my hands up and dropped in defeat. Seriously! I said it before, and I'll say it again, having chores is a job in itself...called 'The Never-ending Story'.

I went to bed without anyone saying a word to me.

The next few days dragged on.

"The school left a message," Aunt Jane confronted me. "They said they're concerned with something they're hearing."

I looked at her, which was unnerving because she was biting her tongue. "What have you told them?"

The silence that followed that statement seemed endless.

Then, just as I was beginning to think no answer would be forthcoming. "I told them I get angry," I blurted.

The sentence hung between us.

"What did they say about that?" Aunt Jane asked.

"Not much," I said simply. "They told me to find the root of it. They have a small anger management thing."

"What a load of crap." Aunt Jane nervously touched her smooth patches of scars that ran down her neck to her shoulder and collarbone. Her strawberry freckles and thin red hair were slightly the same shade.

Aunt Jane sat down opposite to me, her hands folding together. "Whatever it is you're telling them, just stop it." She warned. "I don't want them calling the house. We don't want anymore social jerkers or any more trouble."

I wish I could get her to understand.

She braced herself for a hot denial and slapped her palms down on the table, so we were eye to eye. "Everything we've done, we've done for the better of this family. You got that in your thick empty little head?"

"Uh-huh." I grumped, not knowing what to say. I knew I was stubborn, but that just meant nobody was going to tell me what to do.

Aunt Jane took a deep breath and looked down, "Just shut your mouth." She huffed. Her lips curled in derision.

I gulped.

Aunt Jane sighed. "We just want to grow happily."

Even as a little girl you knew that Aunt Jane was not the kind of woman meant to have five kids. Unexpectedly she took us in; Trisha, me and Michael. Her two girls came afterward; so, we had to know we were asking too much to expect Mother Goose from her.

"There are going to be changes." Aunt Jane's unsmiling scrutiny made me wonder. She called the rest of the kids down to the kitchen.

Minutes later, Uncle Don walked in feeling driven and accomplished. "Kids we have something to tell you." Uncle Don interrupted Aunt Jane's gloating.

"You're having a baby," Sarah smiled.

"God, no." Aunt Jane gasped from elation to disgust.

Uncle Don unfolded a paper from his pocket, revealing a plan. It was a photo of the new acreage.

"We're moving to a chalet," Aunt Jane said impatiently.

"It's far out in the country," Uncle Don interrupted.

"Our neighbours are further out," Aunt Jane couldn't help but rave. "There's even a solarium and a cast iron tub."

"We can make a garden and start growing tomatoes," His gleaming eyes were fixed on me. "You'll love this, Rockhead, there's even a ranch down the street."

My heart leaped at the thought of living near a real working ranch. I always imagined myself riding.

A long silence followed. I had to ask, "Can I stay at John Rennie?"

"No," Aunt Jane answered with a snort.

I remember Trisha upset about moving all the time.

"The Social jerker is closing your file." Uncle Don said.

Aunt Jane smiled at me, "you have to decide if you're staying with us or if you're going to live with your mother."

I didn't say anything.

"This decision will affect your future, so don't be a dumbass." Uncle Don pointed out. "I may boot fuck you but that's because I love you."

"What?" I said with some anxiety at where this was heading. The abrupt subject change took me by surprise.

Some memories were so vivid, and they played over and over in my mind, while other memories I buried away... as if blanking them out completely. It seemed all this time the decision boiled down to me.

My heart beats louder in my chest and my palms sweat just thinking of the question.

"You have time to decide," Aunt Jane said. "Your mom is coming in a few days." She grinned. "You can decide then. No matter what happens, you're always welcomed to visit." Aunt Jane said, leaving me to my thoughts once again.

CHAPTER SEVEN

Not what they seem

"Do you have my tape?" Simona asked me over the phone.

"I haven't seen it?" I replied automatically. I had it but its been missing since Trisha left.

"Are you sure?" she said mortified.

I stretched and yawned loudly; my voice tired as I answered. "I don't think so," I said sitting on the bed without even getting up to look for it. "Are you sure you left it here?"

"I think so," Simona said clearly bothered. "I can't find it."

"Okay, I'll look around."

"I really need it back." She insisted. "It belongs to Crystal and she wants it back."

"I'll let you know," I said firmly.

We spoke for a few more minutes. I listened to her ramble on about her babysitting jobs. How she loved to ravage the fridge and sometimes go through the wardrobe.

"He's really nice, you'll like him," Simona sighed. "I can't wait for you to meet him."

"Who?" I asked briskly, focusing back on Simona. She had lost me after she mentioned the kids colored all over the dog; apparently, the child was connecting the dots with a marker.

"The guy I'm babysitting for," Simona said. "The one with the little girl, Misty, and the baby. The older brother never showed up and their other daughter went missing... remember?"

"Oh." I smiled. I remembered the picture I took.

"Come with me," She pleaded, "It's the last time I'll ask."

"I'm not sure." I gritted my teeth.

"Come on. I finally met the son and he isn't that bad," Simona promised.

"I have to call you back." I chuckled. In no way was I going to babysit with her again. I even let her keep the cash both times. Crystal and Laura at least offered to split their share.

"Come on," She said with a pout.

"I hear someone calling me." I didn't give her a chance to reply before I hung up. I wasn't interested in being sucked into more babysitting. I still haven't told anyone I was moving yet.

"Where are all the fucking socks?" Uncle Don stepped out of the basement with a bang, slamming the door shut. "How fucking hard is it to keep a pair of socks together?" His deep hollering drowned out my thoughts.

I became paralyzed analyzing the different scenarios. Do I find freedom in moving to the country or into the city?

I made my way into the kitchen and for a minute, my mind went blank. The room spun with a foggy fuzz I reached out towards the counter. Sweat formed at the nap of my neck. Lightheaded, I missed my footing. I didn't say anything, and I hoped no one noticed. I bent over the sink and got myself some water.

I turned around holding the half glass of water. Nauseous and feeling warm and in a haze my knees weakened. My legs gave out from under me. I heard a whoosh as I dropped.

The cup shattered with a violent ear-piercing pop. Pieces of glass scattered across the kitchen floor.

Gravity took me down; my hip and my head followed in unison in a loud thud.

I heard a skull-smacking thwack before I blacked out.

Cringing, when I came to, my eyes focused on the peeling linoleum on the floor.

I slowly sat up. Still in a fog, I sat there thoughtless.

"What's going on?" Uncle Don looked baffled. He picked me up and carried me over to the living room and plopped me on the couch.

"What happened?" Michael asked quietly.

"She fainted," Uncle Don said perplexed, he coughed to clear his voice. "You're okay." He patted me on the head like a pet.

"Fainted?" Sarah repeated. Farley pretended to faint onto the floor laughing and Michael watched intently.

"Just leave her be," Uncle Don snapped.

"Augh..." I shivered and turned into the sofa.

I hugged myself. I was morbidly afraid I was going to faint again.

Uncle Don blinked, plainly puzzled.

Farley tugged on my leg. I couldn't help but close my eyes tighter. Sarah moved closer to get a better look.

"Go," Uncle Don roared, waving his fist. "Get ready for school," he ordered the rest of his so-called troops.

"You look like shit." He scratched the back of his head and one of his eyebrows arched. "That's why you need vitamins."

My head bobbed weakly and I felt pins and needles. I firmly placed my arm on the couch and put my chin on my fist to keep my head straight. I deepened my breath and slowly recovered from the dizzy spell.

Uncle Don opened the basement door and called to Aunt Jane, "Burnt out Jane... wake up." While he waited, he decided to whip up some eggs. The smell made me even more queasy.

"Eat up." Uncle Don ordered. "This will help." He handed me a plate of food as though it was the answer. "You're still going to school."

It wasn't long before the kids left. It was unusual to see him in the morning during the week. He usually was out the door before the sun was up.

Aunt Jane rarely woke to see the morning sun. We were left to take care of ourselves, get lunch. We had to get creative. It was about survival of the fittest.

When Aunt Jane woke, she looked like death.

We learned to stay out of her way until she had her first fix of the day: a cup of coffee, smoke and a shower to help her get started. "It's too early for this shit."

Aunt Jane popped one of her CD's in the stereo system and cranked up the volume. She swayed her way into a better mood. "Don't forget the pumpkin pies I made for you."

I hesitated. Just as quick as the dizzy spell came the faintness dissolved. I was left with exhaustion. I looked over at the orange brown pies. I had agreed to bring something into class, I just wasn't sure of my options.

When I mentioned the Halloween party to Aunt Jane, she said I had to bring pumpkin pies. I was thinking more along the line of chips or drinks. Aunt Jane said pies were a better touch and gave me a few forks and paper plates.

I threw my backpack over my shoulder, carrying the two pies onto the bus. Fuming, I didn't want to carry shitty looking pies into school. I wondered if they tasted the way they looked. I thought about throwing the pies away, but I didn't want to arrive empty handed.

Carly showed up wearing her Halloween costume. It was hard to take her serious wearing a tiara and holding a wand. Her large sparkle fairy wings took up most of the couch. "I'm having a party..." Carly smiled with shimmery cheeks. "It's at my house. It's the biggest one on the block." Her speckled nylons went well with her glimmer shoes.

I traded some more of Uncle Don's beer bottles in for some cash and bought some vampire teeth and a tube of fake blood from the pharmacy.

The rest of the stuff I needed... I shoplifted. It was like a small game. Uncle Don likes to drill into me that the apple doesn't fall far from the tree. The rush of sliding something by thrilled me... I took the risk for a night of play. I learned the hustle young. Mom used to leave us in the food court to swipe some shoes for school.

I looked at the clock above the door in the guidance counsellor's room.

"These pies are delicious." One of the students said with a mouth full. I nervously brushed back my short dark hair and watched the big hand on the clock draw closer to the top of the hour.

Cautiously, I stepped into the group, easing toward the circle to sit down. How I felt, or my circumstances, was difficult to talk about. As much as the counsellor wanted me to sit and share, my choices left me indifferent.

"Does anyone have anything to share today?" The counselor asked with a calm voice. "How about you?"

All eyes turned to me and they were expecting me to say something. I didn't know what exactly.

I pictured what I wanted to say. Over the last week I slept on the thought of opening myself up, whether I should elaborate or not.

I shrugged. "There's not much to say... my life hasn't been that exciting." I couldn't help but switch the subject. "I just want some help with my homework."

"We could get you information for that." The counselor drew me back in and maintaining the same steady question. "How's it going at home?"

"Fine." I smiled.

"Just fine?" He looked at me.

Why was he singling me out? I rolled my eyes disregarding him. I was about to shut down and just stay mute.

"It's always good to share," He encouraged.

I paused and then, with major effort, got a grip on myself and managed to continue in a calm voice. I responded with a dejected, "It's all good."

I sighed as I tried to be patient. My stomach sank at the thought of being exposed. I preferred to wait and talk to the teacher after class. In these group sessions, I preferred to be a spectator on the sidelines.

"What are these?" The girl next to me asked, picking up a stack of large pictures. The black ink stain images had no solid lines.

"Those are ink blots. Pass them here," the counselor said. "Let's play a game. I'm going to hold up a card and you tell me what it looks like." He looked at the lot of us and stood in a way we could all see.

The image he raised gave two different answers. Some of us said it looked like a tree, while one or two of us said it looked like a body of water.

"So, those of you that said a tree, you're nourishing, looking to grow roots and reliable," he said, pointing to the black ink and continuing as he moved his finger to the outer white space of the image. "And for those that see the water, you live with uncertainty, but regenerate."

"No way." The girl who found the cards smiled. "Can we see another."

"The cards are used for personality tests. It's all in the eye of the beholder. It reveals how you look at the world, your vision." He lifted another image and held this one up a little longer. "What do you see?"

For a second, I noticed a gorilla, and then I saw the face of a tiger. There were people shouting out one or the other.

My stomach sank as it brought back memories of when I was taken from my family and evaluated... they had used these cards.

"If you're among the ones who see a gorilla; you're characterized as an independent person that values personal space and teamwork," he continued. "If you see a tiger, you're a risk taker and nothing is impossible."

"What happens if you see both?" Carley asked.

I looked at her at once. We both thought the same thing.

"Then you're a bit of both." He smiled.

The inkblots inspired an idea in me. I wanted to create abstract art and evoke emotion. Just like a reader loving a book, I wanted an observer to feel my art.

"Did you make that pie?" One of the guys asked me.

"No," I said. "My aunt did."

"It was good. I had three pieces," he said stuffing his face with chips.

There was no more pie left when I looked back at the table. I got some much needed attention over how tasty it was. I was surprised that even Carly grabbed seconds.

After the group meeting, I caught up with my friends. I walked towards the decor of ghosts, ghouls, black cats and pumpkins. We met in the auditorium for what they are calling 'The Hollows Fest'.

The homemade, do-it-yourself decorations were taped up by students. Cobwebs and orange lit lanterns with hanging bats formed a labyrinth towards the centre of the room.

I headed out towards the double-sized corridor. There's a lengthy line of carved out pumpkins. Teachers, faculty and eager students participate in a fun tradition. Three judges stood aside ready for the pumpkin carving contest.

"Have you spoken to Simona?" Crystal asked.

I shook my head. "No, not today."

She looked at me annoyed. "I think she's avoiding me."

"Why do you say that?" I asked curiously.

"She still has my tape," Crystal cringed. "Whenever I ask for it, she brushes me off."

I pressed my lips tight. I didn't say anything about it for the rest of the day.

My concern escalated when I saw Simona waiting at the corner of our bus stop. The idea of Crystal and Simona confronting each other weighed on me. My anxiety spiked. It's only a matter of time before they figure it out.

Better late than never. I thought while tugging my backpack onto my shoulder. I jumped off the bus before Crystal and Laura. I speed-walked passed Simona shouting, "I'll see you later."

Once at home, I threw my backpack on the ground and I ran up the stairs to my bedroom. The cassette wasn't there. I couldn't find it... I double checked everywhere I could think of. For such a silly thing my stomach twisted. How was I going to explain this? I looked under my bed and under my dresser again... in the drawers and all around. I was sure someone took it.

"Crap!" I couldn't help but start cursing myself. "What the shit am I going to do?"

Aunt Jane shouted up the stairs. "Hey Rockhead! Don't forget to clean your room before going out trick or treating."

I didn't want to miss out tonight. It was my last year collecting candy. My shoulders slouched at the thought of having to clean.

The evening went on and I didn't go back to the corner to confront my friends. Instead I sat back down and pondered about tidying up. It looked like a hoarder lived here. I just didn't know where to start. I got some candy from school and I ate half the bag before I started to clean.

It's Friday night and the lights are on to show we are participating for the big give. You could confuse Aunt Jane's love for the holidays to borderline obsessive. Her favorite activity is throwing parties. She goes all out with the holiday spirit. She hung a sign, 'Happy Halloween' across the front door.

Images of pointy hats and brooms welcomed kids to a coven's brew. The witches' pot was filled with candies and chocolates. Slowly more and more costumed kids walk up the path.

The dark October harvest gives us healthy, hearty foods. Tonight, it's about treats and sweeties and mouth-watering sugary goods.

Aunt Jane sang while wearing her Broadway-style leather costume, looking like the 'Rocky Horror Picture Show'. She wanted to be the creepiest house on the block. Like the Mistress of the dark. She wore a long black wig that made her pale skin even lighter. Flaunting the black stringy dress, she smiled, "I need more web!" She called out to Ebony who arrived at the party with Scott and her kids. Her son was closer to my age and her daughter was the same age as Sarah.

Aunt Jane made sure the last of the decorations and games were in order. The carved pumpkins sat by the front stairs and there was more than enough candy to munch away on.

"Make it believable." Aunt Jane passed me some more spider web to stretch along the front railings.

"This will be our last Halloween here," Aunt Jane sighed.

To my amazement, I had been so worried about what my friends thought about me that I forgot my whole life was going to change one way or another. Where was I going to live, even if I stayed with my aunt and uncle... their moving to a completely new place altogether.

No one was sure what to do with me... It was even a mystery to me. The streetlights lit up as twilight took over. I couldn't even trust myself to make the right choices.

An erratic fluttering flew overhead. It was a moth drawn to the light. I threw my hands over my head and squealed a weird sound I never heard me utter before.

"Didn't I call you this morning, asking you about that cassette?" I heard from behind me. I couldn't help but smile. It was the furthest thing from my mind now.

There was a pause and then a familiar voice, "How 'bout it, Vicky? Any clue to where the tape is?" Crystal asked.

A few others with them threw in a comment. "Thief!"

"What's it to you?" I said. I was starting to get worked up. I had no answer for them, especially now that I couldn't find it. I guess the tape just has that effect. No one wants to let it go.

"Look, I'm sorry, but I'm a little busy at the moment." I didn't want Aunt Jane to find out about something else missing. She wouldn't believe me. She still called me the picture thief.

A group of teens stood on the front lawn staring back at me. Standoffish, they expected a better answer.

I found no comfort in the ghouls and creepy masks. Only one seemed to be a comforting costume with a boy dressed up as Bob from the show 'Reboot'.

"This is between us." I felt eyes on me.

In the living room window, my cousins watched with their faces glued to the glass. Watching all the drama unfold. This wasn't the time or place.

"Well, this sure is fun." I said trying to break the tension, picturing my aunt or even worse my uncle walking in on this spectacle. Why do I get myself into these predicaments?

When people are on this property, they must understand I'm not me. I brought my hand up to her face. "It's just a fucking tape." I groaned with spewing words.

Simona grimaced. "Where is the tape, Vicky?"

"What about it? You'll get it when I find it." The spiderweb bundled up in my hand. "Back off and get over it," I said. Mimicking my uncle and pushing her face back. "All this because you want a tape back." Not wanting to show any weakness, I stepped forward. "Look, it's really not a big deal... I'll find it or I'll pay you back." I wanted to be honest.

"That sounds better," Simona said.

"Why didn't you say something." Crystal carried on. "We could have avoided all of this."

"Now you know. That's that... so just go away." I demanded while shutting the door behind me. I wasn't sure if I was going to get in trouble from Aunt Jane or Uncle Don. But nobody besides the kids noticed. Nobody wanted to leave to tell, they all wanted to watch and see what was going to happen next.

What a strange night. I walked to the backyard to listen and see if the girls were leaving the front lawn. Slowly waiting them out; I could hear them part ways and their voices fade down the block.

My cousins had already come back from the trick or treat walk. Aunt Jane and Ebony went to see a creepy house up the street. They said they were coming right back. They were like kids when they got together.

I leaned over Michael and asked him how much candy he got. Whispering I added, "Did you check it before eating it?"

"Yes," he said with his nose in the sky. "I always check."

The rest of the group came in two minutes later.

"I got four pockets full and I even filled my bra," Ebony shouted stumbling in the front door with Aunt Jane and the others. Laughing like a bunch of schoolgirls all liquored up.

"I get some of that cut," Aunt Jane said as she stretched out her hand chuckling.

"Oh, it's like that?" Ebony took out some tootsie rolls and some chocolate bars and stuck her tongue out and licked all the candies in her hand. Leaving saliva all over the wrappers. Ebony handed it to Aunt Jane.

"I'll still take them." Aunt Jane laughed.

"What is going on? What happened?" Laura asked me the next day when she saw me. I figure she was asking about the tape.

Giving in, I opened myself up. "Simona forgot a cassette at my place. Now I can't find it."

"That's not what I'm talking about." Her eyes narrowed in on me. "I heard your house is a grow op?"

"Eh?" I replied and so she repeated the exact same remark.

I paused for a moment; it was the first time being called out on it. I didn't care. My brain stuttered on what to say.

"Oh! That?" I'm more bummed that Simona and Crystal hated me. I butted heads with some people, but I wanted my friends in my life, even if we have our disagreements. I felt safer at their house. It was like a tragic loss of a loved one. "You think they'll ever talk to me again."

"Stop with that already," she said. "Just replace it."

"I feel stupid," I replied.

"Don't." Laura's golden ponytail swept along the nap of her neck. "They'll come around." Pausing and waiting. She stood there expecting me to say something else.

"So?" she prompted when I didn't respond. "Is the rumor about your place true?" then she added. "Is that why you never invite anyone over."

"Shhhh..." I winced defeated. "That can cause some serious trouble." I didn't even bother asking where she heard it.

"Seems like you already are." Laura agreed, slipping her arm within mine like friends do.

I flinched. I still had to adjust to being touched. I looked over at Laura.

"I have to avoid any questions about it," I told her with a finality. "I can't talk about it."

"I'm here if you need me," she said. "My home is always open."

"Maybe I'll just run away." The thought slipped out.

Laura smiled bleakly. "Don't do that."

I held her gaze, then laughed and turned my attention to the apartments by the bus stop.

"There's no point worrying about it now," Laura said.

The older guys that lived in the building called out to us. Probably to gloat about our lawn last night being attacked by pranksters.

"I'll see you after. These guys are trouble." I emphasized on trouble. I had to get rid of her before they started up their shit again. Vultures! I was hoping to get in the house before they got to me. Smug and full of themselves they ran over.

"Piss off!" I sneered.

One dude leaned into me. "Relax, we're just saying hi."

"Are you going to keep bugging me."

"We were just playing around last time." The guy teased, "It was just fun and games." He protested.

"What's up?" I asked. "I know you guys attacked my lawn."

The guy seemed surprised. "No, we didn't." He smiled. "We have better things to do with our time."

Obviously, something was going on back and forth. "Look let's have a truce." He put his hand out and introduced himself.

I didn't say anything, but I did shake his hand reluctantly.

"I heard you have some pot?" Shit! How did these numbnuts find out!

"No." I dismissed them and didn't give any other explanation.

"Simona said you do," he challenged.

I had to cut off the head of this snake right away. With my finger, I turned around. "You'll get shit. Because I have shit."

"Come on." One guy shrugged. "Don't get your panties in a twist."

"I wear boxers," I said frankly and walked up to the house. "Look just back off."

"We'll talk again," he said in a deep voice and the pack of guys walked off with a rough rider style.

I closed the door behind me. Reminder to self... tell Simona to watch what she says. I could get into some serious heat for this.

CHAPTER EIGHT

Dream Flight

I paused, surprised by the unexpected news. "We won a trip!" I shouted with the phone in my hand.

"Victoria Lafontaine, you better not be pulling any funny business," Aunt Jane muttered from the basement.

"We won!" I shouted even louder.

Aunt Jane glanced out through the open door. She adjusted her eyes to the bright sun filled kitchen. I watched her walk in and cocked an eyebrow at me. Anything more would have taken too much energy. "Stop shouting... giving me a flipping' headache. And don't get too excited. It may be what people call a scam or telemarketers."

"He says he's from some dream flight." I couldn't help but grin.

"Really? Now I know you're dreaming." Wrapping her robe tighter across the front of her with a sigh, she grabbed the phone. I lifted my chin higher.

"Hello?" Aunt Janes voice was a mixture of firm and soft. Her smile faded and her shoulders slumped. "Yes," she said and continued, "Yes. When?" she said, my guts twisting with understanding with what may be in motion. Aunt Jane hung up. "Mm..." She turned to me. "We didn't win a trip. You did." She sighed again. "Apparently you're going to Tomorrowland to the Magic Kingdom. You were chosen or won a contest... something like that."

"Maybe it's like when I got my art in the newspaper?" I continued, "Maybe the school entered me in?"

Aunt Jane just looked at me. "Uh huh. Right." she grumbled.

"Who is going with me?" I ask quietly.

"You're going alone," She said with no explanation. Then Aunt Jane returned to the basement slamming the door behind her. But I've never traveled that far alone!

"Shit! I hope we're not late for your flight." Uncle Don looked down at me with worry.

"Flight?"

He nodded. "How else are you going to get to Florida." I stared into the distance. The signs passed as we sped down the highway. "Well, shit!" Looking around he spoke to himself. My mind still reeling.

We stood in front of the scheduled flights. "Is this the main airport?" He asked, and as if a light went off, he walked to the front desk. His eyes narrowed. "Oh Fuck! Follow me, Rockhead." My feet weren't as quick as his.

A few minutes before leaving the house, I used some of Aunt Jane's makeup to cover up this giant-sized zit on the tip of my nose. It didn't cover and left me feeling ridiculous. My nose a shade lighter emphasizing on this big red target of a pimple.

"Get in the car," Uncle Don said. Did I miss something? "Did we miss the flight?" I asked him.

Slamming the door shut and starting up the engine, "Not if I could help it, now get in!" He demanded.

"It's okay." I said.

"Shut up, kid." He sped up a little faster. "Put your seatbelt on and look out." The vein in his forehead throbbed.

When Uncle Don said to look out, that was code for a look around for the police. It's a game he taught me while on our drives together. He said I had a good eye.

He pulled the car around, and in the distance, I saw it. We entered the building into a small queue designed to look like an airport boarding terminal. I could see one single giant plane with a sign called Dream Flight. We made our way closer to the group of people standing in line boarding the plane. A royal blue carpet invited us in. Some parents had already said goodbye and stood around the buffet table grabbing biscuits and coffee. The sun hadn't come up. I was hoping to catch it rising in the sky.

"Sir? We need you to fill out these, so your son can go." The lady handed a paper to Uncle Don. "It's just a few small questions; who to contact in case of emergency."

"What?" He looked like a child at a teacher's desk. "I thought you had everything."

"We have most of the information, but we also need to know the person dropping him off will know where and when to pick him up." She finished with a smile.

"Okay." The lady had totally caught him off guard.

"Rockhead." He passed me the paper and pad. "Fill this out."

"I'll try." I bit my lip and looked up. "I mean I'll do it." My reading was just starting to come along.

It only took a few seconds.

"They were only asking for some basic stuff and your signature." Patting me on the head for a good deed Uncle Don asked the lady. "Is that all?"

The woman quickly looked over the paper. "You made a mistake." Uncle Don looked at me. I stepped in to see. "Where?"

"Here. Look, you marked female." The lady politely asked us to change it.

"She is a girl!" Uncle Don said. Eyes wide he looked down at me. After a pause. "Why are you wearing all black? And why are you in a sweater?" Frowning he studied me. "Florida is hot you know."

"And it's freezing here," I said.

Turning me around by my shoulder and leaving the lady with a blank expression, Uncle Don walked me to the plane and wished me well. "I'll be here when you get back," he said towering over everyone.

I waved goodbye.

"Your seat is over there in the center aisle." The stewardess pointed to the only empty chair left in a row full of boys.

"Is this your first time flying?" a freckle faced kid asked me.

"Yes."

"Me too," he said opening a package of peanuts.

"It would suck if we crash." He didn't even take his coat off.

"So, you're a Joker, are you?" I said expressionlessly. I turned to face him. "If we crash, I vote to eat you first."

"Suits me." The boy grinned. "The same goes for me," he said and I glared at him. We sat in silence while the lady demonstrated the safety steps.

"Finally, finally, we're moving." He laughed nervously. "I remember you," he said. "During Regatta at camp. We were on the same team and did the three-legged race together."

"Oh yes," I answered. "At girl's camp."

"You're-" he began but couldn't finish his sentence or even the next word. Trailing off I added. "A girl." I smiled.

"Are you?" He looked quickly up and down me and with his eyes round. "If you are say so!"

"I'm a girl." Looking around. "Is anyone else confused about that?" I groaned in exasperation.

"Nope," he said promptly. "Apparently just me."

That stung. "Look. Are you going to bug me the whole trip?" I ask sincerely. Clearly not in the mood for games.

"No." Passing me peanuts. "My name's Lucas."

"My names Victoria, some people call me Vicky."

"Wow, you really are a girl." My face was full of false surprise. "You better believe it," I answered sharply.

"Distracting... I mean discouraging." He grinned.

"Uh-huh!" trying a small glance, I couldn't help but grin back. The air was thick with noise. I can't think right. With no other choice, I held onto the armchairs as the plane started to move. "I have never flown before," I admitted.

The flight landed smoothly, and Lucas and I became friends. We talked for most of the flight after he got past the fact that I was a girl. "Can you believe a place like this exists?" I said softly while imagining living in a magic kingdom. I don't want this day to end. Looking at the famous castle I sighed wondering what princess I may see today.

"We only have one day," A woman in a dream flight shirt called out. "Please stick together and follow the group leader. We will all meet back here at the same time at the end of the day."

"My group lets go." I didn't care about not knowing where I was on the map, I was just happy to be here. Extraterrestrial Alien Encounter had been my first choice. The smoke with heat and special effects were like no other ride I've been on. It came with a story attached to it and some cute fuzzy thing. Then the haunted house with its dancing ghosts in a cathedral hall. It was even better than the time I went to La Ronde with the family. That was a special case on its own.

I remembered everyone brought me to the haunted house. I was six years old and someone got the bright ideas to put me in a cart by myself. A cart that moves through the spooky house with ghouls jumping out at me. Even though the carts were not far spaced from each other. It was hard to see the person in front of you. So, when my cart passed through these black flaps and had stopped. I thought that was the end of the ride. So, I had to make my way out. Looking around for a door with my hands guiding me in a hysterical cry. After a few minutes when I saw a cart go through another pair of flaps I followed. As I eventually walked out Trisha screamed and shouted out, "She's here!"

"You idiot." Was what she said. "You weren't supposed to get off the cart." People in line watched me as I made my way out and around the bars. I wiped off my tears and didn't say much. What really scared me was I thought my family left me; Instead, once they found me, they teased me about how stupid I was to get off the cart. The only comfort I got was Aunt Janes saying, "I wondered where you went. Thought the big spider ate you." Chuckling we shared a laugh. Snapping me back to the present, a tiny lizard walked by my foot. At first, my reaction was to kick it off but then it took everything for me not to pick it up and put it in my pocket. Florida had some cute little critters. "It's like a little dinosaur."

"You're not like the other kids," The team leader commented. I turned and looked at him, wondering if that was a compliment. "Okay."

"You don't say much?" At that, there wasn't much to say. I caught myself gazing at these elegant 4-wheel carriages. A site straight out of a fairy-tale. Like some fairy godmother putting me under a spell. By mid-day, the heat had gotten to me. Laying on a bench I passed on going onto any more rides. "I'm melting." I pointed out.

It wasn't until we reached the end of our day that I found a character I knew. I wasn't even thinking of him until he popped up. A warm fuzzy sensation grew in me. "Pluto."

I pretended I didn't want him to acknowledge me. I knew he wasn't really Pluto and that he was just some dude underneath but when the big lug gave me a hug I didn't hold back. By the end of the day, I had something to hold onto. Like a fairy-tale, that was that it ended.

Pulling me from my sleep someone had a tight grip on my arm. "We're going to crash." Shaking me, my new friend Lucas shouted. "CRASHING!"

Panic struck I jumped up stunned. "Please take your seat. We are about to land," the stewardess said cheerfully. With a puzzled look on my face, I stared at the lady and murmured, "We made it." I didn't see any emergency lights on. I also noticed no one screaming for dear life. Shit, that scared me. "Who does that?"

"Me." The boy teased. Transfixed, I stared up the aisle as if I didn't quite believe we were going to be okay. Then, without warning, the anxiety of the past seized me. "It was just a joke." He said noticing my heavy breathing.

I shut my eyes, hoping the feeling would go away, but when I opened them again the tension was still there. I turned abruptly away with disapproval. "Not cool." I ran a hand down my left arm and strapped myself in. Note to self: Don't fall asleep in unfamiliar places.

It was past midnight when the plane landed. I parted ways with the Dream Flight. It wasn't hard to see Uncle Don when he appeared. A strong distinct frame behind two cookie cutter couples. When he saw me, he nodded for me to follow him. "Did you have fun?"

"Yes," I said, trying to keep up. "I had a good trip." We walked briskly back to the car.

I didn't mean to lose train of thought but as Uncle Don went into another lecture, I started to think about the move. I couldn't bear the thought of never seeing my friends again or the thought of them never talking to me again. Crystal, Laura, and Simona were all I had. They kept me stable. What about my friends? I asked myself. What's going to happen to us four?

"Get out of the way you stupid broad!" My uncle pulled around a woman in her car who had issues merging onto the highway. "Get off the fucking road, cunt." He yelled stepping heavy on the gas and roared forward. Skidding away with his hands gripping the steering wheel. "What a fucking mess." A snowball effect was starting to build up. "Today, people." I could see his nostrils flaring and his face boiled over red with anger. "These fucking potholes and idiot drivers." Traffic had started to form due to construction on the road ahead. Gripping the shift tighter he growled, "Now what?"

I looked at him wondering what the rush was. Without thinking I asked with my most earnest look, "When are we moving?"

Round eyes, turning his whole top body to look at me, stiff as a board. "July." The car horns and the machines drowned out any thought. "During moving season." He said while forcing his way into the lane, Uncle Don stepped on the gas as soon as he saw an opening. "When's the traffic and construction going to end?" I asked him.

Uncle Don grinned, "Never."

I repeated the same words back, "Never." Surprised by the answer, I asked. "Why can't they just make it properly the first time?"

"Still needs maintenance. It goes through seasons." He smiled. "It wasn't built for this much traffic," He said hastily. "We still have cobblestone streets in some parts of Montreal."

From anger to lecture, Uncle Don gave me a history lesson about Old Montreal. Then he headed into the importance of the rules of driving. I drifted back into thought about my friends and how things seem to be changing.

"Chin up," Uncle Don said, "It will be fine, just be a defensive driver."

Next, Uncle Don and I returned home. I dutifully climbed out of the car onto our front lawn. "I want you to help me with something tomorrow. So, don't go far." He said.

"All right!" I answered with fleeting feet into the house. I remembered how I helped him when we lived in Laval. He remodeled his father's unfinished basement into a basement apartment. That's where I first learned about chalk lines and measurements and tiles and diamond tile cutters. He has all types of machines – toys, he called them. I oversaw taking all the airplane and helicopter models down for packing. They hung with lines from the ceiling. Military models and ships sat along the shelves. It was like taking pieces of history out of the room.

It felt nice to take a load off. It was weird laying down in my bed, in this nine by ten room. It no longer felt like home. As if replaced for something new. The grandness of the trip showed me a world outside of my own, out of this box.

I took out my pad and started to draw. In some wild frenzy, I sketched. The sound of the pencil sliding against the grain paper captivated me. I moved my hand without anything in mind. By the time I was finished, the piece came to be one of my best works. I sat there staring back at a reflection of what I call the manifestation of my struggle. An abstract draft that moved me more in an image than words. I pinned this piece to the wall and stared at it until my eyes could no longer stay open. I fell asleep in vindication.

CHAPTER NINE

Simona's Crib

It was quiet in the clean suburbs but there wasn't much to talk about. People thought just using the word 'random' would give excitement to their ordinary lives. People liked their routines.

The skies above were no longer dumping rain on us. Moisture in the air with a heavy morning fog still hung low along our street. It was good for the lawns. Most of the adults were obsessed with their lawns.

No one had woken yet. I decided to take the chance and go to Uncle Don's room. Quietly stepping into the damp dark basement, I made my way to their bedside. Tiptoeing as my heart raced. I knew they had drunk a lot the night before and who knew what else they did. They were practically howling. Clothes laid along the floor and a lingering musky scent of sweat. There wasn't much I couldn't see. Bodies partially covered but mostly bare. I made my way to the end of the bed. With my hands stretched out and fingers spread wide, feeling my way around for Uncle Don's jeans on the ground.

Ah! Here we go. I slipped his wallet out of the back pocket and slowly slid a few bills out. Uncle Don liked to have extra cash in his wallet. Sometimes Aunt Jane had rolls of cash stashed in her adult toy drawer or Uncle Don's underwear drawer.

"Who's there?" Aunt Jane's groggy voice asked.

"Me." I whispered. "I need you to sign a paper." I showed Aunt Jane an old paper knowing very well she wouldn't read it. As she did that I gently and slowly placed the wallet back into his pants. "What's it for?" Her eyes looked glued together. There was no way she was getting up. Let alone being able to focus on anything. Aunt Jane could barely put on her side lamp to grab the pen.

"For a free outing," I whispered quickly.

"Free sounds good," she slurred.

Uncle Don was snoring in a deep slumber. I walked carefully across the floor. After pocketing some cash, I still had to get ready for school.

"You know you're one of my best friends." Crystal said as we stood at the bus stop in the rain. Her presence disturbed me so much that I almost considered going back home. No matter how uncomfortable I was, I wasn't going to run. We couldn't avoid each other forever. "It really bothered me that you lied." I didn't respond, but in truth, I would probably would have said anything to put this all behind us.

I exhaled. "Sorry." The humility oozed off me with a guilty fragrance. I blushed with embarrassment, and then became embarrassed because I was blushing! "I got hooked." I slowly slipped the cassette out of my pocket and passed it back to Crystal.

"Next time just ask," Crystal ordered. I had to walk away before I became a blubbering idiot. Who needs friends Uncle Don would say? While Aunt Jane couldn't live without hers. Like sugar and spice. It was hard to make friends that didn't ask any questions.

I sat on the curb waiting for the bus, feeling awkward and speechless. I really didn't know what to say. I avoided everyone until lunch. I never had any idea of how to be around people.

"Can you spare some change?" The same dude as last time came around to ask again. "Yeah." I said, tossing him some change.

I found a spot where there would be no issues. Away from my friends or any eyes that would make me feel judged or awkward. I sat in a class available for students that wanted to play board games or wanted to go onto the computer.

"You're good at that." A student teacher complimented me.

"I like this shit!" I said.

The bell range and time flew by fast. Some people looked at school as an institution while I looked at it as an escape. I strolled out feeling like I found my own hidden place within the school. Something that I found I was good at.

"Would you have some change?" a student asked as soon as I left the class.

"I don't have." I gestured with both hands that my pockets were empty. I felt bad saying no but I couldn't give what I didn't have.

"You have," the guy accused.

"Dude I really don't have a dime," I said firmly, defending myself.

"Yeah! Okay, you always have."

"Whatever!" Ignoring him, "And I usually give." I snapped giving as much distance between us as I could.

I made it to class just before the teacher closed the door. "You said you would help me with this one, you dissect, and I'll write the answers down." Laura reminded me as I slid onto the stool. "Remember we're dissecting Jim." Jokingly giving the dead earth warm a name.

"Yes," I said. "I almost...forgot!"

"Does the offer still stand?" Laura asked. "I feel like a fool, but I just can't do it."

"It's not nearly as bad as it looks." I smirked, interested in how it all works.

"I just can't!" Ghostly white Laura gasped at the sight of the little slime ball.

"Each of you has a sheet with a checklist. Check off each box as you move along with the dissection." The teacher shouted for the whole class to hear him. "If I see you walking around. You get a zero. So, if you wouldn't mind staying seated."

A worm had been pinned down on both ends. "It says to slice a line from each end." Laura couldn't even finish the words to the sentence. "This is disgusting."

I picked up the scalpel and slowly penetrated the skin. "I didn't want to cut any organs." As I said that, juice spurt out from the first cut. "Juicy mother fucker, isn't he?" I said, ducking back.

"My God!" Laura cried. Looking like the jitterbug, she couldn't stop fidgeting. "Ew."

"Just one piece at a time," I said slowly as her eyes grew larger. It fed my need for attention and I just smoothly acted like I did this before. "You want to try."

"I don't want to pick it apart," she whined. "What do I look like?" Looking at me, she stopped. "How can you be so calm about it?" I restrained a smile.

"I guess because it's strange and unusual. So, therefore, it intrigues me." I looked at the insides. "I like to see how things work." I blinked, "Plus we have to for a grade."

"I know," she answered grimly.

I didn't know exactly all the parts, so in a way, we were working as a team. She called the parts out and wrote them out as I picked. Relieved I wanted to give a good impression. "It says they feed on live and dead organs." The teacher taught as he walked around the class observing us. "As they burrow into the soil to allow air, water, and nutrients to reach deep within the ground, they consume soil, extracting nutrients from decomposing organic matter like leaves and roots." He said wrinkling his nose. "Did you know that worms have no ears or eyes?" he carried on. "They us vibration and light receptors."

Looking inside, I whispered to myself, "What am I looking for?"

"They have more than one heart," Laura said.

Smiling I waited for the others to finish. I wrote a small note for Crystal. I folded and transformed my paper into a secret envelope square. I doodled a heart with wings and a halo with a devil tail. I passed it along to her at the end of class and I finally told her the only joke I knew. It wasn't till class ended that I was given my mark. 100 percent. I felt a twinge of relief.

"Have you decided if you want to stay with us or move to your mother's in the city?" Uncle Don asked me

I gave this some serious thought. Although I rarely considered Uncle Don's behavior and it may not seem appealing living with his tyrant rants, I'm observant enough to know that even though it's a messed up situation. I've come this far and have other opportunities available for me. I still could visit my mother in town. I'd live in the country and see horses, maybe even ride one. I wondered if they have computer classes.

"Will there be computers?" I asked nervously.

"Urgh... What's with the computer shit?" snarled Uncle Don asked. "Don't talk about that crap." Grumbling, "That shit won't get you far! It's just a fad." Pacing Uncle Don complained about the new wave. "Art won't get you anywhere in life either. Just hard work and it takes money to make money. Money, you won't have." He stopped, "Stick with us and you might have a chance."

His eyes dark and his mouth bitter spewing out his dislike for technology, especially devices that threaten existing jobs or interfere with personal privacy. "You have to use your hands. Get a trade," He said while washing down his food with some beer. "It's okay if you are not the college type."

"I could sell art," I responded, a little confused.

"The only artists that are famous are either starving or dead." He threatened, guessing my plan. "Dreamers don't bring in a paycheck."

"Leave her be," Aunt Jane said. "The more you practice the better you'll be." She then added, "It's a craft." Her voice sounded frustrated for some reason I couldn't imagine.

"Be practical, stop feeding her some pipedream." Frustrated and in his own bubble, Uncle Don's venomous view towards computers and distaste for whimsical thinking, had been formed into a single-minded opinion. Which is funny because Aunt Jane lived and breathed in that fantasy world. A flakiness yet creative aura about her. The opposite of Uncle Don. You could see a matter of fact intolerance for flightiness. Where she's flexible, he's inflexible.

"It's possible," I insisted. He ignored me and went into the basement grumbling.

"He just doesn't like computers because he doesn't know how to use them." Aunt Jane headed straight for the front closet and pulled out her different scarves. She reached into her antique wood buffet where the fish tank of angelfish sat; feeding them flakes she added, "Anything worth having, takes work." Giving me one of her withering looks. "You'll learn. Everything's not just fun and games."

"Okay," I said, knowing when it was my cue to leave. I tried to maintain what dignity I could. I wasn't very successful. I wondered about the fate of my friends. I decided to take the night to think about it. I thought about my friends and saying goodbye to them. Who am I without them?

I met up with Laura at the ice cream store. "You look good."

"Thank you." I tugged on my new dark purple and white jersey jacket. "It's new," I said, smelling the scent of new material as if I never owned anything new before.

"You're so weird," Crystal said in a friendly way.

"You better believe it." I winked. "There is no other way," I said stiffly. "The stranger the better."

"Here comes Simona," Laura warned.

I couldn't keep hiding. As soon as she walked up to us, Simona looked over at me. Narrowing in. The guilt was unbearable.

"This is your chance." Crystal pressed.

"Now?" Palms sweaty, I couldn't help but babble. Uncertain, and totally deserving of her disapproval, on top of confronting Simona, we now had an audience to observe me if I screwed up. Just get it over with, I told myself.

Both Crystal and Laura whipped around for a better view.

I groaned and took a deep breath.

"Simona. I'm sorry." Like jumping into a pool, I just went for it and threw myself out there. "I should have asked for the cassette or given it back." I looked down. My cheeks burned with embarrassment and humility. "I want us to be friends."

"Oh, puh-lease..." Simona rolled both her eyes dramatically. "Why didn't you just ask."

I'd asked myself the same question. "I was embarrassed."

"I don't believe you." Simona's pent up annoyance flew freely now.

"What's done is done." My mood shifted. "Sorry."

We stared at each, unsmiling for a moment.

"Are you still mad at me?" I asked.

"Who says I'm mad?"

"It's written all over your face." I sighed.

"You pushed my face back!" She waved her hand.

"It was a reaction." Tilting my head to the side, I softly added, "I'm sorry. Please come sit with us?" When she didn't say anything right away, I added, "I mean it. I feel about two inches tall." I hesitated. "Please." I smiled, blinking at her.

"I can't stay long," she warned. I could see a slight smile. "I'm going to meet a guy."

I shrugged, reminiscing about the day at a guy's house when she came up from the basement. Whipping her mouth while I was waiting in the living room.

At the time, I didn't know what the white trail running down her chin to her chest was. I had to look away from her stare. I didn't want her to think I was judging her. I couldn't speak, so I just nodded.

The girls filled each other in on the recent info between the last time we were all together. From the girls at school to the new shops opening. I realized I hadn't told anyone I was officially moving. I decided to wait a little longer. This way I could pretend I wasn't moving. I watched them laugh under the cloudless blue sky. Finished with the last bite of ice cream parfait, I lifted my cup, and scooped out the remains of pineapple.

As I crossed the darkened living room "Where did you get this money?" Startled by the brusque question from Uncle Don, I answered without hesitation.

"From your wallet."

He paused, surprised at my answer. "I know." He gestured towards the seat. "My wallet was in my front pocket. I never put it there." Shit! Right... I slipped up.

"Why did you need the money?"

"I go to a place called the shops for lunch at school." I clarified.

He scowled for a second. "Why didn't you ask?" His face was abruptly serious. I stood carefully and I was still fine. "I was shy," I said, smiling despite myself as I faced Uncle Don. I didn't think I had to lie. Clearing out the beer bottles had been different than asking for straight cash. He paused and waited another minute. His wide hand covered my cap as he patted me on the head. "Don't bite the hand that feeds you."

When the door opened, I turned my back to Aunt Jane, a little ashamed of my behavior. I hope I hadn't offended either of them.

"Who shut the blinds?" Aunt Jane darted to the living room to let in the sun. "It's like a tomb in here!"

She'd been working on something upstairs in the no zone room all afternoon. Pot plants like warm, damp environments. Uncle Don tampered with the venting systems. He used a variety of chemicals and fertilizers. My job was to water and check the timer for the lights. Aunt Jane sparked up a small pinner as she put on some music and swept the floor.

He coughed, clearing his throat. He sat a tall sweaty glass of beer on the table. "Next time just ask me."

That sounds familiar. "Ask for what?" Aunt Jane looked at me. "Did you take something again?" eyeballing me she scolded me without as much as a word from me. I shrugged cluelessly.

"The banana." Bringing that back up was just childish. I was five and had just moved in with them. For some reason, I didn't consider it stealing. A lady invited me over to her place. She just had a baby and she said I could play in her house. I was hungry. I hadn't eaten much. So, I grabbed a banana from her table and snuck it under my shirt before I left. The lady ended up phoning Aunt Jane and making a fuss. I was no longer invited over. Aunt Jane was talking as rapidly as ever, but what caught my attention was what she said next. "You should be grateful for the sacrifices we make," she told me. "You have stolen pictures and apparently cassettes."

Rats! "How do you know that?" I asked. Someone talked.

"I have my ways." She smiled.

"Rats," I repeated but this time out loud.

"Beg your pardon? The fact is you stole." She pointed out. "And speaking of rats did you talk to the guidance counselor at school again?" Both Aunt Jane and Uncle Don studied my reaction. Slowly it grew quiet. "No." I stepped back into the patchy shade of the hallway. I'd never felt more alone in my entire life. No one got me.

Uncle Don nodded slowly as if it were important. "Don't say a fucking thing to those straights." It wasn't as grand as dividing people between Socs and greasers or hippies and squares. But one thing was clear, apparently. There was them and there was us. And who were they? I don't know. I'm figuring out as I go along.

"This isn't a game," Aunt Jane said. "It's our livelihood. They're fascist pigs."

I answered with a nod as if agreeing to avoid argument. I assumed anyone with authority was a threat. Uncle Don studied me. "You had better get your ass into gear," He stared down at me. "Because we're moving."

"Really?" I wonder if that included me or if I'm going to move in with my mother. I knew why they were doing this. Uncle Don always envisioned himself owning a lot. He says a man isn't a man till he owns some land. He repeats it over and over. A place with a remote outdoor location. Out of prying eyes and nosy neighbors. He had been born with a green thumb. His mothers' side of the family came from a long line of farmers. He took on that strong farmer's mentality of working the land and not asking many questions.

Aunt Jane was a tree hugging granola eating type. She wore her peasant skirts with off the waist belts. She dyed and revived her hair strawberry blond every three months. Though I couldn't see her leaving the city for long, her social butterfly tendencies might get the better of her. "Why is the school still calling?" Aunt Jane stopped what she was about to do.

I stared at them. "What are you talking about?" I asked cautiously.

"Don't play innocent with me! You just tell me why they're calling?"

I shrugged, clearly confused. I hadn't mentioned anything else to the counselor. I was avoiding Carly like the plague. I wasn't fighting at school, leaving for the shops during lunch kept me out of trouble. So, it was Aunt Jane's turn to stare. Clearly waiting for an answer I didn't have. She blinked. "Rockhead," controlling her buzz. "Next time keep what goes on in this house to yourself." It was beneath her dignity, and Uncle Don's unbending principle to admit anything was astray or unlawful. Maybe dysfunctional but not harmful in any way. Aunt Jane would be the first to speak freely on her liberal rights. People wondered why I was so rebellious, yet I lived in a politically rebellious home. "Just trust us and do what you're told. You would think you already know all this." She carried on. "You have food, clothes, a roof over your head and that is all you need." Lifting the dustpan up from the floor.

"What does that mean?" I asked disappointedly.

"It means... Shut your trap," Uncle Don snapped, frightening me. "That's an order." He mentioned with a glare before stalking out of the room.

It didn't seem right to me that there wasn't much of a discussion. It seemed very one sided if you asked me. It certainly didn't matter, because I didn't intend to do anything about it.

As it stood now, Aunt Jane gave me a canny look, reminding me that underneath it all she was indeed a force to be reckoned with. "You walk around with a Goddamn chip on your shoulder, and I'm telling you right now-" she tossed the dirt in the garbage. Then tilted her head back Aunt Jane exhaled smoke up to the ceiling. "Whatever it is you're trying to pull, pull it with someone else because it's just not working with me." She turned around and put her thumb up, gesturing for me to move my ass. "Go find something to do," she said picking through the clean laundry hamper, folding and rolling. Aunt Jane threw all her socks into one basket.

Simona's mom and boyfriend were out for the night. We promised we'd behave. Her brother wasn't far. The odor of food filled the hall and cul-de-sac bags hung under the mailboxes. "You want to go in soon?" she asked me. Her shoulders leaning against the wall. We sat on the hallway carpet while people passed by us. Simona put her feet up on the opposite wall from her and I sat cross-legged beside her. I didn't know how long we sat there but it was nice. It was one of the longest conversations I've ever had with anyone. "Are you sleeping over?" She asked me.

"If you want." I looked in the distance, avoiding eye contact. "It's done. You're sleeping over." She pulled me to my feet. "Let's go. I have something to show you." Simona lead me into her home and down the stairs to her room beside the bathroom. "My mother got me a makeup box and some makeup." She smiled, "First I'll do me and then I'll do you."

I climbed up onto Simona's large bed. Sinking into her thick flowered comforter set. Her cushions buried her pillows, her dolls and stuffed animals made her bed fuller on top. Her side table was clearly a vanity. Perfumes and lotions lined up on a crystal platter. The light gave her a rich caramel glow. Her brown eyes popped with gold eyeshadow, touched up with a showy dark finish.

"Oh, shit!" I jumped and threw my hands up to my chest. "I think I saw someone through your window." It looks like a shadow looking in. "Like a peeping tom"

"What's that?"

"A creeper," I said.

"Yeah. People walk by all the time," Simona said and sat beside me on the bed. "It's your turn." It was strange, she wasn't as concerned as I was.

"Not yet." I looked at her. What difference did it make if I told her now? It's better than never. So, I just said it. "I'm moving." I wasn't expecting to swell up.

"Why?" Simona cried. "Is it far? Is it because of the grow op?" She sighed.

"Well, I don't know!" I said, rolling my eyes. "No." I looked down at my hands. "It's just time," I said grimly. "It's far." Whichever place I chose was far enough. "I wanted you to know," I said automatically.

Simona turned my cap around and gave me a quick kiss. Inches from my face she held her gaze. "I'll miss you," she said.

I tried; I really did. Shit, I didn't want her to see me cry. She knew what it was like to move often. I ignored the voice in my head and carried on. "I just wanted to say sorry for what happened and it's a tough time for me. You're a good friend."

"Remember to call me," she muttered. "Have you ever worn makeup?" Simona asked me. The words were rushed.

"At Girl's Camp." I smiled reminiscing over the time we got ready for the dance. I was terrified that I was going to look like a clown. It was one of the only times I remember feeling like one of the girls. "I surprised myself." Pamela had helped with that transformation.

"Can I try on you," she asked, inclining her head toward me. I wasn't sure what she was expecting but I gave her full facial access. Nervous that someone was going to see me I got up and locked her door. Then I walked to her blinds and closed them. "I don't want any witnesses."

Simona burst out laughing. "You're funny." Smiling she held up an aquamarine eye shadow compact. I shot her one of my disgusted looks. "Ah... Nope." I pursed my lips. "NO..." I said firmly. "Try pink if you want but not that, please."

My jaw just about hit the floor in amazement when I looked in the mirror. It only took her twenty minutes. "You missed your calling." My hair was pinned on the sides and moussed back all over. I gave her two thumbs up. "Very cool." This was a guess, but she doesn't look the way she does by not taking care of herself.

"You'll have to keep in touch," she whined.

We both froze. We heard someone coming in through the front door. "Hay Alguien en casa." Simona got up and unlocked her door. "It's my brother."

.

CHAPTER TEN

Tussle

A security guard yelled in his mic. "We got a runner."

I crane my neck, trying to get a better view.

A lanky fan jumped over the railings and leaped his way into the ring. The wrestler didn't budge. He stood over the other fighter as the fan ran towards him without thinking. He seemed to look smaller and smaller in comparison as the wrestler got closer. The over excited young man hung a sharp right; making a quick ninety-degree angle as he realized the size of the physically cut man.

Two security men dressed in black darted towards him. The pencil shaped guy slides out of the ring. Jumping, waving his arms around but with nowhere to run. His face was pressed up against the ground in two seconds flat. In the center of the ring, the alpha wrestler shouted, arousing the fans, and incorporating the fan in the show.

"Just watching that goof troop get tackled down was worth coming tonight." Excited I expressed to Aunt Jane. "I love this." Nudging her while she ogled the wrestlers.

"I can't wait to tell Pamela about this." Our seats were close enough that I could see their sweat drip; beads and bucket loads. I watched Aunt Jane carefully. I was looking for something, but I didn't know what.

"Too bad we didn't have any props," I shouted.

"Think of the money we save not getting them." She smiled. "It's money we can use at the dollar store." She winked. "After this, we'll go somewhere special to eat."

My mouth watered at the image of Lobster, shrimp and garlic sauce. "I could kiss you," I said playfully.

"No." Aunt Jane grinned, "Someone might think I love you." she winked at me and gave me a small bag with a box inside it.

"What is it?" I asked. Aunt Jane didn't make a peep, she let my find out for myself.

"I opened it up," I grasped the box tighter on the bottom as I opened the lid to see what was inside. "Beautiful." I laid my eyes on a sterling silver necklace with a crowned Jesus Christ Crucifix Cross Pendant. I was confused. "This is for me?"

"Yes. It's from Mama and Papa. They asked me to pass it to you for graduation. I forgot to give it to you. Thought to-night would be the right time." She added, "Don't forget to call and say thank you." The metal of the necklace was cold against my skin. "Nice," I said, dropping the cross onto my chest.

My mind's on overload. It's a quarter after seven in the morning. It was an abnormally unexpected question I was asked. What a predicament, I thought. On one hand, live in the country or on the other hand live deep in the city. I got ready for school in my boxers and extra-large robe. Then, I headed out the door. I needed some fresh air. I don't feel like myself. I felt a little sick and nauseous. How am I going to know if I make the right choice? The question circles around in my mind.

I woke with a jaded sigh. Soaking up the idea of moving in with Mom. It would be sweet to get to know her better. Uncle Don taught us to take orders. When I did something, it was more so a reaction to something else. In this case, I had to decide. I still didn't even know how I like my eggs made.

It's very weird, having this stupid panic thing inside me. Their expectations send my emotions into a tailspin, leaving me in a paralyzed state.

I bow barefooted into the gym; the training hall took up the corner of the strip mall. It didn't take long for the sunny atmosphere to turn into a no-nonsense class. It started with peaceful stretches and then slowly grew to exhaling shouts, grunts, and fists flying. The blows add to the popping sound of people hitting the pads.

THWACK! I knew I needed to come this morning.

"Team up?" Why was the idea as exciting as it was frightening? Right away, I paired up with a higher belt girl. Similar height. I didn't mind. We didn't say anything to one another, just shouted every time we stepped inward with a punch or kick. The material of the gi soaked up my sweat. My aggression burned away. Every muscle was sore

The school halls had been filled with wide giant banners and colorful flyers.

"Who else is going?" Felisha asked, wanting to know. "My mom's driving Donna and me."

"I'm taking the bus," Crystal said.

"I'll come pick you up," Felisha invited.

"Let me see," Crystal replied sternly. "I'm not sure if I'm going to the dance..." She still had to ask her mother if she needed Crystal to babysit that night.

It took effort to explain something without having to say it.

Donna caught on, not knowing exactly what it was. "The offer still stands," Donna added, trailing ahead. "Just let us know." Felisha winked and smiled as she walked side by side with Donna.

I got into a routine as the weeks passed. I thought long and hard about my next step. It wasn't easy but I pushed myself to play the part like a muse. I kept my guard up concerning my heart and instead I opened myself up to converse amicably. High school brought out the survivor mode in me. I rather someone think I was unstable rather than paint me into some corner, like some yellow belly my uncle would say; assuming that they would. It was easier to pretend. If I didn't, they'd notice it.

I couldn't avoid it. It was time for another session. The guidance counselor brought a chair from the room down the hall. He placed the chair in front of us with a slight thud. He began with someone else before he got to me. So, it begins... I notice this time there are two tissue boxes in the room. One on the desk and the other on the table. The books on the shelf all have titles that scream self-help and twelve step programs. Nothing that wasn't said before. Year of counseling and programs, evaluations and tests have questioned my very lifestyle.

"Now," he said, sitting across from me and we sat face to face. "What has your situation been like since we last spoke." An annoyance tugging at me. Can't he see I'm in thought? The frankness in his question made me uneasy. I didn't know what to say. It's been fucking strange. Was he being nosey? My gut tightened and my instinct was to automatically go into defensive mode. I raised my arm and I looked down at my watch, looking as if I had somewhere else to go. You're not going to crack me open. I turned my head away from them for a moment. I waited and wondered what to say. I wanted to say that I live in a grow op and that my foster parents seem to be in their own world. I would like to ask, is it okay that when I killed a few pot plants, I was punished for it? I fought back the frustration and swallowed my pride while everyone rested their eyes on me. I wanted to ask if it was okay that somebody felt like they had the right to choke sense into me, literally. I could see that he knew nothing about me or that situation and really then they could never really help me. I figured I'd share and give them another bite. I wanted to unload a bit.

"My uncle tells me that I'm stupid and that the apple doesn't fall far from the tree. He says that I am spawned from thieves and low-class hustlers." Grimly, I finished with... "He says that art isn't a proper trade and that computers are destroying the world."

"Is that all?" Carly spat out prompted. "Maybe you are." She added, "Someone told me that you live in a grow op." she challenged me in front of everyone with her head bobbing like some bobble head.

"Uh-huh, is that a fact? And you believe them." I grinned. What were my options? I had to play stupid.

"I'm asking," Carly said because she didn't have a clue.

"There should be a rule against lying you know?" Carly couldn't possibly be upset. Shit disturber. Why challenge me? Where was she going with this?

I decided to egg her on. "Who's lying?"

"You have to be honest here," she said with a sly smile.

"What's it to you?" I said with a disappointing scowl.

"You're so fake." Carly rolled her eyes.

"Have you looked in a mirror. You think your unique but you're nothing but what's sold to you." I saw something flicker over her face. Not sure if anyone else caught it but Carly didn't like that comment. Crossing her arms over her chest and tucking her hands into her waist.

"Don't be jealous." Carly said. Turning her head, with her chin in the air, she raised her eyebrows.

That stumped me. "You know, we're here to share about ourselves. And I don't hear you sharing. Only bitching."

"It's not my turn." I looked over at the counselor. Is he getting paid for this? Paid to hear other people's problems. Is this counseling? I thought as he observed us. I shut down for a minute. I had to make the right choice. Decisions, decisions. Not knowing exactly what to say. In most predicaments, I found it was better to keep my mouth shut. I'd rather observe or rebelliously be stubborn and play mute. But in this case, all eyes were on me. I have had enough now. "That's my business, Carly. All right? So, fuck off." Thump, I dropped my foot down, set apart, with elbows on my knees I leaned forward. "It's none of your business." I felt a flare of anger within me. My nostrils flared out. With wide eyes, I gave her a questioning look.

"Why so defensive?" Carly asked. To make matters even worse, I felt like I somehow betrayed my family. Now rolling over all the questions like a thunderous cloud, I was going to implode with worry. Biting my nails down to the nubs. "You don't know shit." It was true but she couldn't prove it. I raised my chin. "It's my business, not yours."

Carly wasn't having it. "A business." she confirmed my worst fear. Not dropping the topic. "A grow op isn't a business." She condescendingly muttered.

"Good thing it's just people talking," I growled. "Do I look like I'm balling? No, so fuck off."

"You look like a criminal," she muttered.

"Ladies," the counselor said. "We don't need to get personal." What the shit did that mean? Personal! So, does that mean I look like a criminal? I looked down at myself once again self-conscious.

"She's no lady," Carly snickered. "More like a jailbird or a spawn of one." I didn't say anything. I took what she said to heart and gave her a death stare. Imagining maybe some Jedi mind trick would work. I tightly clenched my jaw together. My mind began to race leaving me sick in the stomach. "My mom had gone to jail due to drowning in the drug scene and lost custody of us. My dad was known as a thief amongst other things I dare not say. My foster parents are poster advocates for grow ops and anti-fascists and capitalists. They are considered corrupt and in being so that makes me and anyone else apart of it in some organized crime. I was placed into this environment before I even got to the playground by a system that you stand for, and know I'm supposed to say something about it here with these people I don't know..."

"So, this is what it has come down to." I paused. "I'm done," I said grudgingly and decided to shut down. I locked my lips shut, like a switch, I just turned off for a few minutes and sealed myself up in an invisible cocoon.

. When I turned back in from my raging thoughts. Interestingly, the guidance counselor whipped out a yellow handkerchief from his pocket and wiped his forehead and stuffed it back into his pocket. "Think of it this way. When people feel warmly welcomed by you, and they are sure that you won't judge them, in any manner, they allow themselves to open up," he said to us as a group and rested his eyes on me just before getting up from his seat.

What a crock of shit. This guy thinks I'm dumbfounded. "Give it a rest, man! We can't show weakness. We'll be eaten alive." It's lucky for them that I'm here, I added, "I find when you share information with people, they tend to use it against you. It's better just to just shut your mouth." These fresh fish are going to be walking out of here like marshmallows if they listen to this yuppie stuff. "Learn to protect yourself and 'open up' and 'close up' when need be. It helps me to block off the weight of issues." I guessed.

Another student in the group brought her hand up to cover a grin. "And sometimes, it's just better to forget. Why talk about something that reminds me to feel like shit," I yelled, waving my arms frantically.

"Sometimes where we live has gotten so damaged by desire, anger, and fear, that we tend to feel like we have no voice." He leaned into me. "You have rights."

I couldn't help but laugh and not one of those little half-assed laughs. I laughed so hard that my stomach tightened like a crunch and tears welled up and rolled down from my eyes. A hearty laugh from the gut. Rights... yeah right! I needed a laugh. The others couldn't help but be infected with the same laugh. Contagious like a sneeze I couldn't help myself. Once again, I stopped to stare at the people looking back at me.

"You're such a weirdo." Carly snickered.

"Better than ordinary," I said hastily.

Shifted from one foot to another. "Sessions finished." The counselor saved Carly's face once again.

Is this as good as it gets? I didn't even get to talk to anyone about moving. My real issue.

The counselor asked me to stay back while the others left.

Carly smirked as she brushed past me. A soft lingering scent left trailing behind her. Her hair was swept up baring her naked neck. I lifted my hand to the back of my head. I played with the ends of my hair, pulling, wishing it would grow faster. My mullet to a pixie cut, then bowl cut was slowly transforming now into a bob cut. I tried not to undress Carly with my eyes, but her body made me feel I got the short end of the stick. Not only did she have a genetically gifted hourglass frame, but she carried herself like some teen fashionista. Wrinkling my nose, I watched her leave. Too bad her attitude sucked.

"Victoria, if you feel like you are in any danger, or if any of these rumors have merit, please don't be hesitate to ask for help." I imagined him pleading a case and standing face to face with Uncle Don and Aunt Jane.

What can they do? Place me somewhere else.

"We care and you're not alone," he said.

For a moment there was a stiff, awkward silence and I almost believed him. I felt compelled with a strong urge to speak and even ask him his name. The voice in my head told me something else. Trust no one and suck it up. Really, what can this dude do to help my situation? Nada, nothing. I discreetly left the room in agreement that if there were any changes, I would reach out if need be. In all honesty... I hope he forgot me.

Speak of the devil and he shall appear. "Slackers," Uncle Don shouted from the back. It wasn't what Uncle Don would call a productive day. He brought home some two-inch thick pork chops that were presented on the barbecue. He had just turned them over and started brushing on the barbecue sauce. The grill marks lined up along the juicy meat, dripping fat sizzled in the heat under it. The flames just barely danced under the chops.

"Bet you've never tasted food like this when you lived with your mother." At that very sentence, I knew I should have turned around and walked right out. I stepped into it and I was in for the long hull. Aunt Jane rolled her eyes while putting her wind chime up by the overhang.

Was it harder than I thought to ask to go to the dance? My hands began to get clammy. Aunt Jane seemed to be in good spirits and Uncle Don was in a promising mood.

"Can I go to the school dance?" I asked him flat out.

"Who are you going with?" he grunted over the grill. "A boy?" He frowned.

"No." I quickly added, "I'm going with the girls."

He stopped and studied me with an odd expression, "Who and when?" Uncle Don went back into the house knowing I would be right behind him. Aunt Jane interrupted, "I think you're going to your mom's. When is it?" She asked with eyes like daggers.

"It's more like three friends and it's on Friday."

"Is that Mexican going?" Uncle Don asked, now pouring red wine into a glass.

I frowned. "Yes," I said biting my tongue.

He made the word Mexican sound dirty. All I could think of was Simona's mothers and him stumbling on his words if he saw her. Or eating them.

"I'll drive you and the girls to the dance," he said. "What time does it end?" I shrugged not sure. Now nervous how he was going to behave.

"Let me know," Uncle Don told me, "Does your friend know we own an Eagle Talon?" I shrugged again. "I don't think she cares." Uncle Don looked at me with a kind of funny expression on his face, again, I felt a flicker of caution. "They don't drive," I quickly said trying to close the conversation. I sat back on the kitchen chair with relief, as though a tight string held me and then suddenly let go. The green tiles on the table framed in maple wood and topped with plates of food were comforting in a picturesque way.

"You're going to your mother's on Friday," Aunt Jane said coldly.

I grimaced. "Um...I want to go to the dance."

Aunt Jane stared at me. "No."

For just an instant, Uncle Don seemed desperate to change the subject. "Call your mom." He demanded handing me the phone. "Pass the phone to me when you're finished talking. I have to speak to your mother."

I didn't have to wait long to ask. I asked her nicely, but really, Mom offered. We made plans to go for an outfit. "You're going to rock... I promise." She said through the phone line.

Finally, I could do something with Mom. Shopping. I wonder if she wanted me to move in with her. "Is Trisha with you?" I asked. Mom's voice was patient and slightly pitched.

"Yes." She answered.

I mumbled pathetically before I had to hand the phone over. "I have to choose..."

Uncle Don looked over at me and stopped what he was doing. I figured mom knew what I was saying.

"I'm not forcing you to make a choice, but you'll have to make a decision." If mom asked me to move in, I would be out of here before she knew it. "We'll talk about it when I pick you up." I recalled Trisha, saying: "She had plans to go to Oka." I wonder if Mom would move into a bigger apartment or just give me the couch that her boyfriend's mom passed away on. The living room was made into a shrine. A no-enter zone, with wall to wall pink carpet. The furniture came out of the 50's. Small porcelain figurines and live vines run along the ground up to the crown moldings, just framing the windows and giving enough light to the flowers. The buffet displayed a timeless photo of the older woman just before cancer got her. A vase with her ashes resting on top of a long buffet. Remembered for her poker nights, late hours of ballroom dancing and Sicilian foods. "Listen, I hate to let you go but... Trisha's waiting for me."

"Ciao," I said before Uncle Don interrupted me.

"That's not a proper goodbye," said Uncle Don, who was never very polite.

"GOODBYE," I said slowly and clearly, deliberately being a smart-ass. Heart pounding, I gave him a knowing look while passing him the phone. He didn't flinch over my tone. He smiled in amusement as he grabbed the phone from me.

Clearly not pleased, disconcerted I lurked back. Only now realizing they weren't talking about me, but about business. It was on a topic that didn't concern me. I shrugged, pulling my crucifix out from behind my shirt. My held breath slipped from me as I forced my eyes away. Where's the love?

The memory of Momma and Papa, my highly detailed, co-zy-warm-hearted prayer nights. My mind went off on a little excursion remembering what it felt like to have them in my everyday life. I wonder what it would be like with mom. Or if I'll ever get the chance to meet my siblings and have a life with them. What is this life, this stolen life I live?

CHAPTER ELEVEN

Silent Move

Uncle Don turns the volume up even louder. His black sports car hugged the road as it took the corner at what seemed to be at breakneck speed. The dark tinted windows and dashboard gleamed. The engine roared into the parking lot as he drove in, announcing his way to the front steps like some gas gosling brute. He laid on the charm by passing me a twenty in front of the girls. "Just in case," Uncle Don said.

"Thank you," I answered while he handed me the bill. He flashed me a look in the rear-view mirror, looking pleased by the reaction his unexpected gift had caused. The girls distracted me from my fear of crowds without knowing they were my crutch.

"Your uncle is pretty cool..." Simona said. Her full lips pouted in a way that made grown men turn to butter. Her cheeky smile had been infectious. She smiled and then others smiled back, and so one smile made two. I wasn't listening. My reflection distracted me in the side-view mirror.

"You're lucky." Simona began to praise.

I nodded in agreement. He has his moments, I thought. At times, Aunt Jane and Uncle Don surprised me, leaving me to understand not all love is wrapped in a perfect bow, that sometimes there actually may be coal in it.

"Here you girls have fun. I'll come get you when it's done. It's no skin off my back," he said evenly with a faint charming grin. The corner of his eyes crinkled.

Simona leaned forward between the front seats. "Can you honk?" She smiled. He looked down at her. Like some giant meat head, he honked and honked and honked again. Out of his usual uptight self, like a boy showing off his toy, he took out another twenty and passed it to Simona. "You girls have a good night." He grinned.

Uncle Don pulled out of the parking lot with a heavy foot. Some people stared in wonder and others in judgment. They could keep their opinions to themselves or shove it up their ass. I told myself.

The girls and I walked into the gym like we owned the place. I wore the outfit my mom helped me choose; with a biker twist. We went to a boutique and bought some black matted leather shorts with a zipper on each side and a matching V-neck vest. The boots my mother bought me reached just under my knees.

I walked in with the others and stuck out like a sore thumb. A boy with a camera up my ass made me think of being on film. Nobody said anything about what I was wearing.

I even stroked the soft leather fabric. I found it made me look tough in a rock and roll type of way. It seemed to take a long time for people to stop staring. For a moment, I stopped and wondered if all the attention was in my head or it could be toilet paper hanging from my ass and trailing along behind me like some leftover parade. I turned around just in case and looked at my butt.

Nothing was there.

"Who dressed you? You look like a prostitute." Carly said, pointing from across the juice bar.

I wasn't fazed. "Better than a French poodle."

She made her way around the table and stood beside me. "When are you going to know your place." She slung a companionable arm around my shoulder... and smiled as I automatically stiffened.

"Don't touch me." I bellowed.

"Relax." Carly shrugged.

"Hey, weren't you in that special class?" One of the girls asked me.

Carly shot the girl a look.

"What do you mean?" I hope I had misheard her.

"That special class!" She emphasized on special; a gesture of fingering quotation marks. "You know... that slow class?"

"Go eat a dildo." I said firmly and cut my eyes at her.

I looked at Carly. "You need a better class of friends."

She knew her friend was crossing the line. I hated being in special ed, I hated that the other kids made comments and that I was mute.

What's important? Being yourself or being accepted for living up to other people's standards. I felt trapped.

"They have no clue." I said to myself, knowing how hard is for me to control the urge to smash them. I exhaled. "Just forget about it."

"Are you talking to yourself again." Donna teased, grabbing me to the dance floor. The girls made space for me in their dancing circle.

I wasn't going to let anyone break my stride tonight.

"Someone spiked the juice." Simona said.

We stared at each other for an awkward moment and then quickly ran to grab a cup. I could taste a slight tang.

"Imagine it's not alcohol but instead piss." I said curiously.

Simona spat out the liquid in response. "Gross!" She said as her nose tingles and leaked out.

One of my songs come on and I just about lost all self-control. I couldn't contain myself; I ran to the dance floor replicating my dance moves from home. I tend to break out and bust when the beat takes over.

When I clean my room and do my chores. Sometimes Sarah and Farley watch me; giving me an audience or shadowing me. I soaked up the music channel. They play video after video, giving me an idea for what's in for the season.

From pop to jazz to house music and rap, the songs kept coming. I recharged through the tempos and beats of music, transferring my emotions into art.

When the dance was done, the lights turned on. Nobody fought and I called that a good night. Or a boring one. I rolled my eyes to the comment in my head.

When I woke up in the morning and saw my reflection. I didn't recognize myself at first. At first glance, I thought I was sick, then I recalled all the makeup the girls touched up on my face last night in the girl's bathroom. I look like a horror show.

Aunt Jane opened my door before I got a chance to wipe the dark smudges away. "Ew, you look like crap."

"Thanks," I said lethargically.

"I have something for that." She left and came back with Tylenol and ginger ale.

"Everyone in the car," Uncle Don ordered. "We're going on a drive," he said smiling.

Aunt Jane gave me a pill for motion sickness. It gave me an idea of how far we were going.

I didn't ask any questions.

We all climbed into the van that Uncle Don got from the shop. It was nothing special, the same one we took to Niagara Falls together. It still seemed run down. I assumed it was a before repair vehicle, considering the small bubbled up rust and flaked pieces stained along the trims of the windows and doors. The dents on the sides were just an accessory compared to the deeper damage.

Uncle Don drove us out of suburbia. It wasn't long after we pulled off from the four-seventeen that we drove up these thin narrow roads.

"Pretty." Sarah pointed out the window to the tunnel of canopy trees we drove through and under. It was a maze of roads and maple trees, pines and all sorts. We drove up the mountain and I crossed my fingers, hoping, I wouldn't get sick on these whiney roads.

The sky was still a bright blue like a summer day, but the trees were no longer green. Instead with rich fall colors, with leaves that could barely hold onto the branches. The cool breeze became even colder with an electrical charge. Leaves broke off dancing in the wind; as if something invisible played with them, scattering autumn colors everywhere.

The speed of the van disrupted the golden shades as we passed through with an electrical charge. The leaves are lifted, and they swirled into the air to rest back on solid ground. Pink, magenta, blue and brown with a touch and wisp of purple poked through trees and shrubs. There were colors I never knew existed in nature.

Only once my leg fell asleep had I realized how long we were gone. We passed a large horse ranch with long white fences patched out across acres. The four-legged animals flickered their long tails side to side, slapping the flies away as they ate. Some horses had covers and other did not. I wondered why that was.

We pulled into what looked to be a chalet. Is this heaven or what? I thought as we drove deeper into the driveway under a canopy of color. What are we doing here? We stopped in front of a golden orange maple, yellow birch, and red oak forest, touched with evergreens and white ash. I opened the door to the van. I didn't expect to be welcomed by the sound of birds and a creek. A single giant boulder stood in front of the house. I stepped onto the gravel, walked down the long spaced out flat stone steps. Drawn out towards a rock garden on the left and solarium entryway in front. Leaves scattered everywhere covering whatever plants were around on the right. Moss slightly visible. A large rectangular wired fenced in an area once used to breed giant Newfoundland dogs.

Whose place is this? I thought. And what do they do for a living? I wondered about the owner. How at any time they could walk up the street and see the ranch? I wouldn't even want to go away on a vacation. I would just want to hang out at home. "This house is empty?" I said to myself as I peeked into the overwhelmingly wall sized windows. I have no idea what we're doing here but I was starting to question 'why?'. "Oh!" I said, staring up at the high ceiling.

Uncle Don strode to the French doors, opening one of the pairs. "Follow me," he said as the bronze handle turned. The wood framed glass panels that extended most of its length had an aesthetic appeal that achieved an elegant, timeless charm. "Look around," he said, marching ahead of me as he made his way up the stairs.

"Come see," Sarah yelled from downstairs. Michael tagged along through the open concept living space. The rich dark paneled walls were freshly stained. The brick fireplace was more for show than for heat. "There's no neighbors," Farley stated suddenly, staring through the front windows overlooking the rock garden.

"Further out," he answered, and he was smiling. "Get used to it because this is our new place." He stood inside the empty, custom designed house that was to be our new home.

"No shit," I said quickly. I didn't expect anything like this.

"This is just perfect," Aunt Jane said, looking through the back-patio doors.

"Rockhead," Uncle Don interrupted brusquely, "This could be your room."

"If you stay with us," Aunt Jane murmured. Farley squeezed my hand. "Maybe we'll take this wall out and re-place it with an island."

Interestingly, Uncle Don swelled up and grinned. My cousins, who'd been exploring the split-level floors shouted with excitement to the news. "We live here." Farley sprinted off as I trailed Uncle Don.

"So, it's done." He said, looking pleased. "We're moving."

Sheesh! I wondered if that included me. What was the worst that could happen? If I moved with them and changed my mind, I could always find a way out. Trisha did. So, I didn't say anything else.

"Everyone gets a room." He said with great dignity and disappeared downstairs, showing the kids around the bricked basement room attached to a large furnace room. He then headed out the side door to the shed. I stepped back into the solarium with cathedral ceilings. The crafty house settled into the nature around it, as if rooting itself in. I always wanted to live in the country. I thought.

"The deck will be transformed into a small greenhouse," Aunt Jane said. "The lady before had the house full of plants." I didn't know what it was about this place that com-pelled me. I stood at the window mesmerized by the woods.

A few moments later, a car horn blew out front. It was time to leave. Across the room, I was still staring into space. I probably wouldn't even have noticed that the family was leaving, if I hadn't heard the horn.

Tap, tap, tap! I had fallen asleep on the drive back. There was nobody in the car except for me and Michael.

I opened the door on my side.

"Vicky! Michael" It was Sarah. "Come."

"Just a sec." I unhooked my seatbelt and made my way out of the car. Aunt Jane stood in the doorway with a worried look on her face.

"Come here." This wasn't the first time Aunt Jane got that expression and as usual, all I could do was a shrug. "What?" I said, a little uncertain.

"This fucking school called again." I didn't know what to say about that. "They think you're having some trouble."

I shrugged, trying to find my words. "I think I'm doing fine."

"Who the fuck cares what you think is fine? If things don't change, you're going to be fucked like your sister." Aunt Jane explained, impatiently. "Get your act together."

My act? I thought. What did that mean?

I was relieved beyond measure the day I woke up with anticipation, of course and remembered that it was the day before the move.

It happened so quickly, the house in the west became bear with piles of boxes. Fall was almost finished. Crystal and I spoke for a bit. She took on a new babysitting job. The group of them were being called The Local Babysitting Squad.

"Don't forget to call." Crystal demanded. "And get out of your room once in a while." I fought back the twisting ache in my gut, knowing time was getting shorter. "If you ever need a friend." Crystal said again. "I'm just a dial away."

We moved from Pierrefonds, Quebec that past autumn. I said goodbye to my friends and John Rennie High School.

CHAPTER TWELVE

Rigaud Mountain

The new house came with rules. Uncle Don didn't waste any time.

"You brats are going to have to rake." He was in command now. Keeping us under his thumb, his critical eyes examined us. His glare always provoked the same nasty feeling in my gut.

"All of it..." I murmured, almost too shy to speak.

"What about a blower?" Aunt Jane suggested.

"There's no blower." Pointing along the side of the house. "Don't forget the driveway, the lawn, and whipper snipper around the shed," he said in his low, hard voice, which never failed to make me shiver in obedience. "Do you understand?" He asked. I was too mad to care. "Don't get bent out of shape. Just do what you're told," Uncle Don advised, starting the engine to the lawn mower, which kicked over with a rumbling purr. Why hire a gardener when you have kids? I pictured him saying.

"You think you would love to play in the yard." He finally blurted out shaking his head. "Keep your hands out of your pockets. No one will hire you looking like a slouch." He grinned and his eyes glimmer with a boyish twinkle. I replied with a frown while I forced a smile on my face. "Now that's a happy camper." Uncle Don went on to call out every area that needed to be done.

Uncle Don complained of slackers and how the generation today was going nowhere. "It's because of these fucking computers." Clearly, not into the new wave. I paused and listened for ten unproductive minutes of ranting.

"What a disaster," I said to myself while I nodded, even though I wasn't totally in agreement. Looking at the dead leaves being plucked off the trees by the wind. Fucking guy. I thought as I stomped up the pathway; I had a solid grip on the weed whacker. My hands already becoming numb from the vibration.

Relief washed over me when I finished the last of the lawn. At that same instant, Uncle Don opened his mouth. "Okay people, we have shit to do." Where was he going with this? "uh..." I was starting to get a bad feeling. "It's time to earn your keep. I own your ass," He said and jested with the other kids. "We need to get all these railroad ties together and make garden beds." Uncle Don continued, "Maybe even a pond bed." The man was impossible. "When spring comes, we'll be able to fill it." This will take us all day, I thought.

Sarah and Farley were given the shovels to dig, Michael and I had to help carry the logs and rocks to the garden plot. Uncle Don began to walk back to the house, so I asked, "how long do we have to do this for?"

Uncle Don flinched. "When it's finished," he answered. I blinked a couple of times, managing a smile.

"Of course," I said, distraught. Tyrant!

Uncle Don hated people and he could be so mean when he felt like it. I could feel his eyes on me as I lifted the end of the big railroad tie. Half showing off and half afraid to look weak and be made fun of, I held my breath and lifted with all my might.

"Don't be afraid of getting your hands dirty or some challenging work," he said. "I'm helping you." I held tight to the beam. Who was he kidding? I'm breaking my back over some principal.

You could leave, I thought. Why did I choose to stay in foster care? Seems like I was there to serve. His burly shape in front of me tossed the orders over his shoulder, he didn't stop, and neither did I. Isn't this child slavery? I thought. Or just tough love?

It hurt to run the water over my hands, it stung, leaving me in pain. My legs and arms were sore, and I just dropped on my bed like a hammer. I wanted to explore the backwoods, but my legs slowly took on the form of jelly and my body didn't respond to my brain telling me to get up. I inhaled deeply and my upper body hurt painfully. I changed my position; It didn't stop the aching.

"Rockhead." I jumped back to my feet and quickly poked my head out of the room. I didn't know how long I could handle this. "Yes?" I acknowledged and answered his roar from the dining room.

"Did you close up the shed?" I hadn't really had time to think about it. I leaned back and looked through my thin long bedroom windows. "Uh, yeah." I guessed in a shaky voice. The doors to the shed looked closed from where I stood. "Yes," I said at once. "I also closed the gate to the garden," I said with fake enthusiasm.

"Good," Uncle Don said. I didn't close the door until I knew he was done. I waited a moment.

"Get rest... tomorrow is another day." He sounded preoccupied. I closed the door slipping away, hoping he wouldn't call out for me again that night.

I telephoned the girls from the West Island. Crystal and Simona had a babysitting job and Laura was out with her family. I found myself staring once again at a set of four walls. At least the view from the windows was different.

Like a windup toy activated by a switch, I stalked over to the window, cranked it open, and took a deep breath. Instead of suburban parks with people, homes, and lawns. I could see endless woods and a garden bed. The sun began to set behind the shed. The sky turned a yellow-grey. The air was still and calm, even the birds stopped singing. An eerie silence rippled through the woods, leaving no sound. Nothing, not even the movement of rustling leaves.

I was just about to back away from the window when the sky suddenly opened with a crackled bang. I froze. There was someone out there. I could see someone standing behind the tree peeking at me through my window.

I turned to hide, but something inside me made me stop. Out of the corner of my eye, I saw him walk closer to the house. I just stood there in my room, mesmerized by this guy I was seeing. The rain poured down on him, slapping off his shoulders. I pressed my face up against the glass as I watched him walk around the path to the front of the house.

I waited to hear the doorbell ring. I wasn't about to go looking for him. I sat down on my bed wondering who that was. He never rang the bell or came to the house. It was as if he was never even there.

The phone startled me and not a moment later Aunt Jane called out to me from the kitchen. "Rockhead, pick up the phone."

The enticing smell of olive oil and sauté onions made me think of my grandparents.

"All right." I rubbed my nose reminiscently and picked up the phone. "Hello?"

"Hola."

"It's Simona." Her voice was distinct, with a soft accent. "You're hard to get in touch with."

"I haven't been anywhere but here." I shrugged. "What have you been up to?" I slumped down in the chair.

"School and babysitting," Simona replied.

I heard someone in the background, a young girl. "Where are you?" I asked.

"I'm babysitting Misty." Simona explained. "And did I tell you... Brandon goes to my school."

"The guy who wasn't there when we babysat?" I remembered his door being locked. We waited up for him to see if he'd show.

"I've been talking to him; he's been coming around more. A little strange but not much stranger than you."

"HA. HA." I remarked dryly.

"You know he was there that night we were here watching the kids. He was in his room." Simona said as she spoke slower. "He was too shy to come out."

"What do you mean?" I asked. "He was there?"

"Yep." Her voice didn't falter. "The parents didn't know he was already dropped off before we arrived."

"And how do you know this?"

"Brandon told me." The words out of her mouth sounded creepier by the second rather than comforting.

"You're telling me he was there?"

"Yes." She said. "The reason the order got wrong was because he ordered the pizza."

"Oh." That information didn't sooth my racing thoughts at all. "And that doesn't freak you out?"

"No," Simona said. "Not everyone who locks themselves in a room is a threat." She continued, "I lock myself in my room to get away from my mom. She has no problem butting into my life."

She got me there.

I'd lock my bedroom door if I could, instead I hide in the closet and scratch out my thoughts with a calming madness. I liked being alone. Nobody really cared what I did, as long as I didn't break their rules or seemed like I do.

I preferred one-on-one over a large crowd. My nerves always got the better of me in an unruly way; twisting in my gut. Entering a large gathering was only achievable if I was with friends. The West End Girls had been my shield.

I enjoyed talking with Simona. I imagined my old neighborhood without me. Our conversation took me out of this house. Cabin fever was very much real.

"There's this guy..."

I just listened; I wasn't surprised.

I gazed into the mirror on the wall. I was expecting to see something different, but my hair was still the same mousey tone, with no real style. My all too natural look wasn't doing me any justice. I looked like a giant hacked-up hairball. Still, I looked better than I did.

"He's older."

"I'm missing something." I clued in.

"It's the guy I started babysitting for. He says his wife and him are divorcing."

"Does she still live with him?" I asked.

Simona sounded relieved. "She is staying with her sister." She carried on, "It's just weird because his son goes to me school."

"Are you talking about the house we babysat at again?"

"Yes."

"Simona, he has kids?" I asked puzzled. "He sounds like a creepster." My uncertainty didn't go unnoticed.

"You mean creeper." Simona corrected.

"No, I mean what I say and I'm saying, creepster." It just rolled off my tongue easier.

"No," Simona said. "It's not like that. He gives me gifts."

"Gifts?" I rolled my eyes. I already have an idea where this was heading.

"He gave me a charm bracelet," she said cheerfully.

"Okay." I didn't elaborate.

"It's just a gift, but I find he's growing on me."

After a long pause, I wanted to know the bottom line. "Do you want it to be more than just a gift?"

"No." Simona assured me. "I just thought is was cool that even an older man wants to date me."

"Then make sure he knows that," I said rolling my eyes.

"I can take care of myself," Simona said.

That answer stumped me.

"Oh. And how are you going to do that?" I asked her sarcastically. "Do you have a stun gun."

"No." Simona chuckled and tried to reassure me. "I just won't accept any more gifts." She neatly avoiding any more questions. "I just won't babysit for him anymore," she said. "That's it, isn't it?"

I rubbed my temples. "Maybe." I shrugged. I learnt early on in life that nothing is free. There was debt over me just from being born.

"Oh, err, Vicky, I got to go," Simona said tersely.

"Okay," I answered. "Call me later."

"Later?" She said. "I have to babysit," She said flatly. "To make sure it's just a gift."

"Hmph" I began, "and if it's not?"

"I'll have to stop going." She bitched. "No matter what he offers." She said with a nervous laugh. "Uh, I got to go."

"Okay, call me tomorrow." I rolled off the chair and practically knocked the lamp onto the ground while I hung the phone up.

At the table, I found Uncle Don, Aunt Jane and my uncle's cousin Matt seated in the dining room. Aunt Jane was sipping an Irish cream liquid from a delicate, long-stemmed glass.

The table had been set up and dinner seemed to be displayed with some thought.

"They're not going to fucking care about your napkins." Uncle Don called out to Aunt Jane who was on a mission; folding cotton and linen. It was another form of art for Aunt Jane. Origami was one of her many proclaimed talents. Uncle Don slurred out mocking comments. "Savoir Vivre, these guys won't even notice that shit," he said, his tongue slid across his lips. It left them moist as he pressed the edge of the bottle securely to his lips for a swing. The velvety pungent liquid drained out; pouring into Uncle Don's greedily welcoming mouth. "Where the hell have you been?" he asked after he finished the last malty drop of beer.

"In my room," I answered. I notice Aunt Jane had made centerpieces. I sat down slowly beside Uncle Don knowing he preferred me to sit close by him. He rotated his head on his shoulders, irritably, like someone trying to work out a kink in their neck. "Kid, get me another beer," He ordered Michael. "Do you like your room?" he asked.

I nodded back, "Yes." Honestly, there are times I just want to run away and then there are other times like this. I adjusted myself on the walnut wood chair. The new harvest table didn't have a bare spot on it. Set up like a feast from a thanksgiving ad. What's the occasion? I thought but couldn't bear to ask. As if answering myself I looked up at our guest.

As if on cue, Matt looked up with a smile when he saw me staring at him.

Uncle Don held up one finger. "Rockhead! What did I tell you?" He said with satisfaction. "Owning land means everything." He commented dryly. I shook my head in wonder. "A person is fuck all without it." Uncle Don was having his usual effect on me. I dropped my smile and I hadn't noticed the plate of food placed in front of me.

By the time I emptied the last of what was on my plate in my mouth. I was still trying to calm down from the scare I'd just had. Stinging, from an insult to my feelings. "It's not your fault you'll always be poor." Uncle Don said, Aunt Jane simply stared at him, coldly dispassionate now. "It's because you come from uneducated people." Impulsive and impatient Uncle Don said one more comment before Aunt Jane stormed away from the dinner table with a look of disgust. "The apple doesn't fall far from the tree."

He ignored Aunt Jane as she walked away shouting, "Yeah, Yeah, we all heard you before."

"What?" with a hearty laugh Uncle Don was enjoying the fact he hit a nerve. "It's true, the only way you have a chance of bumping up a class is what I do."

"Is that why you do it?" Matt's face hardened.

"No." Uncle Don stopped smiling and his face became straight with seriousness. Relaxing both cheeks he said, "I do it because I'm fucking good at it." With an arrogance he bellowed out, "I have an inheritance coming my way." Straight faced he then added, "You don't have an inheritance. You have fuck all." I let out a big sigh. "If you want a place at this table, it takes work." I allowed myself to be led, trying to see the point in this charade.

"Go think about what I said." He stepped to the ledge of the patio door and opened it. Sliding it aside. He let in the fresh cool air of the night. Then he unzipped and took a piss. I couldn't help but wonder what Matt thought about all of this. Why didn't he say something? He just sat there with a blank look. "And get your ass ready for school tomorrow."

"Yes, sir," I responded, but the connection was already dead. I slipped quickly back into my room while Aunt Jane swayed back and forth in her room with a lit-up joint. She wore a long gypsy skirt and a waist chain/hip scarf, perfect for belly dancing. With her boho-chic style, and added gold accessories, Aunt Jane was in her own state of mind.

Again, I sat wondering what I was going to wear tomorrow. The first day of school wasn't something I was looking forward to. How many times must I go through this? Always the new kid. Looking through the pile of clothing on the ground and the few items still stuffed in my drawers. I found some flare legged jeans that I got from mom and her boyfriend. He wore his dress shirt open showing off his chest hair and his flared pants while he walks with a cane. He collected a stack of them, some were used for self-defence he claimed.

The pants fit me perfectly. Now I just had to find a shirt and play with my hair. Maybe I can steal some hairpins from Aunt Jane. The night's young. I thought looking at my watch. ten twenty. Or maybe not. I chose to wait till the morning, then I'd decide. I couldn't do much till then anyway. I switched off the light and laid down and listened to the familiar voices in the distance and Aunt Jane playing her music faintly in the next room.

CHAPTER THIRTEEN

Hudson High

Is this like a Cosmo mag or what? In the first few moments here, I've noticed that the students weren't just arriving on school buses, bikes or walking. Instead some of these teens were parking cars and scooters. The outfits weren't just what was in for the season but seemed to be more like Valley trendsetters.

I wasn't sure what I was doing there. The red brick building with stairs to its grand head office, seemed overwhelmingly structured. I peered down the hall of Hudson High School, known as HHS. The school's intention and purpose were written on a banner. Our motto was: "Achievement and character. Challenge yourself to fulfill your academic, intellectual, creative, and social potential," I read the sign hanging from the cream-colored walls. This office was even larger than the one at the courthouse. The room smelled like newly laid carpet. It demanded a certain type of quality and author-ity. There were pictures of its founders on the walls.

Blah, blah, blah, I thought recalling my beginning at all the other schools. I stepped forward and approached the first desk and with my arms tucked in, I waited.

It's okay. I calmed myself. I wondered what it would've been like if I was never taken and separated from my family. I smiled thinking of my mother and her long hair. With ele-gance, she always made me feel special. Even if it was just for a moment; like a blink of an eye. I told myself it was just about finding a way for us. Just to be able to talk...

Scanning the room, I read another sign that said boldly, "we engage in real world challenges while preparing students for the workforce and encourage active citizenship, and life-long learning." Everyone around me seemed to be smiling. Again, I felt like an alien. I found myself staring at everyone intently. My cousin Michael came with me to grab his courses and he was even more withdrawn then I was. I stood there getting sucked into another daydream when finally, after a brief explanation the woman behind the desk sat down and gave me and Michael a list of our classes.

"Here you go!" She said and impatiently eyed another stu-dent beside us. I cleared my throat, meaning to say thank you but it came out more like a mumble. Michael and I didn't know anyone there. Suddenly, I felt nauseous. Michael and I were on two separate floors. Shit! My fingers felt the jeans under my shirt. I looked down and saw a few small holes on the side. Crap! I'm full of holes, like some hobo. I hardly re-semble myself. It didn't seem important wearing what I chose last night before bed, but today when I got up, I just wasn't in the mood. I felt like wearing something completely different. Something that said think twice before talking to me. I had to work with what I had and that wasn't much. My wardrobe seemed to be an ongoing battle I had, and I wasn't winning. I wanted to be left alone. I wanted to hide. I want a superpower that made me invisible.

"You're new here." A girl with deep brown tight curls from roots to tip smiled. Her hazel center eyes fanned out into a green gray. "I'm Julie," she said with a firm hand. She stood beside me and gasped, and her eyes widened as a guy with red dreadlocks named Leaf joking placed his cold water bottle on the top of her bare back. Making her jump forward.

"Brat!" Julie shouted.

The moment I saw this guy down the hall, I immediately recognized him. It was the guy I saw outside of my bedroom window. The one in the woods. I found myself strongly drawn to him, almost as if I were going to question him. Julie watched as I attempted to walk towards him.

I just had a few more steps to his locker, when he paused and smiled at me, then was pulled away by his friends the opposite way. His brown hair swept over his forehead. He turned away and kept going. It seemed like he read me easily in a matter of seconds.

"Punch me." I whispered.

Julie leaned in and gave me a punch in the arm. "Hey." I rubbed the spot and corrected, "I meant pinch me." Then she went to pinch me, "Stop that!" I slapped her hand away.

Julie smiled, "Carlos is advanced and was bumped up a grade." She cleared her throat, while I wondered why he was around my house. "What's your name?" Julie asked me.

"Vicky," I answered and sat down. I leaned back in class and put pen to paper. I doodled out some characters and scribbled some lyrics while I coasted through the first few classes. By the lunch came around Julie and I already exchanged favorite colors, movies, songs and even went to the washroom together.

Winter had finally arrived; Large snowflakes fell over Hudson high bringing with it the promise of a white Christmas. The snow just barely covered the ground, leaving footprints behind as the students stepped through it at the end of the day. Like walking into a book, the first pages to my new life were being drawn out. I could get used to this. The first day was one of my better days. "See you tomorrow," Julie yelled out to me before going onto her bus.

"Tomorrow," I said. Making friends had never been easier and Julie didn't seem to mind my lack of words. I had to tread lightly – school politics had taught me that much. I never wanted to be a part of the gossip pit. I didn't realize it this morning, he must have gone on the bus before me, but Carlos was on my route home. It was a long drive back, waiting in anticipation to see where he lived.

The bus stopped just before my house. Carlos walked past me from the back and as he went to step off, he looked up at me quickly. He caught me googling him and I couldn't help but blush. My face flushed as I made my way off the bus and down my drive. I adjusted my shirt as I walked in.

As Matt led his dog out of the house, I could see why I had a crush on him. His snowboarding gear waited by the door for a chance to hit the slopes. His slick sunglasses just shyly sitting on top of his forehead. I couldn't help but compare him to Carlos. My mind kept slipping towards my new neighbor as I made grilled cheese sandwiches aside with a tall glass of chocolate milk.

A ripping roar broke the silence from out back. "F-U-C-K," with a loud thump I heard a crack. I looked out the window and Matt stopped what he was doing when he heard a dog cry. From the glass patio doors, I saw our dog run passed and then Uncle Don chased it with a two by four stick. He circled the house twice before he got the dog straight across the back.

"Oooh." I thought about that for a minute. I wanted to go see the dog but wasn't sure if I would get in trouble for checking up on her.

Matt's jaw clenched. He opened the door and called his dog to him. While Uncle Don chased the dog for one more thump. "Does he do that a lot?" He turned and asked me, but what could I say?

"What?" I answered, I wanted to hear it for myself from someone else's lips. "Discipline."

"That's not discipline," Matt answered and took his dog and things out to the front. I watched Uncle Don come in from the back with his face burning red. He looked like a mad man. "The fucking dog ate all the hotdogs on the barbeque." Shouting he tossed his hair over his ear like he does when he's agitated. "I'm going to kill the fucking thing." I wasn't sure if he was serious. I turned to look in the other direction, unable to face his raging glare. My eyebrow rose as he turned to look for more meat in the fridge. "F-U-C-K-E-R."

Striding boldly through the front door, Matt looked straight ahead. "What the fuck is wrong with you?" Matt shouted as he walked into the kitchen. It was the first time I saw a guy yell at Uncle Don.

Uncle Don stood over Matt by a few inches, "Listen, the fucking animal ate our dinner." He said firmly.

"Well, you didn't have to hit her," Matt said coolly. Having his own dog here made him nervous and edgy.

"It's my dog and I can do whatever the fuck I want with it," Uncle Don snapped.

"Well..." Matt spread his hands apologetically. "It's not right." Matts face went still. "It can seriously hurt the dog. It's a living thing." He corrected. "Just keep a better watch on your barbeque."

Something more was going on here. It looked like Uncle Don was just pissed on. "Thanks for the tip," he growled. I knew it was a lost cause for Matt to try to make sense of the situation. Uncle Don was on a roll. Like a snowball effect he rants on... "No dog is going to get away with eating my meat." Uncle Don wanted to show who the boss was, while I sat still and slightly shaken. Matt stayed around for a little while but kept his dog away from Uncle Don, who looked annoyed. His anger echoed through the house.

I was slightly excited and happy to see Uncle Don's attention elsewhere and to see a challenge. It was like live television. Matt could see he was getting nowhere with this. It was almost as though the reason for Matt being here had been forgotten.

Aunt Jane was in her own world in the solarium decorating for Christmas, sprinkling fake snowflakes loosely around the massive Christmas tree. Around us, everyone else enthralled with the situation unfolding at the table... everyone but Michael. Things aren't going to turn out the way Matt had hoped.

Uncle Don looked up, reddening, "You don't know what the fuck you're talking about." Matt stood, and Uncle Don stared down at him. "The dog will learn." Matt didn't budge and stuck his chin upwards. I thought that was the worst thing to do besides turning your back. So, they say at the gym.

Matt said nothing as Uncle Don continued, "The dog will be okay."

Matt rolled his eyes, "No thanks to you." I couldn't help but smirk. I pictured Matt being thrown out the front door without even touching the ground.

"You mean, it's all thanks to me." His grin was more than just a grin. I wasn't surprised to see Uncle Don finding amusement in what I call the pissing contest. Enjoying himself, he knew exactly what he was doing. As if defeated, Matt changed the subject, while Uncle Don found something for us to eat.

By the time Aunt Jane was finished decorating everyone was off to their rooms and the table had been cleared. The moon shone bright in the blackened sky. The freshly fallen virgin snow heaped along the outside of the window frame. Tiny white bulbs on electrical strands hung overhead along the wood beams, creating a fairy-tale canopy with sparkly lights. A star sat on top of the Christmas tree with a warm glow. I was hesitant to enter. Aunt Jane had created a place in the home where you can turn off the world. I sat down in an antique rocking chair Aunt Jane found at a flea market. I sank within the wood arms of the chair and wrapped myself in the large sheepskin blanket. The great gauzy popcorn texture gave a touch of luxury, encasing me in its soft coziness. My head bobbed and my eyes kept closing. I tried to find the strength to rise. Defeated I sank even deeper into the chair.

The French doors opened with authority and the bottom brush seal lightly scraped over the solarium tile floor. A deep voice echoed within the large space. "Hey Rockhead!" I woke up at once with a numbing chill. My arms wrapped around myself from the cold. I hugged the throw over as tightly as I could while Uncle Don stood at the front door. I closed my eyes and willed myself back to the present. "Get up," he said sliding his feet into his boots. "Come on." He put his jacket on and his trapper hat and took his gloves out of his pocket. His large hand gripped one of the shovels and walked out the door.

The winter wonderland that I fell asleep to wasn't what I woke up to today. A glacial skin piercing breeze swept over me when Uncle Don opened the door. My now red nose and ears were as cold as ice. "Eh," I really didn't want to get up. Uncle Don seemed to take pleasures in my discomfort.

Not one bird chirped and not one bird was in sight. I put on my black winter jacket and red toque. My scarf wrapped around my neck and lower face and my mitts were slightly larger than my hands.

"Your birthday is coming up," Uncle Don said as we started to shovel. "How old you are you going to be?" That was something that I hadn't even begun to think about.

"Fourteen."

"Did you want to do something?" His question took me completely by surprise.

"Yes," I said at first. Then, "No. I mean, maybe a sleepover." I answered breathlessly while we finished clearing the walkway. "If that's okay?" My nose hair stuck together as I inhaled the air.

"Yes," he said dryly. Uncle Don and I were birthday buddies. I was born on the winter solstice and Uncle Don just after Christmas. He seemed to take a liking to that. As much as he didn't give a shit about birthdays he didn't forget about mine. Maybe it was going to be a good year after all.

The light brightened around me as the sun reflected off the shimmering white snow. "Do a decent job," His eyes bored into mine, "Finish this driveway." The emphasis he put on the last couple of words was unmistakable. I looked up, following his gaze, shrinking at the thought of shoveling all this. I studied the narrow driveway. The branches had been covered with heavy snow and curved from one side to another. Trees and shrubs bent but didn't break. I wondered what time it was, but last time I checked it was still two hours till school started. My active start to the day caused a ripple effect throughout the rest of the morning. Once the bitching and complaining was done... I was good.

I emerged from the bus, throwing my bag over my shoulder. I didn't have long till my ride came. Julie invited me to go with her after school for a recreational swim at John Abbot College.

"You'll love it." She said, and, before I could say anything, it was planned. "It's very large."

I didn't know how to explain to her about my fear of swimming, first almost drowning at the water park, then the stadium and I still wasn't fully over what happened at camp.

"I go with my family every chance I get," Julie persuaded. "We'll pick you up and drop you back home afterwards."

I couldn't understand what Julie saw in me. All I knew was that I wanted to see what her family was like. Curiosity got the better of me and I tried to swallow my fear.

We stopped at Julie's house for a moment. Her family grew their own food, including their meat. I got the picture of Charlotte's Web as I saw the barn next door and the white picket fence. She told me about her stepbrother and how he was shot with a nail gun by his friend. It was an accident that took his eye. Her stepsister looked like Goldilocks and her parents like farmers. As sweet as pie and right as rain.

"You want to try some?" Julie offered me a snack stick, like a pepperoni stick. "It's lamb." I winced, looking at the meat stick. Julie wasn't interested in my protest. "You'll love it," she said and hummed the tune for Lamb Chop's Play Along.

I heard the best way to overcome someone's fear of water is to learn how to blow bubbles. I wet my feet and slowly entered the shallow end of the giant pool. When I got deeper, I splashed water on my face and slowly dunked my head under. To Julie it was just another swim but to me it was conquering something within. Pushing past my comfort zone. Especially when I saw the guys. If my friends from the Pierrefonds or Pamela were here, they would be eating up all this eye candy. I wondered why the students looked enhanced with a quality that stood out even in their walk. In an instant, I answered myself. I knew that's what I wanted – confidence.

Julie had been a natural swimmer ever since she was a baby. "Have you ever wanted to swim like a mermaid?" She asked me.

"I never thought of it," I said. "I'm more like the type to pretend I'm a galloping horse." I stretched my legs out and let them float while my back was up against the wall. Julie's long legs were placed together, and she held her breath and went under. Smoothly, her body moved like a wave under the water. She couldn't be bothered with the guys swimming; Julie was fully immersed in her water play... to the point where I was playing as well.

"Do you want to sleep over this weekend?" Julie asked me as we climbed out of the pool. Her damp hands shook as she gripped the towel to dry herself off. My hair still streaming wet and my body creating a small puddle around my feet.

"Sure," I said without thinking. It was only a second thought when I realized I had to ask if I could go. Aunt Jane and Uncle Don seemed to be in better spirits since we moved.

It's worth a shot. I shrugged. Julie made the plans as they drove me back home.

I took the chance to ask Uncle Don if I could sleep out. He said yes but not before asking me how my swim went. He gave me a lecturing on swimming and even told me about his experiences when he was younger and about being a part of the swim team. An hour and a half later, I called Julie back with an answer.

I continued to draw in my sketch book until supper was served. When I got to the table, same as usual, there was a disagreement going on. Matt fed his dog by the table; Uncle Don didn't agree with feeding human food to animals.

"It's my dog and I can do what I like," Matt said in a voice rife with warning. Cutting a piece of his meat he threw a chunk to his dog. Uncle Don's reaction was swift, he moved across the dining room, his nerves were clearly on edge.

"It's not a big deal." Matt ignored Uncle Don completely, examining his dog for a moment. "She's more than just a dog to me."

"Moron," Uncle Don spat out.

"What's wrong with you," Matt challenged.

Aunt Jane and the rest of us stopped, I straightened, looking at the situation with surprise. Uncle Don raised his voice and put his fist up to Matt. "It's just a fucking dog." As if his dog understood, Matt's dog growled and dropped its head. The closer Uncle Don got, the deeper the dog growled, until Uncle Don booted the dog in the face. As he was going for another blow, Matt bull rushed Uncle Don but to no prevail.

Matt stood up to Uncle Don, but it wasn't more than a second before Uncle Don was choking Matt over the dinner table with both his bare hands. It took both Aunt Jane and Matt to get Uncle Don off.

"Cool it." Aunt Jane tried to separate the two.

As soon as Matt was freed, he left with his dog. That was short lived. I was hoping this one would have lasted longer. It seemed to be a turnaround, or revolving door for workers. At least he didn't gas himself like the last dude I remember working with Uncle Don. His bud killed himself over a broken heart.

"Everyone go to your rooms," Aunt Jane yelled. The evening was done... the show was over.

CHAPTER FOURTEEN

Chocolate Chip

I'm going to kill myself, if I can't express myself. "Tell me what I'm doing here?" I demanded and gripped the phone tighter, as if daring someone to hear me, I raised my voice a little louder. My hands were sore all over.

"Vicky, please, if anyone understands you, it's me. I had to stay at a foster home and trust me, it's no picnic." Pamela carried on, "Uncle Don cares in his own way."

"A fucked up way."

"An old fashion type of way."

"No..." I dragged on, then lowered my voice and hissed through my teeth. "You only say that because he's nice to you."

She laughed and then said. "He could be worse."

Perfect, I thought. Not only am I being worked to the bone, but now I'm supposed to be grateful.

"Okay," I finally said, letting out a relieved breath. "I'll stay here until I graduate, then I'll move to the city."

"You can stay at my place," Pamela offered. "I'm sure my parents won't mind."

"Thank you but I'll move in with Mom," I said. "She lives near Vanier college."

"Fine. But you have to come and visit," Pamela told me. "A bunch of people are coming for my birthday," she said in a hurry. "You better not miss it." She insisted. "It's my sweet sixteen."

"I'll be there." A horrified feeling came over me. My anxiety spiked. "Do I have to talk to anyone?" I asked mildly.

"Oh, no." Pamela said calmly, almost serenely. I always thought that living in the country would be mystifying and relaxing, but really what was mystifying was the amount of work I was expected to do. Pressed, I agreed to be at Pamela's party.

I dropped my head when Carlos stood at the front door to drop off his sister. Apparently, Sarah and the neighbor are now friends from school. His dark eyes looked me over from head to toe. I turned away from him, my stomach fluttered at the thought of him so close.

"Rockhead will bring her back," Aunt Jane said introducing me with a nod. I gave a slight wave and disappeared as quickly as I could. How would she like it if I introduced her as Burnt Out Jane? I felt claustrophobic and needed to get out. I slipped into my winter gear and went out the back. I sat on the four-wheeler and placed the key in it and turned it on. Then I played with the gear with my foot and pressed the gas with my thumb on the handle. I drove up the driveway and down the mountain to the store. I bought an egg sandwich and stopped to look at the horses by the ranch. I couldn't help but try to pet one, but with no such luck. They kept their distance from the fence. My hands were frozen by the time I got back home.

It wasn't long till I had to bring the neighbor back. She didn't want to stay anymore because Michael jumped out and scared her in the washroom. He shoved her to the ground.

I was forced to face the parents and brothers, including Carlos, to explain to them what happened. Even though I wasn't there and really didn't have a clue as to what happened. Carlos' family were all in the kitchen around the island with all the food on it. His mom was cooking while his dad helped with the studying. His brow was creased with concern.

"Please let your parents know that our daughter cannot go over to visit anymore, but that Sarah is more than welcome to come here."

I shrugged and answered, "I'll let them know." I exhaled slowly and glanced wearily up at him. "Sorry about that." I sighed.

When I told Aunt Jane what they said, she wasn't impressed, she shouted at Michael and smacked him across his cheek. "You're a piece of work."

Uncle Don didn't care, he figured it was better they weren't around anyway. "Calm down," he managed to say.

I took the opportunity to ask to sleep over at Julie's. Both Uncle Don and Aunt Jane allowed me to. Trying to head off any more insults, I steered Michael towards his bedroom door.

"Honestly, I was just playing," he said.

I couldn't help it. I laughed. For a few moments Michael looked at me as if waiting for an answer.

"Some people can't take a joke," I said. "I mean, I hope you can understand. They see it differently."

He looked down at the ground a moment, then up again, and his pale blue eyes stared into mine. Without a word, he closed the door to his room between us.

The rest of the week, I tried to dodge Carlos and his brothers at school. I didn't know what they thought about me and the family. The week dragged on, but once Friday was here, I couldn't get to Julie's fast enough.

"We'll pig out all night and watch movies," Julie said, laughing as she chose the chips for the night. The pull-out flowered patterned couch was opened for us. I looked at the clock on top of the television set. I automatically grabbed a handful of VHSs to look through. For a few minutes, we were both silent. Then Julie jumped to her feet. "Did you hear that?" She asked.

"No." I stopped to listen but heard nothing but Julies foot-steps walking to the window to check.

"Have you heard from Kerry?" Julie asked about another friend I met at school. But I haven't made any plans with Kerry yet besides talking on the phone a few times and hanging out at the shops near school. Hudson high shops... the store sold individual candies and marketed around the teens. It seemed to be in a heritage house, but I wasn't 100 % sure. All I knew was that the buildings were old with charm. It appealed to my interest, the character and story of the building. Most homes or places had a story or history. Most of the places in Hudson had a reason for standing.

I didn't know how to approach my first sleep over at Julie's. It seemed to be a different life unfolding here. I laid across Julies couch and soaked up the peace. I wondered what it was like living off the land. I guess we are all beholden to our parents. What if I wasn't raised by my parents. This was what ran through my mind while Julie slowly picked the right movie. Is my fate to become slowly like my parents or to take on this identity with my foster parents? Expectations of others painted me into a corner. I found myself slowly losing my mind. Not for the first time, I wish to see and meet my other siblings. I'm afraid I'll never meet my youngest brother on my mother's side or my other two brothers and two sisters on my dad's side. I know social services called to speak to Trisha, and the fact that my siblings were placed to other foster homes, gave me an idea about the conditions. I wondered if Pamela was right. Should I count my blessings.

Maybe, but I also know that I had to keep moving, to keep growing. I watched Julie in her pajamas and I couldn't help but smile. She wore a turquoise and purple onesie. I didn't know what to say. So, I didn't say too much. The house smelled like flowers and oak. It felt safe. It felt like a real home full of love and care. The smile on Julie's pale face seemed genuine. I wondered if she wore a mask like me. The invisible one that I sit here with, one way in public and another at home.

What if I didn't care about the rules anymore? I just wanted to be me, whoever that may be. I knew I wasn't going to find out who I was by hiding. I didn't want to paint myself into an image of someone else's ideal of who I should be. They didn't define me. But I did like the way Julie made me feel important. And I had no idea why she took me in as a friend, but she did. Shit! I barely spoke to her, unless I'm spoken to.

"So, what's your favorite thing to do around here?" I asked, attempting to strike up a conversation. Maybe Julie could be a way for me to practice social skills without her knowing it.

"We're doing it," she said. "Besides cooking, eating and watching a kick ass flick, I don't see what else. Maybe tomorrow we can feed the neighbor's horses."

Horses! Now I knew I was in heaven. Finally, I looked over at Julie smiling ear to ear. Waiting for her to finish, we made eye contact. I whispered, "Thank you for inviting me."

"No problem," Julie said. "Maybe I can come to your place at one point?"

I agreed but wasn't sure if it was possible. Though Uncle Don did say I was allowed a small birthday party. Aunt Jane wouldn't mind. She liked parties of all ages. I didn't think she would miss a little tea party with toddlers, to teens, to adults, to old timers. "Do you want to come to my birthday party?" I asked Julie.

Intrigued, she lifted a brow. "Yeah." She looks at me and her face was already glowing. "When is it?"

"It's the weekend Christmas break starts," I said with care, nervous that no guests would show being so close to the holidays. I looked down at my feet. I hadn't even noticed the holes in my socks. I curled my toes. At least this time my socks matched.

"I'm up for it." She turned to study me. "How about Scream?" Julie grinned and slipped the cassette into the VCR. "It's new." Julie pointed out.

"Sure. I love Drew." I referred to the cover of the movie case.

Maybe we should have thought twice about watching a scary movie while we were sitting in the dark. But in some way, it was also nice.

"Come on!" I shouted, forgetting for a second where I was. I looked over at Julie and back at the screen. "Is that it?" I slumped back into the couch and dropped my hands. I wasn't sure if I was more mortified to have screamed or to have just realized Drew wasn't in the rest of the movie. "What a bummer." I mumbled. Why would they have her on the cover if she was just going to die in the first few seconds of the film?

"Don't worry, it's still a good movie." Julie said.

Tonight, I discovered Julie and I were kindred spirits when it came to our taste in movies. When you're a child of the eighties and early nineties, there's no shortage of movies.

We stuffed our faces and as the scenes unfolded, I ate my nails down. By the end of the second movie, Romeo and Juliette, even with Leo, we passed out. The blank television screen lit up the living room and left us with a faint humming sound. I turned around and snuggled into the fluffy cushions and big comfy couch.

"You girls want some breakfast?" Julie's mom asked. She opened the curtains and the sun crawled across the floor waking me. "I'm making some French toast."

I heard that. I raised my hand and sat up. "I would." My eyes were half closed and my hair was a mess. I stretched. I had held my pee most of the night. I didn't want to get up. I was cozy tucked away. I tried to nudge Julie awake. I wasn't going to miss an offer for French toast and melted butter with maple syrup. I hope I didn't seem overly anxious when I grabbed for thirds.

"So how long have you lived in Rigaud?" Julie's dad asked me as he poured a glass of orange juice.

I sat up and rested my elbows on the table. "Just a few months."

"Where did you live before?"

"The West Island and before that Laval and before that Lasalle, then there was Little burgundy." I rolled my eyes and shrugged "All over." I was getting tired of repeating myself, but I figured they didn't know me and for some reason I didn't mind answering. I stared down at my plate.

"What do your parents do?"

"Grow plants." I said as plain as day. I usually avoided this question like the plague, but I answered without thinking. I couldn't even come up with a good lie. I remained silent, stumbling over my thoughts to their stunned reactions. "He grows vegetables."

Julie's family blinked back at me. Julies father's eyes never left mine. I knew he could see the truth in my eyes, could feel that I wasn't lying to him. For one second, for a fraction of a second, I saw understanding between us. He didn't push the subject. I could have mentioned the body shop, but it was too late now. I'm such a bone head.

When breakfast was over, Julie and I went out into the courtyard and carefully pet the horse standing at the gate. Julie gave me some apples to feed the four-legged beauty. We stayed out in the cold and watched a majestic rich sunset. The golden glow reflected off the horizon.

I watched a full moon rise slowly. We also ate freshly baked chocolate chip cookies.

"Take this home." Julie's mother gave me a batch to go home with. Nothing else was said about my little comment about the plants. So, I left it as it was and just went with the flow. I waved Julie goodbye as they left me to walk up my driveway. From afar the house looked peaceful and full of warmth. As I got closer, I could hear Aunt Janes Christmas carols playing from inside the house. In addition, I could see Aunt Jane dancing by herself in the frosted bay window. The family albums were laid out across the dining room table. I picked up a picture among the layers scattered on top of the table. Without warning Aunt Jane told me to drop it. "Don't touch, you picture thief."

"What?" I raised both my hands. "I'm not taking any-thing."

Her answer on that was a grunt.

I narrowed my eyes as she rummaged through a box.

"Here," she said. "This one you can have." She glances at me and then at the picture. Curiosity had me reaching out, warily, my eyes riveted on the picture.

It was the family I had with mom and my siblings before we were taken. My mother was younger in the picture and her hair was still the same, long, chestnut brown. Trisha and I sat on the sides with our hair done up for Sunday service.

"It's before your haircut." Aunt Jane smiled. "Before the round brush got stuck in it." I looked around the table to see if there were any other old pictures. Like puzzle pieces, I wanted to see the images that may fill in the forgotten spots of my childhood. Fanning my hands away, Aunt Jane said, "Wow, you'll get a chance to see all them when I have the al-bums finished." She sent me a quick silent signal to head to my room. "Go," She ordered, then waited until my footsteps faded away. I placed the picture in the shoebox I found and placed it alongside the necklace Derrek gave me from camp and a blueprint of a house I wanted. I kept it under my pillow when I lived in the West. I saved some money, in hopes of one day being able to create my own exhibition.

I fell asleep to a dream, imagining several large canvases hanging with my paintings of children in dark mind sets. A welded sculpture sat as a centerpiece in the large cathedral room. It was made with metal, rock, clay and wood. Words were written in calligraphy along what looked to be a cement shaped ribbon. Even one of the pieces were interactive...where the sculpted child held out in the palm of her hand a plasma globe. I walked up to it and touched the globe with my finger, and the small colorful currents grounded to my flesh. The metal ribbed child, with a small hanging rock within the chest cave, gave depth within the soft smooth detailed clay on the outside. She had been placed as to be stepping up wooded roots growing from within the earth. When I looked up to her eyes, I saw something shine and then move. As I leaned into them, I realized her eyes had coin shaped mirrored eyes.

When I woke up, I sketched it out as fast as I could. To someone else it may have looked more like scribble then art, but as for me, it was art that came to me in a dream.

CHAPTER FIFTEEN

Higher Standards

The long narrow hall wasn't designed or decorated like the other schools. This one seemed to have the festive energy without plastic ornaments. Only a personal item left on a teacher's desk seemed to be visibly different. Near the office they placed a Christmas tree decorated with gold and red ribbons softly circling around the outside of it, from top to bottom. There were simple round balls to artistic creations and a lettered gold sign across the door that said 'Joyeux Noël, Merry Christmas'.

"Hey, you want to buy something?" A guy asked me as he walked up on me. I stepped back and declined. "No, thanks."

"Oh, come on... You're missing an opportunity," the blond-haired guy asked me. He wore a clean cap with a Capital "D". "It's just five dollars." He continued; his baby-face smile stopped me.

"No," I answered. I wondered how he lasted this long trying to sell so openly in school.

"You don't know what you're missing." The guy started to say and pulled out a disk from his pocket. "It's got original beats and the lyrics are solid." I looked down at his hand and he had a small pile of CDs.

"You want me to buy music." Relieved, I let out a breath. "Are you allowed selling these here at school?" I asked him with a straight face.

"It's my work. Plus, I'm selling them for next to nothing," he said defensively. His voice echoed down the hall.

I noticed he resembled a cousin of mine, and I smiled, but I wanted to make sure I didn't give him any cause for optimism. "Let me see what you got." He gave me a disk from the pile. "If you like it, pass me the five dollars tomorrow." I placed the disk in my pocket, and I watched a girl rush up to him. "Hey, can I use your studio for my photo shoot?"

"He gave you a CD," Kerry, a friend I met during English class, said. We were to do the Shakespeare skit together.

"Yeah," I continued. "I'll check it out tonight." I started to feel accepted by some of my peers. They knew I wasn't old money and they didn't care. The only ones that seemed to be bothered were the prissy, stuck up, self-centered, all-knowing, hard to please biatches.

The one rad thing I noticed was that we have an actress that attends our school. I recognized her from the television show Are you afraid of the dark. She was the doll on the other side of the mirror. It took me all day to get the courage to talk to her after I followed her to her locker. "I just wanted you to know that I loved that episode," she wasn't snobby like the other girls in her grade. She seemed well put together. I didn't want to seem uncool even though I had a thousand question of what it's like to be on the show. I got a smile out of her and that was enough for me. I think I'm going to like it here.

I slipped in and out of the ladies' room before math class. It seemed Home Economics wasn't as important as Math. So, for some reason, I had two math courses a day, which suited me just fine. The teacher had a rather memorable style of teaching. As soon as I walked into the class, Kerry jumped where she stood.

"Hi, Vicky." Kerry said, swinging her bag on the back of her seat. "Hey," I nodded. It was going to be a long day. I already found myself looking at the clock.

A few minutes before math finished, I could see Julie at the door trying to wave me down outside the view of the teacher. It seemed urgent. Her hands were waving around, and her eyebrows almost touched her hairline. "I think I'll go check what Julie wants," I mentioned to Kerry, who also noticed Julie's weird behavior. I raised my hand and asked to be excused.

I strolled out of the class light-footed and I said the first thing that comes to mind. "What's wrong?" I asked in a whisper, "Are you okay?"

"Your agenda is all over the girl's washroom."

"Really?" I said nonchalantly, aware that I was hoping it was a mistake.

"I went into the girl's washroom and saw your agenda ripped up and scattered everywhere."

I did hiss this time, my face hard. "Err..." I almost fully ran down the hall and when I saw what Julie saw, I felt like throwing up. Someone ripped out the pages I wrote of my notes and doodles of Carlos. Hanging onto my heart I wondered who would do this. "What the fuck?" I quickly picked up the rest of my stuff with Julie and threw it out. I even had to wipe off the mirror, someone wrote Vicky's a bitch on it.

"Someone stole your agenda!" Julie asked.

"No," I sighed, "I probably forgot it here this morning." I groaned, "Mother fuckers."

"Who would write that?" Julie pointed to the words.

"I'm guessing someone that doesn't like me or may even like Carlos." I shrugged. "Who knows?" I was surprised, I didn't realize there was a problem. I do now.

"I responded with a nod. I wanted to cry right there, in front of Julie, but I'm not that type. It was hard to go on with the rest of my day. It really pissed me off and caused a chain reaction. Left to my imagination I wondered if I was missing something. An image of a show I watched with my grandmother of Matlock came to mind. I smiled at the memory and pushed through the rest of the day.

From school to this, I kept my mouth shut, having learned the hard way – not that Uncle Don was more than happy to spend hours talking about himself. The sooner I could get my letter written, the better. "It takes work to be in the will,"

Uncle Don slurred out. He stuck out his chest proudly, "Think of it as good works."

I felt like I couldn't leave the table, like I was trapped. Driven by dollars, he explained that the government finally cut off funding.

Crumpling the paper together, my frustration was being taken out on the documents. Left on the table in front of me. It said file closed in big bold black writing. It was like being kicked in the stomach. What does that even mean, file closed? Like an expiry date, my case was just closed. The choice I chose was to stay living with my uncle and aunt and cousins, but at what cost?

"Go to your room." Uncle Don shouted to my cousins and then shot me a look and pointed to the shed out back. "Follow me."

I admired the set up. He built a shed in the backwoods, hidden from the sky under the trees, and out of view from the house. He made his own automatic watering system and had the lights on a timer perfect scheduled every twelve hours. It proved to be important. Uncle Don never refused a challenge and expected the same for me. "Your mom and her boyfriend aren't giving us anymore cash for you." Uncle Don started to say. "It's not a problem," he said. He laughed as he said it, though, the ass. "You see, we care about you and I want you to learn a skill."

He didn't waste no time, he taught me how to make multiple clones and plant cannabis babies. I put on music and just did what he said. I tore right through it. I didn't understand what the whole issue was. The public had one view, while we had another. The little green plants seemed to be a type of therapy for me. No harm, no foul, I thought. It was like taking a walk. I didn't like all the fucking lying all the time. I was tired of playing the fool. I sat there like a brown noser, even asking obvious questions. I knew how much an ego liked to be fed. If the beast was fed, I figured then so was I. Kind of like don't bite the hand that feeds you. The rest of the night I was doing one thing or another.

"Those people driving in their nice cars or wearing their nice fancy clothes and accessorized to the hilt, looking like they own a house, are in debt. It's like you're borrowing from the government to be their slave overall." He continued, "There are student loans, but you still have to pay them back and try to live." He grinned, "Some people need a to cut corners every so often to get ahead."

I nodded in agreement, he sighed impatiently, "So, what did you do after school today?" he asked me.

"I helped you," I said.

"No. No you didn't." He blinked and gave me a darting glare, "Don't be stupid."

I hate that word...stupid. "No. I guess I didn't." He didn't want me to repeat any of this to anyone. Plus, it was more like he taught me rather then I helped him.

I wasn't sure what his lesson was really about this time, but I figured it was an explanation to why he does what he does.

"Well, Rockhead." He leads me out the shed, almost breezily. "I'm coaching you."

Coaching? Flabbergasted, I gaped at the back of him as we walked to the house. It was ridiculous, a foolish career choice that had nothing to do with me or plans of being a recognized artist.

Yet he seemed to think I could do it. I had to change the subject and fast.

"Is it still okay for some friends to come over for my birthday." I knew he got anxious over the word party, once again, one too many parties of Aunt Jane's turned him off from the word.

As we entered the house Aunt Jane joined the conversation. "So, what's the plan?" she asked, grinning. "How many people are coming for your party this weekend?"

My throat was suddenly, uncomfortably dry. "Four," I tried to look convincing. The truth was I wasn't sure yet. I only told a small handful about my party. I wasn't sure what Uncle Don's mood would be in, so, I wasn't even a hundred percent sure if I was going to have a party or who to invite.

"You better get on it then." Aunt Jane said, "We need to know exactly who's coming and how many people."

"Okay." I said, acknowledging the deep need that dwelled within me. I didn't just need some time that was mine; I needed my friends, all of them, a moment with us together. Merged in laughs before everything faded into memory.

I called my friends before bed and got a few answers. The rest of them I'll have to try again tomorrow. It was too late to think about it. Some were meeting for the first time. I invited friends from the West End and from Hudson and then there was Pamela. There was always Pamela. If she does miss it, it's most likely because she's grounded.

The last week of school seemed to drag on, between exams and trying to pass them, I had hoped for more multiple-choice questions. It seemed most of the students here had an above average I.Q. or they walked around as if they did. There seems to be a drive to be the best and a lot of the kids here came from what they called old money.

I read more than I ever had before. Sometimes I would read out loud, I found it helped with my speech. I discovered words I had never heard before. It seemed the only books you would find in my house were Buddhism, Zen, mechanics, bodybuilding, healthy eating and these encyclopedias based around cannabis. How to grow, what was the best and all the different strains, how to distinguish female to male.

As far as I could tell Uncle Don has been collecting these books for years. Just like his boxes of comics. Some being first editions and some dating as far back as to the forties. Uncle Don allowed me to have a few heavy metal magazines that had erotic graphic stories. I much preferred looking at the pictures.

I was almost sure that they would disqualify anyone who arrived late. I sat next to nobody that I knew, peering toward the clock in the gymnasium. The exams were almost done. The students sat under the bright lights with the desks even-ly wide enough apart. I studied all the way across town this morning on the bus. Conjugating verbs in English was one thing but conjugating in French was my kryptonite. I broke out into profuse sweats and sat on the edge of vomiting.

"You look nervous," Julie whispered to me. "You don't think you passed?"

I looked back from the exit doors. I didn't leave any question unanswered. Now it was up to them to determine if I passed. Thank God, my French oral was done.

"Hope so," I answered. "It's not my best subject." I almost fainted when I had to stand up in front of everyone for a presentation last week. I stood there like a dope for a few moments and covered my mouth and didn't say anything. My bangs covered my eyes. After introduction, I stated the topic: Sharing a family memory. I said about four sentences and looked at my feet the whole time and then rushed back to my seat in the back of the class. I refused to answer any questions.

Julie now shrugged wearing her oversized V-neck knit sweater, leggings with slouch socks on. "You'll be fine, though," She said casually with a scrunchie holding up her hair. "This time next year you'll be passing French with flying colors."

Early before the school buses were ready to leave, Julie and Kerry whisked me away over to Main Street. I bought a handful of sweets. It's how I liked it, in a paper candy bag. The street ran parallel to the Ottawa River and today the river was frozen over.

"What are those?" I said during our stroll. "People put sheds out there?"

"No, you dope." Julie smiled and Kerry cackled. "Their ice fishing shacks."

"Are you serious?" I cleared my throat again, with my cheeks already red. "You mean people actually go fishing out there...?" I replied wearily. "Why?"

"Because fresh fish taste good." Julie said. Kerry added. "You should see the river in the summer, the sailboats and bike paths line the waterway." She continued and pointed out to the iced scenery. "Now it's littered by makeshift shanty town shacks."

A few moments later, I found myself being invited to an event in town, just further down Main street.

"I'm not missing it." Julie said now putting her mitts on while walking. "Apparently everyone from school is going." She gasped, "A known hip hop MC is coming to town and that's a first for around here." She smiled. "Apparently, he lived here once before moving to Little Burgundy. He was adopted and started rolling out beats in the metro."

That caught my attention, like me, he lived in both places. "I didn't know you liked rap, I thought you more of a country music type of girl." Julie paused and looked at me. "Whatever music my body responds to, I like."

I thought about it, thought about bumping into Carlos, or just hanging out with friends and living a normal social life. Why couldn't I go and have some fun with the girls?

"You're on, babe." I grinned; I was adjusting to this new life. I just wanted to spread my wings. "Let's do this."

CHAPTER SIXTEEN

The Buzz

A knock at the front door wasn't something we usually heard being in the woods. "Do you have a dog?" A nervous man asked looking over to the road. "It's a German shepherd."

I only said five words, "Nope. Check across the street." I knew Carlos' female cousin lived across from us. She was a bigger girl, tall with a mushroom cut. She never spoke to me but always looked uptight.

It was about five minutes later when I saw Uncle Don walk in carrying our dog. Looking at her I guess she looked like a shepherd, but she was mixed with Collie. Uncle Don laid her down in the sunroom and the kids and I stood around him and Aunt Jane.

"It'll be okay. It's just a dog." Uncle Don bent down on his knees to help her, and he could see rips in her fur off the side of her, revealing her flesh underneath. Her eyes were rolled

219

back, and her tongue laid out, her breathing became shallow. She slowly faded to just a whisper of breath. "Dogs are tough."

Uncle Don gave Aunt Jane a look and she took my cousins and I out of the room. Uncle Don wrapped Jesse up and carried her outside.

"What happened?" Sarah and Farley asked simultaneously.

"She got hit by a car." Aunt Jane said, "She didn't stop to look both ways."

Michael turned around without a word and went downstairs to his room, he was in the middle of a galaxy battle that he put on pause. Shrugging off the dog as just another specimen.

I remained hidden in my room until Uncle Don arrived with a new dog in tow. He wasted no time in getting a dog. This one looked like Matt's. The dog was black and brown, an obvious characteristic of a Rottweiler. I held the cat as they brought the dog in.

"Ow, Shit!" I howled as the cat leaped out of my arms. I took a brief intake of air and I held the cat tighter. The cat bit right through my thumb nail, even getting her long canine stuck. I could have yelled out anything but instead I held my breath. I couldn't spit out a word. I squeezed my thumb tight with my other hand, creating pressure to try and relieve some of the pain. It was a poor attempt to try to stop the bleeding. I walked briskly to the washroom and turned the sink on. Running my finger through the water made it sting even more. I finished by quickly bandaging my thumb up with a square Band-Aid. The new dog was already full grown and at my feet as I stepped out of the bathroom with my thumb in pain. I see the cat was nowhere in sight. What was I thinking? Introducing a cat to the dog like some animal whisperer. Sometimes I surprised myself. "She's from the shelter," Aunt Jane said. "Her name is Devo."

Whatever it took, I just had to make it through tonight. So far, our dog died, the cat bit me and we got a new dog all in the matter of three hours.

"Rockhead," Uncle Don shouted for me. I pushed the already opened door open more, to see Uncle Don demanding a massage.

I made a face at the back of Uncle Don's head. "Just start at the shoulders," He said, exasperated with his refusal to answer any other questions. Sarah and Farley wanted to know more about dogs going to heaven. Uncle Don didn't feed into that, he just casually said that the dog was taking a dirt nap.

"Use this." Uncle Don passed me the tiger balm. With my fingers, I started to rub the cream into Uncle Dons shoulders. It took a few seconds to register but as the stinging in my thumb worsened, I realized the balm soaked through my bandage and is now irritating me with every rub. Like pins burning and poking me, my thumb was in bad shape and I couldn't stop or say anything, I felt like I just had to take it and wait till Uncle Don said I was done.

"It's 99.9 The Buzz, and we're wishing everyone a rocking start to this sunny day with a new hit." The throaty voice over the radio was hard to ignore. His upbeat energy came through the airwaves every morning on my radio.

The school wasn't big enough to not notice the snobbiest crew to ever walk the halls of Hudson High. "Stay away from my cousin, Carlos." The wide shouldered girl looked me up and down. "You're not his type," she said firmly. "He's not interested in the underprivileged."

I envisioned her in a chokehold. I bit down hard on my tongue; on the brink of tasting blood. I took a deep breath. "Whatever, I think we'll leave it up to Carlos to decide if he wants to talk to me or not. Not you," I said with my face twisted in a stilted expression.

The second that I mentioned his name, her face flared up with insult. Her expression made me follow her gaze behind me.

Carlos approached slowly and paused at the mention of his name.

I walked around him, through the corridor chewing my thumbnail. My cheeks burned as we made eye contact.

It's clear that Carlos was clueless about his cousin.

Exposed, I fought the choking feeling of feeling vulnerable. I wanted to throw punches. This is 'why' I don't date. I warned myself. Just do yourself a favor and walk away.

Spinning, I grabbed the door handle and jerked it open. I dove into an empty classroom, slamming the door behind me. "Idiots!" I shouted, turning to look out the window.

I took deep breaths as I watched the rugby team on the field.

"Why am I bugging out?" I quickly asked myself.

My breath hissed in through my nose. It was unusual for me to have a confrontation with no fists flying. Only now I was aware of how unnatural it felt. The more I accept the fact that I'm not normal, the more I look around and realize that none of us are.

I sat on a desk by the door and listened to the students rushing in the hall. Their voices carrying over each other like verbal waves. Defeated, I decided to reset myself.

I never promised... I was normal. I thought. Words played back and forth in my head, taming the criticizing voice and remembering the lessons from the counselors about having to remove my defensiveness. The frustration made me want to bash my head on the wall but instead I had to learn to be soothing when in conflict. It was all just too much!

It sounded nice engaging with people, but how could I without getting unnerved and wanting to open a can of whoop ass on them.

By the end of the day, I just wanted to be alone. People were exhausting! I thought.

Aunt Jane picked up a few of my West Island friends for my birthday. She said I needed to get out of whatever funk I was in. Pamela couldn't make it. But some of my new friends were dropped off by their parents.

"Wassup?" I threw my arms around Crystal and Laura.

"I noticed a few rules have changed since you moved." Simona pointed out, gesturing to the fact I had people in the house.

"Just a few," I grinned.

I sank into a giant beanbag and drank my first homemade glass of vodka and juice mix.

It didn't take long before the girls put some music on and sang happy birthday.

"We all miss you back home-" Crystal started to say after the cake, but Simona cut her off.

"It's not the same," Simona pointed out.

"I'll have to come visit, but..." I hesitated, wishing I'd never spoken, but unable to keep from pouring out my words. "I have nowhere to stay."

All three friends from the West invited me over. Laura also mentioned Donna and Felisha said hi.

There were a lot of people I missed from the West; I didn't really stop to think about how many people I had gotten to know. It was nice to hear that they thought of me.

The mixture of friends at my party meshed well. They got to know each other over a game of darts. But the louder they got, so did my anxiety.

Plagued with my teeth chattered at the vision of Uncle Don barging in and kicking them all out, or worse, flirting with them. I had to think of something else to create some space between us and him.

The darts were getting further and further away from the dart board and more around the wall.

"How about we go for a hike?" Julie suggested.

"Are you mad?" Laura grumbled. "If you want to become a popsicle stick... It's freezing out!"

"Maybe a small walk isn't that bad," Crystal suggested.

"I know a place not far from here," Mel suggested.

"What place?" Skeptical, I didn't want to explore too far. I always preferred to plan.

"There's this house not far from here. My mom says that the bank owns it now." Mel added. "It's been vacant for a few weeks, something about a divorce."

"Let's go see it." I stood up quickly. Sometimes during my walks I'd stare at houses and wondering who lived there and what they did for a living.

"I agree, let's go." Julie grabbed her scarf.

"It's a nice place." Mel reassured us.

The other girls didn't seem thrilled to go out into the cold. Especially when we opened the door and were welcomed by a winter breeze.

"Grab some scrap paper to burn." Mel quickly zippered her jacket up and put her mitts on. "If they still have wood by the shed, we can use the firepit out back."

Even though we were a distance away we still could hear the music from the house, echoing behind us. The snowflakes fell slowly over our footsteps.

"Are we there yet?" Simona hissed as we walked up the mountain. Snow wasn't her friend.

Then, as if out of nowhere, Mel and Julie stood beside a driveway that lead up a curved path. I couldn't see five feet in front of me.

"Are you sure about this?" Crystal muttered.

Laura agreed. "Maybe we should go back."

"We're already here." Julie claimed. "Let's at least check it out." Without a word, Mel led the way.

"Let's go." Kerry jumped at the chance to explore.

The small gang of us made our way up the walkway.

"Hey, who's that?" Laura looked surprised; her blue jacket thinner than the rest of us

"I don't see anyone," Julie said.

"It's unlocked," Kerry called from the porch of the house, squinting into the darkness. "Why is it unlocked?"

"Is anybody there?" Laura shuddered.

Mel surprised me yet again by not making light of any concerns. "The house is supposed empty."

"Wait!" I said without having to think about it. "What's that?" I pointed to the large boot prints on the ground, none of us could have made them.

Mel paused for a moment. I noticed she didn't dispute my comment. "We won't stay long."

The rowdy wind growled down the hallway through the house like a funnel. The footsteps in the empty house echoed.

The other girls went to check out the house, while Simona and I went to check out the kitchen.

"Do you want to sleep over next week?" Simona asked.

"I don't see why not." I answered.

BANG! BANG! BANG!

Both Simona and I jumped.

When I turned around; fear stabbed me.

We froze at the sight of a large silhouette in the doorway. "This is my house." The man shouted. He was more than just a bit irate.

I swallowed hard. Adrenaline zinged through me. From the corner of my sight I saw Simona's mouth hanging open.

Mel drew in her breath.

"Get out." He roared again. "GET OUT!"

He didn't have to tell me twice. I got up and quickly walked to the back, the other girls got the same idea.

"This way." Mel lead the way through the back. We were knee deep in snow, but no one cared; so long as the guy didn't run after us.

He didn't, instead he stopped and shouted from the deck. "This is my house."

We made it back to the road. We didn't intend to tell any of our parents what happened. I know I wasn't telling Uncle Don or Aunt Jane.

"What was that about?" Julie said.

"I thought you said nobody lived there." Kerry breathed.

"Um, nobody does, I think that man is trespassing," Mel muttered under her breath and added. "My mom's the realtor for that house and she hasn't sold it yet."

"You could call her," I mumbled as we walked back to my place.

"I can't. We weren't supposed to be there," Mel admitted. "If she finds out, I'll be grounded throughout the holidays."

"Well, she'll eventually find out," I said dryly. "He'll probably be there when she goes to show the house." I tucked my hands into my pocket. With every exhale, a small misty cloud would appear in the cold air.

Mel began to wheeze and cough. She held her chest as she slowed down. She sounded like she was breathing through a straw. It was a similar occurrence I saw with Trisha.

I slowed my pace; hoping she'd catch her breath. The cold air didn't bother me as much as some of the others. I seemed to be less sensitive to it. A few of the girls sped up briskly to get out of the prickly forming frost.

"You want to jump on my back," I said with a wry smile. "I could carry you," I said half joking and half serious.

"No." Mel couldn't catch her breath. The snow hit our faces like small needles.

I knew I could pick her up. I looked at her and weighed out the options. Just in case if she needed me, I stayed close with her until we got to the house. We were the last ones, but Aunt Jane noticed we were out.

I was worried I'd get in trouble but instead she made us all hot chocolates with a dash of brandy, topped with whipped cream, shaved chocolate, and garnished with a candy cane.

It felt like I was in the twilight zone. What was she up to?

The night carried on in front of the tube.

We fell asleep sprawled out across the room. There were bundles of blankets everywhere. You had to make sure not to step on anyone for a bathroom break.

The sound of the furnace rumbled.

It wasn't long into the next morning that a drunken spin knocked me off my feet. I wasn't a 100% when I decided to go four-wheeling on the Big Bear and not long after I found myself leaning headfirst in a ditch.

"Argh, NEVER." I wiped my mouth. You say that now but wait and see. I thought of a smartass remark. "Never again," I told myself.

I snuck back in from the side basement door and found myself dry heaving on the bathroom floor. The room spun.

When I finally got the energy to leave the bathroom, the girls smacked me down with pillows. It felt more like bricks.

What a wakeup call. Monkey see, monkey do, I took Aunt Janes ritual of Tylenol and ginger ale before we drove into the West Island to drop the girls back home. The others were picked up at the house.

Now I know why Aunt Jane said one bottle with that Irish smirk she does.

"So, what do you want to do?" Aunt Jane asked. "I'm sure you want to see your mom."

I nodded and stared at her for a moment.

"Okay, so, I'll drop you off there." Her voice sounded genuine, but I wondered if there was a motive.

"And I'll see you back at the house tomorrow for Christmas eve." She said as she nearly missed the light.

I got a chance to sit with my mom's boyfriend who finally introduced himself by name.

I never knew which name to use or what to call him, since he is a man with many names.

"Just call me... Angel." He advised.

My mother handed me a cup of tea and cornbread.

The apartment wasn't large. It was packed full of objects. Angel's mother had lived there for forty-two years. The layers collected throughout the apartment told its own story.

"Are you hungry?" Angel asked with a stiff posture. "Let's bring her downtown."

He walked with his head up, his nose and chin to the sky. It was different to Uncle Don's leering glare and having to always look down at our feet or dish.

Mom and Angel brought me down to Saint Laurent street to La Cabane restaurant. It's an urban bar/eatery since 1983 with late hours & a neighborhood vibe for Portuguese tapas & mains. They were friends with the owner and regular customers. They knew the waitresses and waiters by name.

Even as we walked, people would wave.

"Do you come around here a lot?" I asked.

Both Mom and Angel laughed.

"As much as we can," Angel said, waving to the waitress for a refill. He didn't eat, but he did like to drink.

I had my first barbequed chicken breast served with giant potato skinned fries. Not far from a place called the Frappé. Where mom and Angel introduced me to a game of pool.

Surprisingly, my mother whooped my butt.

"You're a talented artist." She grinned. "But a lousy pool player."

"I got game." I hopped on the other side of the table and grabbed the chalk cube as if I knew what I was doing. I then stepped back and studied the table and saw my shot. I leaned in and focused. Lousy huh! I hit the white ball into the lined ball and instead of it disappearing in the pocket, it flew off the table.

"I need practice," I said faintly.

We didn't stay much longer; the restaurants and stores were closing early tonight.

I was happy the day was ending. I needed the sleep.

My mother and I woke up late. It was abnormal for me to sleep passed the sunrise but my mother wakes when afternoon transitions into evening.

Angel cringed. "They want more money from your mom," he muttered, placing his carved cane aside. The sun's rays peeked through the wooden blinds across the counter. "Your mom is heartbroken."

I looked around.

She wasn't up yet. It was just Angel and me.

Angel's silver hair hung down to his lower back. He wore mostly dark clothing and walked with an odd cane, not that he needed one. My mother was there when his mother passed.

"You should think about staying," Angel said silkily.

I looked at him without words.

"Just know your welcomed here." He paused. "It's home."

I winced. "Really?"

"Yes." He toyed with his jewelry; his ears were pierced from top to bottom. He wore rings, watches and gold chains. His shirt was unbuttoned with a large collar, exposing his chest hair. He looked like he was from a 70's flick when he wore his fur coat. A complete opposite of Uncle Don; who just wore a jean jacket most of the time.

"Just keep this between us." He smiled and replied his favorite song 'Whiter Shade of Pale'. In a trance-like manner he continued, "You could be closer to your mother."

It's an ideal offer, but I pictured graduating in Hudson.

"It's an option." I said, uncertain what to say.

"You could start going to my friends' gym downtown." he loved the idea that I was interested in martial arts. "His name is Philip Gelinas."

"That would be cool." I said, recalling my experience with sensei Lee.

Décarie boulevard was bumper to bumper. The city never slept. I thought as I watched the hustle and bustle from the passenger seat.

My visit was cut short and mom drove me back to Uncle Don's and Aunt Jane's. Trisha needed some help. Just like that, Mom informed me that I was going to be an aunt.

CHAPTER SEVENTEEN

Predator

"Why do we put out cookies and milk for Santa?" Sarah asked Aunt Jane.

"It's our way of saying thank you." The answer was sweet and simple.

Sarah sat by the smaller tree in the living room. "What if he doesn't show up?" Sarah asked eyeing the chimney. "What if you have the fireplace on? How's Santa going to get in?"

"Why can't he use the door?" Farley flat-out asked.

"He'll get in. He has a Christmas key," Aunt Jane whispered to them. "Have you been naughty or nice?"

Both girls shouted nice... Michael and I just watched.

"You're allowed one gift." Aunt jane smiled, leading the tradition. "And tomorrow we'll see what Santa brought."

There was no holding back with Aunt Jane. The new house inspired her.

By the time morning came, both my feet disappeared in fluffy grizzly slippers. Warm and snug, I softly made my way out of my bedroom.

The warm cherry panelled walls wrapped around the living room. Our individual stuffed stockings hung low over the fireplace. All the colors of Christmas invited us into our own Christmas story.

I looked down the stairs in disbelief; on the other side of the French doors, gifts stacked up to the door from across the room. It was like walking into a dream. The French doors opened; welcoming us into a white Christmas. The snow encased solarium reminded me of a snow globe. The giant-sized Christmas tree was the focal point.

"Wow." Sarah swelled up with anticipation.

"Is that all for us?" Farley eagerly asked.

"We have to wait," I said, noticing this Christmas was the biggest one we've ever had. The room was so full I could barely see out the window.

Trisha would be kicking herself for missing this. I knew she always wanted to live in the country. She loved the time we spent at camp, just to get away.

"I don't see a telescope?" Michael sighed and turned back towards the kitchen. "I'm getting some cookies."

"Cookies!" Sarah ran to see if Santa ate his.

"He didn't even leave a crumb." Farley bounced.

We all knew better than to wake Aunt Jane and Uncle Don.

We sat, itching to ransack the room. The urge was great, but the sight of Uncle Don's temper was worse. Though, today we all hoped he'd get up soon.

"Merry Christmas!" Aunt Jane shouted as she opened the door. "Coffee first," She said as we all tried not to watch her make her coffee. Sarah's leg twitched in anticipation.

"Brats, come here," Uncle Don shouted as he made his way to the solarium.

The two girls sat by Aunt Jane. Michael sat on a rocking chair. Aunt Jane and Uncle Don sat together on the bench with their spirited coffee, and I handed out gifts.

We opened our gifts with sounds of 'oohs' and 'ahs'.

Once the big unwrapping was done, we sat around the table and ate a large Sugar Shake style breakfast. It was going smooth until Uncle Don was triggered by a comment.

"Don't get wound up." Aunt Jane smugly took another sip of her drink while making gingerbread cookies. "Christmas time is supposed to be a happy time."

"I like Christmas... It's Christmas nitwits I have a problem with." Uncle Don added in an odd, as a matter a fact tone. "You don't see people all year but then they come around for Christmas to get sauced."

"That's called family." Aunt Jane smirked.

"It's full of crap is what it is. Just a way to get tanked on your dime." He boldly howled and dismissed Aunt Janes romantic imagery of Christmas.

"Don't get bent out of shape." She glared, with daggers in her eyes, cursing under her breath to his smugness. It didn't take long before she was in her room with one slam of the door. "Why do you have to shit on Christmas!"

No one made a peep. Uncle Don was on a roll.

His howling laugh rose louder as he dug under her skin. His words rubbed off like salt on Aunt Jane's festive heart. He enjoyed shredding her plans and getting under her skin.

I snuck into my room to escape any bickering. There's no closet to hide in, so, I slide my earphones on and escaped. I wanted to keep my distance from the crossfire.

Not long after Aunt Jane came out of the master bedroom, refusing to let him get her down. Humming a song and tuning him out; she basted the turkey to keep it moist and took a few more sips of her wine.

The scent of food lifted the energy in the house. My stomach opened with mouth watering anticipation.

How much time had passed; I couldn't say.

Without knocking, Uncle Don quickly entered my room. "Where did you...." In mid-sentence he stopped; something caught his eye.

I froze.

Rage boiled into bulging veins and a throbbing forehead. A slumbering dark shadow creep out from within him. His eyes flicker over my wall with a dark veil.

My eyes searched for the error.

His presence reeked of alcohol and his reaction drips with disgust. Beads of sweat ran down his temples and his cheeks burn with a triggering warning.

"What is this shit...?" The large bulky figure smacked his hand on the wall like a bull banging his hooves in the narrow pen. I couldn't bear it, but again, all I could do was stand still as panic and worry consumed me. "You should be grateful," He said stone-faced and tight-lipped. I man-aged to sum up some courage, I wasn't sure what set him off.

"What?" I asked trembling. I backed away from the furious glare. He stormed towards me and spun me around while at the same time slamming me into the wall.

I fought to get loose, but with no prevail, his grip tightened around my neck. He held it there; squeezing me, as if to prove his strength and then he threw me on the bed.

This is so messed up. I thought, looking for a plan of escape. He can snap me like a twig. I surrendered.

"What is this fucking crap on my wall." He marched towards my poster and violently ripped it off the wall. He tore it apart and threw the crumpled image across the room as he growled hatred. "I don't like niggers on my wall." His remark stung, as he'd meant it to when he looked at me and said it.

Now I find myself in pain. My throat burned and I felt dizzy. I breathed in deep and held it there. He acted like he did me a favor. It gave him absolute power over me. It wasn't about learning; it was about him being "smarter" than I was, and proving it by emotional blunt force, shattering any hope of returning back into the world as a normal teen.

"Clean up this room." He leered over me.

You want me to clean... I can't even breath. I thought.

I felt like I was punched in the gut. Nauseous and on high alert, I couldn't believe such a trivial thing caused so much anger. Puzzled, I stood still as his fist waved within two inches from my face.

Things will never change, I thought. There isn't enough flattery to get me out of this one.

I praised his strengths to keep him from finding faults with me. The flattery, combined with sidestepping sensitive subjects, created a workable dynamic between us most of the time.

I looked at him in disbelief. I couldn't help but think that there were some deep seated issues. Based on the unpleasant alcohol stench. I decided to be mute and just nod my head. Answer with one word or short sentences. I told myself.

"You're moving downstairs..." He shouted.

I nodded slowly. I guess I'm bunking with one of my cousins. I sighed.

Rubbing his forehead, he added, "by the furnace room." His words were daunting as he closed the door. "I want this room cleared out by tomorrow."

The new terms had me cornered like some field mouse. I had to share a room with wolf spiders that crept out from the furnace room. There wasn't a door, and anyone could walk in at anytime. I'd have to go to the bathroom to change.

The next night, Aunt Jane and I cleared out what was left in the room and placed it downstairs in the family area. The furnace made me uneasy with it's crackling clanging sounds.

I piled my clothes into cubed milk containers and stacked them up beside the pull-out couch.

"This is a bigger room; you'll like it here." Aunt Jane left the last of the load on the coffee table.

I was reminded that I never really had a choice at all.

"Am I staying down here?" I asked, not sure if I was just being punished for a period of time or permanently.

"Your ungrateful attitude has to stop." Aunt Jane mumbled. "It's not just about the room, but you can't just skate by here or coast, you have to work."

I slouched over wondering where I went wrong. I bit my lower lip hoping for divine intervention. I might... I might... I might just as well move in with Mom. I'd probably get my own room.

I took out my art pad. I didn't bother unpacking anything else. I sat on the couch and thought of the only thing I could do ... draw. I felt safe; making a world within two covers just for myself. I escaped in blank pages, exposing different stages. Illustration manifested into a world of creation.

"Can you come in tomorrow?" Simona asked.

I held the receiver to my ear, already knowing the answer. "Yes."

"Are you sure?" She asked. "I don't want to make plans and you cancel."

Pleased, I shifted my shoulders. "Of course." I knew Aunt Jane wouldn't mind getting rid of me for the weekend and when I asked, I was right.

The afternoon sun was warm on my face. I didn't want to leave. It seemed as if nothing had changed in the West Island while I was away. Simona's home still had the same aroma and her brother still had that dashing smile.

"I just got called into babysit," Simona grumbled.

A grimace crossed my face, and I turned my attention onto her. "Are you serious?"

"Don't blame me," Simona retorted. "How about you come with me?"

I would have tried to find a way out, but she looked desperate. "Okay, but I'm picking the movie."

"Yay." The little girl answered the door like we were old friends and gave Simona a big hug.

"This is Misty." Simona introduced us.

"We've met before." I shook her frail hand. "Remember we babysat Misty and her sister once before." I continued, "And her brother never showed up."

"Oh, yes, he was in the other room," Simona giggled.

"Sorry about that." Misty's mom hung up the phone. "I was just called into work last minute."

"My mom's a nurse." Misty said with a smile ear to ear. "She helps people."

"That's nice." Simona walked over to the couch.

"Brandon will be back." She started forward. "But please wait for my husband to relieve you."

"What about the little one?" Simona looked around looking for the baby.

"She's at daycare." The lady said with dark circles under her eyes. "My husband will be bringing her back with him."

"Okay, so it's just us, eh?" Simona smiled at Misty.

We sat at the table with crayons and coloring books. I slipped in a movie. Misty raised the volume to one of the songs.

I'm sure it was louder than her mother allows.

Simona and I got carried away, talking about Brandon

We found our way into his room. Simona just wanted to see what he was about.

Misty didn't want to come in. "It's haunted," she said.

"Noooo." Simona looked around. "No such thing."

"Why do you say that?" I asked her.

"Brandon says that the banging on his walls are ghosts and that they're mad that I'm in his room."

I rolled my eyes, looking over his desk.

"More like your brother doesn't want you in his room." Simona breathed, her words ruffling Misty.

"He keeps trying to bring me here at night. But I don't want to." She hugged herself and looked down at the ground. "He says it's safer."

"Why?" I asked.

"My sister got stolen and disappeared." Misty replied with broken words. Her shoulders slumped and Simona and I knew we brought it too far.

"Let's do something else," Simona suggested.

"He doesn't like anyone in here when he's not around." Misty added with a frown. "I think the ghost is my sister."

"Why do you think it's your dead sister?" I asked and Simona eyeballed me. I shrugged, I needed to know.

"Because I hear my brother talk to her at night." Simona paused, and the grimace grew more terrible as Misty finished the sentence. "And sometimes I hear her."

"Okay, that it's." Simona grabbed my arm. "Let's go."

BANG. There was a loud thud just before we closed the door. We all looked back into an empty room.

I looked at Misty in question. "Is that the ghost?"

"Yes," Misty squealed under her breath.

"Do your parents know about this?" Simona asked.

"Yes, they said it's probably the neighbours." I looked at the wall.

Simona's shoulders eased, "They're probably right."

"You said last time that Brandon was in the room when we were here?" I wondered.

"Yes. Why?" Simona asked, impatiently.

"Last time his door was locked," I recalled.

"Yes. And this time it's not." I looked at the lock on his door and the size of his stereo and drums. It's odd to have so many things going on in here. The small fish tank in his room had a loud filter and his computer fan sounded sick.

"Why?" I asked myself. "Why leave it open now?"

"Because mom opened it," Misty said. "He got in trouble for locking it. Next time, Mom said she is taking off his door."

BANG! The wall shook again. But this time I thought I heard something. I put my ear to the wall. "I hear music."

"It's the neighbours." Simona said.

"Where's your brother?" I asked Misty.

"Mom sent him to the store."

Simona shot me a look, "So, let's get out of here."

Misty pulled Simona out of the room and I reluctantly followed. Something wasn't right. I placed the door to how we found it. While I went to walk away, I noticed the nanny cam doll by his dresser.

The front door opened, and Simona and I jumped away from Brandon's door.

Brandon walked through the front door casually, his long arms placed the bag of milk and bread on the floor.

"Looks like they sent you on a mission." Simona joked.

Brandon was puzzled to see us.

"Where's my mother?" He asked.

"She was called out for work." Simona sat beside Misty on the couch.

"And who are you?" he asked me.

My stomach curdled at his voice.

"I'm a friend," I answered, meaning to say a friend of Simona's. I looked at Misty and than at him. They didn't look like each other at all.

"I have something to do. So, please don't disturb me." Brandon drew in another ragged breath and walked to his room. He shut the door behind us and locked it.

"He's not supposed to do that," Misty said.

"Let's just leave him alone and your mom and dad will deal with him later." Simona opened a small bag of chips. "Let's finish watching our movie."

I couldn't stop looking over at his door. I could see his shadow pacing back and forth under the door for the first few minutes.

"When is your dad going to be back?" I asked Misty as she dipped her chips.

'He never comes in to stay and I don't know when he'll be back." Misty's shoulders slouched. "But the daycare closes at five-thirty."

"Satisfied?" Simona eyed me to stop with the questions.

I got up to go to the washroom and on my way back to the living room, I heard Brandon moving furniture.

"Your brother is moving furniture around or what?"

"No." Misty whispered, "He says its my sister, Stacy."

"The one that died?" I don't think I've ever asked anyone this many questions, but I was starting to think there's a whole story behind this image. Something was definitely up.

"Stop with the million questions already!" Simona said, her gaze shifting between Misty and me.

"Okay... Okay." I sat down and didn't whisper another word of it.

It wasn't long after the movie that Misty's dad showed up with the baby and a box of beer. Brandon never came back out.

His father seemed different than the last time I saw him; he looked like he was tired and drained. He didn't resemble that guy in the picture anymore.

When we got back to Simona's house, I couldn't shake the thought of Misty and her brother.

"You get weirder by the minute." Simona teasing me about all the questions.

"What's weird is that family," I said.

"I didn't want to get into it in front of Misty." Simona began to explain. "I babysat once and heard him talking to someone in his room, but nobody was there."

"Was he on the phone?" I answered sarcastically.

"No. But I did hear a little girl." Agitated, she focused on me. "Did you know that Brandon was the last one to see his sister before she disappeared."

My eyes got wider as I listened to what my friend had to say. "Wow," I said when she was through. "How'd you hear about that?"

Simona lifted an eyebrow. "Misty told me."

"Next time ask Misty how the nanny cam works and see if you can record Brandon in his room." I was curious to know if it was a ghost or just our wild imaginations.

KNOCK... KNOCK! Simona jumped off her bed and peeked out her blinds. "Go Away!" Simona waved. "I have company."

"Who's that?" I pulled myself forward.

"It's nobody." Simona ignored the last knock.

I gave her a look.

"It's just my brother's friend." Simona gave in. "We've been seeing more of each other."

"Does your brother know?"

"No."

Simona and I spent the night talking and our plans and goals, values and passions. I learned a lot about her in the last few hours than I did living down the street from her.

Seeing that we weren't going to see each other again for awhile, we waited till the last possible moment to say our goodbyes.

When I got back to the house, I thought of all the people I met and missed. I sat in my bricked room with the thumping fireplace. But not even wolf spiders can get me down. A new perspective was exactly what I needed.

CHAPTER EIGHTEEN

The Letter

IT TOOK A FEW DAYS TO FIND THE RIGHT WORDS. The new year rolled in, bringing with it a crisp pea soup fog. A crawling chill lingered along the ground. It could have scared me, the unknown. *"It's never going to change."* I whispered to myself.

Dear Aunt Jane and Uncle Don,

I am grateful for all that you have done for me. I have decided to move out. I didn't realize how much I miss my mother.

My hand shook right up to the last period. I placed the letter on their bedroom pillow and walked out the house for some much needed air. My clumsy feet led me up the trail.

The long path split into two directions. One path went to the house, the other appeared deeper into the woods.

I wasn't sure where exactly the property line ended. I was half present and half in my own little world. My legs carried me deeper into the fog.

The path twined to the back of our neighbor's property. I sank with every step into the knee-high snow. I didn't go for a walk to cry, but to gather my thoughts and patience.

"Ahem."

My pulse quickened at the sight of Carlos. Where did he come from? I asked myself. He fell out of the sky. My cloud nine eyes ran over him.

"You're on private property." His voice ran smooth.

I wasn't sure how to respond. I paused for a moment and turned around to head back to my place.

Carlos shouted. "Hey!"

"Sorry." I waved. "I didn't realize I wandered this far." I mumbled and sank my face into my scarf. I started to back-track over my steps in the snow. I could feel myself blush over my red chilled cheeks.

"No. That's alright." He smiled. "It's Vicky... Right?"

My breath stuck in my chest. He knew my name. I stopped and looked back. He was walking towards me, stepping in my footprints.

"Sorry about that. I was just joking around." He scratched the back of his head. "I was meaning to catch up with you... I wanted to apologize about my cousin," he said softly. "She gets protective."

My face went blank.

"Don't let her get to you." Carlos grinned.

"Has she done that before?" I asked fishing for more info.

"Yes." He rolled his eyes. "Look, I can't speak for her but I'm sorry."

Once again, my body tingled, almost paralyzed. It started at my skipping heart and down to my torso and below.

"I was hoping to see more of you," he said.

I quickly became lightheaded. The last thing I wanted to do was faint in front of him. Or did I? "I got to go." I spit out before insanity took over.

"You could drop by anytime." Carlos smiled.

I looked at him a second time, his eyes never left mine. I quickly walked back home. I rubbed my hands together even though I had mitts on. My fingers started to num from the brittle cold.

The woods got darker as I made my way back. I was a little scared at the thought of facing Uncle Don and Aunt Jane. Maybe they want me to leave. Angel said they had a problem with money. Who was going to pay for me?

I peeked through the patio doors before opening one side.

A flickering flame danced with a warm glow. I could see Aunt Jane sitting in the livingroom by the fireplace. The lights were dim and there was nobody but Aunt Jane and our Tom cat. The house was quiet, but even silence had a sound. The tension in the air allowed me to hear my thumping heart.

"I have something to tell you," Aunt Jane warned.

I observed her weighted down expression.

"Uh... Vicky... your friend Simona... is missing."

Puzzled, I looked at Aunt Jane as she stared back at me.

I cringed. "What?" I didn't think I heard her right.

"Simona never made it home." she repeated.

"That's not funny." I grumbled, appalled.

"I'm not joking," Aunt Jane said. "She's missing."

I stared back stupidly. "How can that be... I just seen her a few days ago." I murmured, refusing to give in to what I was hearing.

"They think it happened after she left a babysitting job," Aunt Jane continued. "Laura called about an hour ago." She sighed. "Just go sit down for now. We'll talk about the letter later."

I forgot about the letter.

"I'll call you when it's time for dinner." She said waving me down the stairs.

I was beside myself; falling into silence. I looked at where I was sitting with Simona the other day when she came to visit for my party. I thought about the time I spent with her.

I rubbed my temples. I wondered where she could be.

Tap...Tap...Tap... I couldn't tell what it was that woke me. The wind was fierce tonight. I let the sound distract me from thinking about my missing friend. I made a mental note... I have to be there when they find her.

I closed my eyes, in desperate need to detach. I had hoped it was all just a bad dream or a poor excuse for a attention.

A dazzling array of Christmas lights run along the bricked wall. The musty scent of old wood and earth tickled my noise. I closed my eyes and laid still, smelling the freshly chopped logs in the furnace room that were piled around the corner. I sank deeper into a soft handmade granny square blanket. My eyes sealed with tears.

A cold draft swept in. The tiny hairs on my body prickled outward on my skin. I curled up and hid from the chilly air. The seconds turned into minutes and left me in the border-lands between wakefulness and rest. It was a strange place to be, as I fell into a slumber. I nodded off with my eyes shut.

BAM!

A jolt shot straight through me and I quickly sat up-right. The air pressure in the room changed and I could tell that the basement door was opened. The heat from the house funneled through the hall and seeped out the door, while the frozen nose-haired air flooding in.

"QUICK!" I heard a deep voice.

Multiple heavy boots, bull rush up the stairs. They headed straight to the master bedroom.

"WHAM!... CRACK!"

I heard thuds and shouts followed with howls and grunts. It was more than a scuffle, or a tussle.

The lights were still out when I jumped to stand along the wall. I wasn't sure what was happening; a home invasion or was it a police raid, either way Uncle Don wasn't going down without a fight. And yet... and yet...I heard the thrashing of flesh being bashed in.

Helpless, I was unable to move.

Just as I made the choice to confront the situation... a man stood in the doorway. Oh...Shit! I thought and in the same moment an ice stabbing wave woke me up.

My eyes shot opened, and I was relieved to see it was just a dream. But the pain in my head was unbearable. My drained face was washed out by the sweat trickling down my forehead. The dark smudges beneath my eyes looked almost like bruises...I could feel a pulsing throb pounding in the front of my head. I found that even the silence hurt my ears.

It's not fair. I threw a pillow over my head and buried the tears. AHHHHH! I got to leave and go... I can't stay here. My fists ball up and my own voice is giving me a headache.

Only once Uncle Don started shouting did I sit up.

I could hear Sarah and Farley playing in the next room. My grapefruit-splitting headache took a few hours to pass.

The pressure grew so bad that it rang in my ears and messed up my sight. I had to lay myself out on the bathroom floor. Nauseous and powerless, I just wanted to end it... the pounding in my head. My sanity wasn't on the cusp of shattering... it's already over the edge of a mental meltdown.

Finally, I crawled back to bed. I couldn't focus of anything before I passed out from the pain.

I woke up mentally battered. I looked like I had a wicked hangover. I felt a lot better though... no more mind twisting pain. My emotions were on another level. I slipped out of bed; my stomach urged me to eat. Oddly, I grumbled with a fierce craving for sour and sweet.

"You're both nuts!" I bit into a salted sweet gala apple.

"Come on." Kerry hurried over the telephone.

"You don't want to miss it." The girls were all meeting up for the party in town.

"I'll come get you." Julie offered as Kerry and I listened on the line. Three-way calls seemed to be our thing now.

The girls talked me into going, I couldn't decide. I found it hard to think through the fuzz and fog... I hadn't been sleeping right.

"I'll go." I said, hoping I was allowed.

It helped that Aunt Jane was fed up of seeing me in the house and Uncle Don kept telling me to stop slacking off. He started filling in the time with work. "Don't lollygag." He'd say. "No excuses." He growled.

I felt disgusted thinking of anything else, while my friend was still missing. I rubbed my forehead and closed my eyes. I inhaled a long deep breath from my gut. I hope they'd find her.

The fireplace crackled and the essence of rosemary, pine and a dash of sage enveloped the room. I got up and opened the fridge and took a big gulp of maple syrup.

Once we were too broke for honey, and now our fridge is filled with fresh farmers 'market goods such as honey, maple and fresh produce. We went from living on an almost nothing budget, eating plain puffed-wheat cereal to organic eggs and baked bacon.

Yet, I still didn't have an appetite. Nothing could make me stop thinking of Simona.

When Aunt Jane and Uncle Don arrived at the house, they asked me to watch the kids while they went on a hike. They wanted to try out a new trail up the mountain.

"We shouldn't be long." Aunt Jane had to unpeel the girls from her legs. "We'll be back soon."

I sat on the couch talking to my friends on the phone as Sarah and Farley played downstairs. I was stuck to the wall in the living room where the telephone was mounted.

A few minutes later, I realized I didn't hear them. I didn't hear my cousins or anyone for that matter. "I'll call you back later." I hung the phone up and went to check on them.

They weren't there.

I checked all the rooms and the whole house and still no kids. Only Michael and I were home.

"Where's Sarah and Farley?" I asked Michael.

"They're playing outside," he answered casually.

I looked out the front, side and back windows. I saw a full view of trees and branches weighed down with snow. My imagination ran wild and I ran outside at once. "Did they say where they were going? Or mention anything?" I shouted to Michael.

"No." Michael shrugged.

"They're gone." I called outside for them but still no answer. Panic set in and adrenaline cranked me up. I lost the kids... how did I lose the kids? I thought as I wondered how I was going to explain this one.

As I made my way up the driveway, all these thoughts ran through my head, making my head spin.

Oh God! I hope they were alright. Looking up and down the road on the mountain, my heart pounded rapidly and my palms sweat as I trembled with a shortness of breath.

I paused to faint voices carried over the distance. I waited for a moment as the group appeared laughing.

Familiar shapes made their way into my vision. It turned out to be some neighbours with Uncle Don and Aunt Jane. My jaw dropped in relief at the sight of Sarah and Farley walking with them.

Oh shit! Fear crept up again as they got closer. I expected them to be cross with me, oddly they were all smiling as they approached the driveway.

I gulped.

"The kids found us," Uncle Don glowed. "They followed Jane's footprints."

I looked down and saw clovers from Aunt Jane's footwear left behind. The girls followed the prints in the snow.

"I bet you didn't think of that," Aunt Jane remarked.

No one mentioned the fact that I lost the girls, or that they snuck out without saying a word.

"They're natural trackers." The neighbours smiled.

I made a mental note, working out what I learned. Two lessons: first don't look away when babysitting, second look at tracks in snow... prints matter.

I mentioned Kerry's invitation after dinner during Uncle Don's captivating audience time. I asked after his third drink. Once he jumped to red wine... stay clear, it was better to be invisible; he started to bark that children should be seen, not heard.

"Can I go out with Julie and Kerry in town?" I asked.

"I don't know... can you?"

I quickly corrected myself, "May I?"

"You may go," Aunt Jane answered. "You'll be able to say your goodbyes."

"Goodbyes?" I questioned.

"Your mom is coming to pick you up." Aunt Jane reminded me simply, surprising me. "Didn't you want to move?"

There was a long pause.

I found myself staring at her blankly.

"You have to say your goodbyes because you won't have another chance later." She said firmly.

My shoulders slumped, and I cleared my throat. "Okay."

"Done." Aunt Jane bristled. "And don't you leave with any of my things." She said with a deep frown and didn't bat an eye when she told me to pack. "Stay away from my pictures."

My eyebrows furrowed even more.

"Rockhead... Phone." Uncle Don called over to me.

I picked up the phone. "Got it!" I shouted before I spoke to whoever was on the other end. "Hello?"

"Hi." I knew the voice right away.

"Laura." We haven't spoken since Simona disappearance.

"What's going on? I called you and Crystal but there was no answer. There's nothing on television about it and nobody is telling me anything."

"There is an ongoing investigation. Some of us were questioned." Laura replied. I could hear from her scratched voice that she was crying a lot. "Has she ever said anything to you?"

"She has a few admirers but that's about all." I shrugged gesturing, even though Laura couldn't see me.

"Yeah, the officer's looked into it." Her voice drifted off.

"Do they think she's alive?" I asked lifting my feet and tucking them under me. I spoke quietly, so, Uncle Don didn't butt into my conversation.

"The police said they found a burned-up corvette not far from here in one of the fields." Laura muttered, "But we still don't know if she's dead or alive."

"I have a picture of the dude that was bugging her... he's standing next to a corvette!" I suggested. "Do you think it will help?" I asked.

"Maybe. Either way the police are looking into it." Laura cried. "I really hope they find her."

"So do I."

As soon as I hung up the phone, it rang again, I had no time to panic about the police. I picked up the phone and it was Julie, "Okay, So, what are you going to wear tonight?" She asked without even saying hello.

I swallowed back a lump of unshed tears and tried for a smile instead. "Not sure yet. I'm going through them." I answered.

I had to pack my belongings, so I figured I could find an outfit in the process. My mind kept going to Simona. God, I hoped she was okay.

"You haven't found one yet?" Julie sounded surprised.

Uncle Don came into the living room I was in. His eyes bored into mine. "Why are all these people calling for you?" he asked annoyed.

"They're filling me in about Simona," I answered in hopes that it didn't set him into a rant. Julie could hear everything. I didn't think Uncle Don gave a shit who was on the phone.

Uncle Don's eyes were dark, his large dark pupils were absorbing all the hazel from his eyes. "I want to know when you get off." His curiosity of the case got the better of him.

"I was just about to get off." I commented, hoping he would leave me be.

He turned to look at me. "You better hope your mom gets you a line when you move."

I covered the phone. I hadn't told my friends about moving yet.

"Just go find something to wear and call me back." Julie butt in. "No rush."

I hung up with the dread of being questioned. But that wasn't what was on my mind now. Now, I was starting to think of who would harm Simona?

"Everyone's here tonight!" Julie shouted.

I pointed over the crowd. The guy that gave me a sample of his music was up front recording and filming the MC, knee deep in the beats.

The lightshow blinded me. The smoke show caused Mel to fall into a coughing fit. But the rest of it was extraordinary.

"Ready to have the time of your life?" His silky voice echoed with a solid presence to his listeners. "You're listening to BNB." It was like he let off a beat bomb and every inch of me couldn't stay still. First my head bobbed, then my shoulders, right down to my hips.

Alongside the music, there's an unexpected fashion show. The runway ran around the room in a U-Shape.

"I want that." Julie squealed.

"The clothing or the girl?" I said with a little smile.

Julie knew I was joking, though she didn't correct me.

"Oh crap!" I said to myself.

Carlos's cousin stood a few feet from me. I could tell she hadn't noticed us. Her shifty eyes hadn't narrowed in on my presence.

I quickly turned my back, avoiding a confrontation. In a fight you're not suppose to turn your back on your opponent, in this case I couldn't be bothered.

We watched the light show and met the MC.

"Found him." Kerry ran up to me. "He's in the rec-room playing Ping-Pong..." A smile stretched over her face. "What are you waiting for." She said, secret laughter lurking in her dark eyes. "Go on!"

What did that mean?

It was clear that Carlos was cute - not enough to run after him like a bitch in heat... I thought for a moment, but enough to distract me.

"There's not going to be a better time." Julie nudged my arm. Kerry stepped into me and grabbed my arm and walked me towards him.

"Eh, I don't know..." I said unsure of myself.

"Don't be scared." Kerry grinned.

"I'm not scared." I just wanted to leave our last memory of us talking alone in the woods. I wasn't about to let my guard down with his cousin here.

Instead, I decided to blurt out to the girls I was moving and let them focus on that.

"What do you mean you're moving?" Julie shouted.

Kerry put her juice down. "You just moved here!"

"I'm moving in with my mom." I confessed.

Julie knew some of my back story, but Kerry was shocked.

Again, another group of friends promising we'd keep in touch and see each other.

I know life is about adapting and rolling with the punches. When I was younger and lived in the heart of Montreal. I was able to spread my wings. I stood fearless on top of apartment buildings. In Lasalle, the best times were playing with my friends in the alleys, in the West Island it was the shops. In Hudson it was this.

I had to face my academics and start learning how to learn and build study habits. I got a chance to live in a beautiful house wrapped up in nature. I had the opportunity. I reminded myself, but now, it's onto something else.

It was eleven o'clock when Uncle Don came to pick me up. The Hudson Village still had its rustic charm even after the event was done.

As soon as we got in, my head hit the pillow like a sack of rocks.

The next day, it was afternoon when we left.

"ROCKHEAD! Move your ass and let's go." Uncle Don shouted like a mindless machine. It was exactly his ranting and raving that made me want to leave to begin with. My heart raced with fear of the unknown.

We headed to Ville Saint Laurent. The largest borough in Montreal. I used to bus to Mom's on the 120 to 68 from the West Island. But now, it was close to a 60-minute drive from

Hudson. I started to wonder if I'd ever see my cousins again. If, I'd get visiting weekends there.

Before Uncle Don dropped me off at home, I had to stop in at the police station. He found out yesterday that they wanted to ask me some questions. Uncle Don didn't want the police at the house, so we went to them. Especially, since he just started a new nursery for his plants.

Uncle Don sent me in alone.

All choked up, I found out it was just a formality to answer some questions for Simona's case. It was no longer a missing person... it was a homicide.

I glanced up at the officer in disbelief.

"The RCMP Serious Crimes Unit took over the investigation and consultation by Major Crimes Unit," he said.

I swallowed hard, "Homicide." Isn't that ...murder?

"Where are your parents." The officer asked looking over my shoulder.

"I don't have parents and my uncle's outside in the car." I rubbed my eyes, hoping that would do the trick to hold back the tears. "Does that mean she's dead?"

"Yes." The officer said. "She was found dead earlier in the week. She was found in a dumpster not far from her residence," he studied me. "Do you know anything that may help our investigation?" he questioned. "Maybe an argument with someone or was she planned on running away?" He looked at me intently.

" No." Emotions bottled up in my face.

He stood tall and looked at me while I racked my brain for a clue or thought. I didn't want to cause trouble unless I was sure. She had a few guys bugging her.

"Anything at all." His carefully built calm eased me.

"I may have something... a picture." I said, "But it's in the car." I added, "There was a strange family she was babysitting for."

"We questioned a few, mostly the ones she recently sat for," The officer said. "We checked all the ones on her callers list."

My mouth moved before I second guessed myself. "You should do a house search at the last one she went to. Their son was a little weird and the father creeped me out a bit... but he did have a cool car."

"I'd like to see that picture." The officer asked.

"Sure." I offered, but now I had to get it from the car.

"That's it?" Uncle Don asked as I headed back to the car.

"Uh... I just have to give them something from my bag." I informed him.

"What?" Uncle Don barked. "Don't be a dummy."

"The officer wants it." I shrugged. I didn't know what to do. I could see that Uncle Don was ghastly against it.

He got out of the car and walked back into the building with me.

I grabbed the picture from my bag.

"What do you want from her?" Uncle Don questioned.

"We just need some more information." The officer replied.

"What kind of information?" Uncle Don barked profusely sweating. "She's a minor."

"That's fine." One of the officers said, "She's free to leave once she gives us the picture." He prompted.

I slowly gave the picture. "That's it." I hesitated.

"What's that?" Uncle Don asked hastily.

"It's a picture," I mumbled. "From when I babysat."

Uncle Don growled under his breath.

"I liked the car." My voice came out childlike and flaccid.

The officer reassured me. "It's probably nothing, but we'd like to have the picture."

Uncle Don's eyes narrowed in on me. "What car?"

"A corvette." The officer answered looking at the picture.

"Can we leave now." Uncle Don guided me to the door.

"Yes," the officer said. "If there is anything else, we'll be in touch." His attention was drawn to the picture.

"Let's go," Uncle Don demanded.

I walked out of that building feeling satisfied and wishing I could do more. I hoped that the universe and the officers found the truth, like that show Matlock I use to watch with Momma and Papa.

"You really are a dumb ass, eh?" Uncle Don glared. "What makes you think giving them anything will help."

My caress provoked a long, guttural gnarl.

The drive to my mother's apartment was filled with Uncle Dons lectures. "Police and the military are the spawn of Satan." His voice echoed. "Those pigs don't need your help." He growled itching for a drink. "and American cars suck, German is the best way to go."

I turned my head and bit back a laugh at how serious he was. Didn't he love his Eagle Talon? I questioned. Isn't that an American car? Though, I haven't seen it around lately. As far as I knew he traded it in for a John Deere Lawn Mower.

I was raised not to trust the police.

If anyone would hate them it would be me, with my first memories of them busting down the door and separating me from my family, rewriting my future for the rest of my life. I was happy they were hunting down Simona's killer.

The anger I had towards Uncle Don didn't compare to the anger of the lose of my friend. I thought of her being lowered into the ground.

The more Uncle Don ranted on, the more I prayed for justice. I sat back in the passenger seat. I thought about who it could be. The deeper I dug in my thoughts, the more twisted the mystery became.

CHAPTER NINTEEN

Crawl Space

I half expected Uncle Don to put up a fight. What a bruise to my ego. After almost ten years of living with my aunt and uncle, it was time to say goodbye.

I knew early in life; before I even knew the words to articulate it, that people looked out for themselves. I figured it was wiser to adapt. The odds of getting through the 80s and the 90s unharmed were just as good as getting through them without a bad haircut.

Uncle Don's arrogance slipped a notch. "You could have stayed."

I didn't say anything. I kept my eyes on the road ahead of us. Not sure of his reaction.

At this point, it's more important to stick with my decision. Plus, Uncle Don couldn't face the ugly truth. He had pushed me too far. His good side is like a giant kid sharing his toys, but his other side is an unpredictable madman.

I sat long and hard thinking of these moral values he beat into me and the others. His self-righteous judgments alongside his skillful advice.

I found myself asking what are these moral values? I had to look at it with a clear sense. I've learned that it was about right and wrong. It's not based on how I feel at the moment. Rather, it was founded on a firm set of principles that act as a guide – even when others aren't watching.

"You should have waited to move out until you graduated," he said bluntly. "You're going to be a dropout."

I felt like I was left with no other option. The only choice I had left was to move away. I felt bombarded with his challenging moral code. Whether it comes from him, the people I went to school, music, movies or television shows. Influences have challenged my beliefs about what is right and wrong.

My vexatious allowance spilled out. "You don't even give a shit about school." I sat in the passenger seat very still, looking ahead. "You keep calling me stupid... you break everything down, like I'm too dumb to understand anything." I rubbed my nose and held my breath. I didn't want to show him that my body wanted to run and that my heart was racing out of my chest.

"I just want you to have a better life than I did. And I do like school, that's why I help you with math and other forms of skills, you may not have any use for now, but you may in the future."

His grin caught me off guard.

"My father's a professor. I come from a line of teachers."

I took a few deep breaths to calm my scattered thoughts. And held an image of him in my mind.

Nothing happened.

"You say the apple doesn't fall far from the tree?" I pointed.

"Oh..." he said with a poignant sigh. "I'm just saying that in hopes you don't become like them, not meaning that you are like them." He grumbled and held the steering wheel a little looser. "Look kid, just be careful." He gripped the shifter to change gears in yet another new van from his Bodyshop.

"I just want you to understand the pressure."

"Me? You want me to understand pressure." I said a little too sarcastic. My stomach tightened.

He looked over at me like a growling bear but instead said, "it's understanding it all, media pressure to be popular and accepted. You need to learn to make decisions consistently with your own values and choices, even if that goes against your family or friends."

Clearly, I misunderstood him. The hurtful words like the ones he pierced me with from his explosive temper were bitter and now, I wondered who he is.

I reminded myself that he built respect through fear, and loyalty through breaking a person down first. If I'm allowed to make my own choices. I think maybe, just maybe... if you are honest, others will trust you or if you are kind, others will like being around you.

"Girl Behind the Wall; Teen brother who hid sister in custody dispute pleads guilty." The radio announced interrupting my thoughts.

Uncle Don kept talking, but my ear tuned into the radio.

"Pierrefonds, Quebec - A teen boy who authorities said hid his younger sister, often in a crawl space, for nearly two years as part of an attempt to keep her safe has been ordered to spend two years on probation, without more jail time.

"Brandon Lang, 17, pleaded guilty Monday to five misdemeanors, including obstructing a peace officer.

"Brandon's mother, Diane Lang, pleaded not guilty. She denied knowing that her daughter was there. A prosecutor said the case-closing plea deals came with the blessing of the boy. Brandon stated that his mother didn't know, but that it was important to keep his sister away from his father.

"Brandon insisted he hid his sister to protect her from abuse. Authorities say Brandon began hiding his sister in his room, stashing her in a crawl space - roughly 5 feet by 12 feet, about the height of a washing machine – whenever anyone was home or when visitors came over.

"Authorities raided the home, finding the missing girl, and arrested Brandon. The other children are in mother's custody, and child welfare is looking into it. The father Mr. Lang is still on the run. Videos have been found in the apartment linking to answers to another case. But officer have refused question at this time."

I looked up at Uncle Don, he didn't skip a beat. He hadn't noticed the change in me. But I did.

"See you around kid," Uncle Don finally said while pulling in front of the apartments.

I looked at him one last time as my stepfather. "I'll see you around, Dad." I closed the door giving him a wink.

He pulled out and drove off down Décarie Boulevard.

I lifted my bags and a box and walked up the cement path to my mother's apartment.

Saint Laurent was highly diverse.

Just because I went through a storm, didn't mean I wasn't headed for sunshine. My heart pounded with the promise of freedom. It was more important than family squabbles.

When all was said and done, I thought the answer to Simona's death rested on finding Mr. Lang.

Full of questioning speculations about Simona lingered. I hated the question what if? Or Why? Because the thoughts that ran through my head kept me from sleeping at night.

ABOUT THE AUTHOR:

Roxanne Pion

Roxanne Pion is an *indie author.*
Primarily writing and publishing, she's the creative director,
from concept to completion and beyond.

Her 2nd Novel 'The Shops' is the
second of a five-book series titled
'Vicky's Witness'.

Dear Readers,

I'm not saying I was running wild in the streets, but I was. I enjoyed a kind of freedom that no longer exists. I spent hours playing outside with friends and didn't come in until the streetlights came on. I was rarely inside, and when I was called in for the night, I would draw. When I wasn't riding bikes in the street or playing ball in the back yard, you could find me at the nearest swimming pool with my friend's eyes burning from chlorine.

Back in the day, we wore ponytails with scrunchies and used Sun-In or Lemons. We kept a Cosmopolitan magazine next to our beach towel, and we listened to music from a boom box. When our friends wanted to talk, they called the house phone, and we'd drag the spiral cord down the hall, out of earshot of our parents.

We lived for junk food. Sometimes we ate pizza, just for a change of pace. We had MTV memorized and stayed up late watching movies our parents told us not to.

We called our crushes at slumber parties and played games like M.A.S.H. and Truth or Dare. We fearlessly summoned spirits with our Ouija Boards and then stayed awake for hours, because we were too scared to fall sleep.

It wasn't unheard of to light fireworks for fun. Maybe we snuck a sip of our parent's drink when no one was looking. Maybe not.

When children are placed in foster care, it can be very stressful. You may feel angry, overwhelmed, or worried about safety and well-being. You may be confused and scared.

No one can tell you exactly how long you'll be in foster care; this will depend on your case and the circumstances that brought you to the foster care system. Reunification does not happen overnight, but everyone agrees that the first goal is to reunite youth with their families as soon as possible. Research suggests that, if children must be placed out of your home, living with relatives can help them thrive.

An image paints a thousand words and a thousand words can unravel a soul. There is something about putting ideas into motion that brings us closer to grasping what we need to grasp.

I look at my life as chapters and see my future painted on canvases. A person is a walking, talking story and if you watch them long enough, they will let their guard down and expose their soul. I enjoyed writing this book and I hope I poured a bit of myself into these pages. I taught myself to adapt and to take in the good, the bad and the ugly. Writing is a way for me to unravel all the emotions that were tangled up inside me.

R. Pion

Made in the USA
Columbia, SC
27 March 2020